THEY'RE GONE

THEY'RE GONE

A NOVEL

E. A. BARRES

CROOKED
LANE

NEW YORK

Published in the United States by Crooked Lane Books, an imprint of The Quick Brown Fox & Company LLC.

Crooked Lane Books and its logo are trademarks of The Quick Brown Fox & Company LLC.

Library of Congress Catalog-in-Publication data available upon request.

ISBN (hardcover): 978-1-64385-555-4
ISBN (ebook): 978-1-64385-556-1

Cover design by Melanie Sun

Printed in the United States.

www.crookedlanebooks.com

Crooked Lane Books
34 West 27th St., 10th Floor
New York, NY 10001

First Edition: November 2020

10 9 8 7 6 5 4 3 2 1

To Michelle Richter,
Thank you for lighting the path.

PART ONE

A NEW DAY

CHAPTER

1

Winter 2019

D EB LINH THOMAS didn't understand how she'd slept through the
night. Something should have woken her.

The sounds of gunfire, no matter how distant.

Her husband's soul ripped away.

The abrupt, violent, permanent change to everything she knew.

But Deb had slept peacefully and only woke when she drowsily
heard the sirens outside her home.

Instinctively, her first thought had been about her daughter, Kim,
at Washington College.

In a panic, she turned toward Grant's side of the bed.

And that's when she realized he was gone.

Minutes later Deb stood barefoot in her kitchen, wearing a robe
hastily thrown over the thin T-shirt and shorts she'd worn to bed,
numbly listening to two cops tell her that her husband had been killed
in a robbery.

This wasn't something she could have imagined—or accept. Now
in her early forties, Deb was of an age when tragedy was striking her
friends: rapidly moving cancer, the slow death of parents. But not violence. It felt like the worst kind of horror, one that Deb thought she'd
been spared.

And not Grant. He wasn't a small man, or a passive one. He'd boxed in and after college, and although he didn't have a temper, people knew better than to test him. For the most part, despite a rueful middle-aged softening, he stayed in shape. He was popular, respected by colleagues and neighbors, always in control—physically, emotionally, professionally. When change happened, it was because of a decision Grant made.

But now that notion seemed hopelessly ignorant.

And terrifying.

Grant had been murdered, and he'd been powerless to stop it.

Men who kill, Deb realized, make their own rules of law, even nature.

And now the laws of her reality were unwritten.

Friends and family soon filled her suburban Northern Virginia home, but Deb was very much alone. She had to be reminded to eat; her eyes were raw from constant crying; her ribs ached from ragged breaths. Her voice, hoarse and grief-stricken, sounded distant to her ears, as if coming from somewhere buried underground.

Her nineteen-year-old daughter, Kim, returned from college to stay with her. Deb knew she needed to be there for Kim but, for those first few days, the most they could do was cry in the same room and hold each other, as if desperately trying to stop themselves from dissolving.

Deb had known Grant was going to die someday, the same way she understood she would also die, but it was impossible to accept.

There, but for the grace of God, went others.

Not him.

CHAPTER

2

Two young cops pushed through the doors of Baltimore's Fells Gate Tavern, eyed by everyone in the dark, dingy bar, then ignored. Most uniformed cops took control of a room when they entered it. But the moment these two walked in, the room had them.

They stayed in the doorway. One cleared his throat and asked, "Is Cessy Castillo here?"

No one in the sparsely crowded bar replied. The bar wasn't large—nothing more than a handful of tables, and only about half were occupied. It was too dark to see everyone clearly.

The cops approached the bartender, a short twenty-something woman wearing a tank top, with tattoos running down her right arm.

"Do you know where we can find Cessy Castillo?"

The bartender drank from a shot she'd poured herself. The glass knocked loudly on the wood when she set it down.

Her voice was guarded when she spoke.

"You know what she looks like?"

The other cop shook his head. "Her neighbor just told us she'd be here."

"Why'd you go to her apartment?"

"It's about her husband. Hector Ramirez."

The first cop glared at the second. "But we really can't discuss that with anyone but her."

The bartender's eyes widened. "Hector? Hell, I'm Cessy. What did he do?"

"You're Cessy Castillo?"

The bruises Hector had left on Cessy's back and stomach earlier that evening ached. She wondered if a neighbor had heard Hector, called the police.

"What did he do?" she asked again.

"He died, ma'am," the second cop blurted out.

The first cop—slightly older than his partner, but only in his serious face, the premature stress lines around his hooded eyes—nudged the second. "I'm sorry. My partner's new."

"Hector's dead?"

For a moment, the pain from her bruises was forgotten. Everything was forgotten. Cessy felt the room darken, her mouth dry. First grief, then relief. The two emotions wrestled inside her like darting flames, each trying to devour the other.

"I'm sorry," someone said. One of the cops.

Cessy was gripping the edge of the bar. She relaxed her hands, shakily poured herself another shot. Drank it.

"If you can," the older cop asked, "we'd like you to come with us. We have some questions about your husband."

"Yeah? Like what?" Her mind raced to figure out what had happened. Natural causes wouldn't have brought the cops. An accident would have to be suspicious.

A killing.

"We'd prefer not to discuss the incident here," the older cop told her.

Cessy had suspected there was something shady in Hector's life— the way he took phone calls in another room; the late nights when she woke to discover he'd returned to the apartment and was in the shower—but she'd suspected he was having an affair.

Had some enraged husband murdered him?

Or had it been something else?

"Okay," Cessy said. She slammed the shot glass down on the bar, called to the back office, "Will! I'm out. Hector's dead. See you tomorrow!"

The younger cop said nervously, "Um, you probably don't want to broadcast . . ."

Relief was winning out, the first giddy realization of freedom. "Let's go, amigos," she said. "What are we doing? You need me to identify the body? In the morgue?"

"We don't do that. Just show you a photograph."

"Well, damn." Cessy grabbed her purse, the quick move igniting the pain in her back. The pain that would never be there again. "How am I supposed to dance on a photograph?"

CHAPTER

3

D EB KEPT SEEING flashes of men.
She first noticed them one morning when she decided to finally clean the house. People had come and gone over the last week, and the house was in disarray. Glasses randomly left on tables and countertops, throw pillows tossed on the floor, clothes tangled under furniture. Like a family had fled their home in the middle of the night.

Deb straightened out the living room until she reached the mantle over the fireplace. She paused at a picture of her with Kim and Grant. It was from their trip two years ago to Hawaii. Kim stood between them, the same uncertain smile Grant had. She'd been given her father's height and, at sixteen, had already surpassed Deb's sixty-two inches.

Grant stood on the other side of Kim, wearing a polo and shorts and sandals, squinting at the camera through the sun. His arms hung uncertainly at his sides, like a novice actor waiting to be told what to do with his hands, and the polo strained to hold his chest. Back then he'd always been clean-shaven. It wasn't until the past few months that he'd let his beard grow. Deb could still feel it tickling her face when they kissed, under her fingertips when she touched his cheek. The beard was bristly when it first emerged, then turned flower-petal soft.

Movement in the picture glass.

Deb turned, stared hard through the window behind her, into their backyard. The gate leading into it was open. A man was walking away. Deb watched him until he disappeared, hand over her heart, failing to control her breathing.

She tried to remember if she'd shut the gate before she left. Had it been open? She thought it'd been closed—it was always closed—but couldn't remember. Deb couldn't be sure of anything, given her foggy grief the past few days.

And that man could have been anyone. A neighbor, a gardener from the HOA, someone who mistakenly opened the wrong gate.

A gardener, probably. That's what she decided. A gardener.

Her breathing slowed, calmed.

"Hey Mom."

Kim walked into the living room, wearing a long T-shirt and flannel shorts. Her eyes were exhausted, half-lidded. She leaned against the wall, arms crossed over her chest.

"Did you take your medicine?" Deb asked.

Kim nodded. The Xanax usually hit Kim hard, left her sleepy. For Deb, it was more soothing than anything else. The pain was there, and the pain was raw, but not overwhelming.

"You want to go out for breakfast?" Kim asked.

Deb had always enjoyed cooking, even something as simple as breakfast. But she hadn't turned on the oven since Grant's death. He'd always been fond of her food, and preparing a meal seemed like too much of a memory.

Besides, since that night neither Kim nor Deb felt hungry. They ate when they remembered, maybe once a day.

"Let's go."

Kim gave her a thumbs-up, ran her other hand through her long dark hair. Grant had thought Kim could be a model. Deb agreed that their daughter was beautiful, but privately knew he was wrong. She was tall, but not tall enough. Thin, but not thin enough. Not that she would ever deny her daughter's soft beauty, her lovely face and effortlessly long lashes, her black rope of hair, the naturally unbroken skin that Kim's friends (and, to be honest, Deb) openly envied.

"Mom, stop staring at me."

"Sorry."

Deb had always worried about her daughter, and occasionally that worry nearly overwhelmed her—the first time Kim went out at night with friends, her first date, the night she hadn't returned home until three AM. But Grant's murder had thrown Deb's emotions into turmoil. Her worry and love for her daughter had always felt like a balancing act, imaginary thoughts and gnawing fears fighting against Kim's strain toward independence.

And now all those fears were real. There was no separation.

Violence had come.

Deb wondered again about that man in her garden.

*   *   *

Deb had lived in Northern Virginia for twenty years and still didn't understand it. She'd grown up in a small town in Southern Virginia, where the cities and towns were spread apart, divided by mountains or wide stretches of flat land. Northern Virginia was split into almost a dozen different cities, and the borders were indecipherable, without geographic demarcation. You could drive from Vienna, where she lived, to cities like Fairfax and Arlington, without leaving a business district.

But it was nice, compared to the remote town her mother had settled in shortly after her adoption, to live someplace far more diverse. Deb had been the only Vietnamese child in that Southern community, and that was a lonely feeling, a sense that she never completely belonged, that there was a deeper association inaccessible to her.

Kim had never known that feeling. It was hard to find an ethnicity not represented in Northern Virginia, DC, or Maryland. Kim's friends in high school, and now college, comprised a wide range of races.

But the DC region was famously expensive. Grant's enormous salary had paid for all their expenses on its own; conversely, the money Deb made freelance writing for nonprofits couldn't even cover one month. And it had been three months since she last worked.

That said, there was enough in their checking account for a year of expenses. It was a relief not to think about it. Looking into Grant's life—even at the confusion of his insurance policies and finances—felt too much like staring at a photograph of him. Deb could function when Grant was floating in the background of her thoughts, but distantly.

She couldn't do a thing when his presence was brought forth any further, was paralyzed when she heard Grant's voice, or his footsteps on the stairs, or the sound of his car pulling into the garage. When she smelled his sharp aftershave in the morning.

And even though Deb knew she'd imagined those sounds or scents, grief still struck like arrows thudding into her heart.

She and Kim pulled into the IHOP parking lot, expecting to see a Sunday morning crowd, but no one was waiting at the doors.

"What day is it?" Deb asked.

"Wednesday, maybe?"

They parked and walked to the restaurant. The weather was chilly—sweater weather—Grant's favorite time of year, which, in

Virginia, only lasted for about a week. Summers were too sweatily humid, winters a bitter dry freeze. Every year, spring and fall merely peeked out before vanishing.

Kim ordered a stack of pancakes. Deb wanted something with more substance.

"You're getting chicken fried steak?" Kim asked after the waiter left. "From IHOP?"

"Why not?"

"When you're at IHOP, you should stay in their lane."

Deb smiled at that. The sensation felt nice, but foreign.

Those muscles hadn't been used for a while.

Kim took a sip from her water, swallowed.

"How are you, Mom?"

Given everything that had happened over the past week, the question came off as odd. But Deb and Kim hadn't talked much about what had happened, or how they felt. Those first days had been stunned silence or body-shaking tears.

Being outside the house felt like a much-needed change.

And talking in public seemed to make things more open.

"I really don't know," Deb answered, and regretted her honesty.

She wanted to be honest, but she also wanted her daughter to think she was strong.

Deb had never considered herself emotionally withdrawn, but she was nowhere near as complicated as her daughter was about her feelings. Furious teenage years, marked by angry arguments and frightening periods of depression, had led Deb and Grant to enroll Kim in therapy. Kim had been surprisingly receptive to the idea, and it had helped. Deb would occasionally overhear Kim's conversations with girlfriends, listen to Kim analyze her young relationships from a psychological perspective Deb hadn't known at that age.

"I just feel," she once heard Kim say, talking about a boy who had asked her out her sophomore year in high school, "that his values are more subjective than shared. You know?"

She and Grant had always supported Kim, even if, privately, her approach to life confused them. Grant had adopted much of his widowed father's attitude—reserved, unmoved, the generational stereotype of a male baby boomer. When Grant's mother had died, Deb had comforted Grant as he fought back tears. And she'd watched Grant's father stoically pass through the funeral arrangements, the service, and the reception, distant, seemingly disinterested.

It was fitting behavior for Grant's father, the same man who had never told his only son he loved him; had merely quietly shaken hands with Grant when he and Deb announced their engagement; never smiled for photos; and who, grimly, briefly, held Kim after she was born.

Deb had felt horrible for Grant's mother at her funeral. She hated the men's reticence, their pointless resistance to grief.

Grief is a monument. And they were doing their best to make the memory of Grant's mother smooth, undisturbed land.

But that resistance was inside her, part of her. There was something that prevented Deb from taking her friends' advice to seek counseling after Grant's murder, to shy away from calling a therapist or finding a support group.

In a strange way, it seemed like taking the grief on herself honored Grant.

Kept him close to her.

She wondered if Kim felt it too, that pull to isolation. She'd noticed her daughter's reluctance to leave the house, to talk with friends. Even to talk to her, aside from offering to share her Xanax, an offer Deb had—surprising herself—accepted.

"I don't know how I feel either," Kim said now, her hand wrapped around a glass of water. "It changes so fast. Like any moment I might suddenly be, like, lost?"

Deb touched her eyes, trying to ward off tears. Saw Kim do the same.

"Sorry," Kim said after a few moments. "Maybe we shouldn't talk about this here."

"No, it's okay."

Kim nodded. "It's hard to sleep. I feel too much. Scared and angry and sad. And I miss Dad."

"I can't feel anything without being sad," Deb said. "I miss him too."

The waiter brought their food, set it before them.

Deb touched her chicken fried steak with her fork, could barely push it through the hard, overcooked meat.

"You want to split my pancakes?"

Deb pushed her plate to the side, took her daughter up on the offer. They ate from the same plate, the pancakes sliced into small triangles, islands poking through a dark lake of syrup.

"Have the cops said anything else?" Kim asked.

"Just what I told you. It might be some gang who's doing this. There've been other people, all men who died the same way." Deb paused, spoke past the lump in her throat. "Shot the same way. The police don't think it's a coincidence."

"Me neither," Kim said.

The women were quiet.

"Sometimes I think Dad's in the house. Like I forget he's gone. Or I see someone and think it's him."

"That happened to me this morning. I saw someone near the backyard, but it was just the gardener."

"The other day I saw someone walking to our door, and then he turned and left. For a second, I thought it was Dad coming home."

They both dabbed napkins to their eyes.

"When are you going back to school?" Deb asked.

"Like I told you, they excused me from my classes for the rest of the semester."

Deb didn't remember. "You were doing pretty good, right? With your grades?"

"Pretty much."

Deb believed her. Kim had an easy affinity for school and studying that Grant shared, but that ease had completely bypassed Deb. She'd been a good student, but only because of how intensely she studied. Kim and Grant could glance at their notes the night before a final exam, show up late, walk away with an A.

Grant's confidence.

God, she wished she had his confidence.

"I don't want you to feel like you need to stay here with me," Deb told Kim.

"I like staying with you."

Her words warmed Deb. Prior to this, her relationship with Kim had been defined by those volatile arguments. Spats that started, seemingly, the exact moment Kim turned thirteen, as if she'd realized at a young age that there was only so much control her mother had over her. She'd grown worse in her rebellious high school years, and by the time Kim left for college, they'd spent days without speaking to each other.

Now that distance seemed immature, something she and Kim had the privilege to play with, the kind of problems created from boredom, from the arrogance of boredom. When real tragedy struck, Deb had felt helpless. And needy. And she'd never felt that way before.

"Thanks for coming home," she said.

Her daughter reached across the table, held her hands.

And there were those tears.

Those helpless, endless, shared tears.

4

CESSY USED THE couch to stand. Nausea touched the back of her throat, grudgingly stayed down as she stared at a pillow and blanket on the living room floor, trying to figure out what had happened the night before.

And why she was naked.

She spotted an empty bottle underneath the coffee table.

Vodka.

Vodka had happened. And so had Anthony Jenkins.

Cessy sat on the couch, considered that an accomplishment. She didn't expect to do anything else that productive today.

She crossed her legs, rested her feet on the coffee table and slouched, trying to ease her stomach. She found the remote control buried in the cushions and switched on cartoons. Watched SpongeBob SquarePants cheerfully bounce along the ocean floor.

The shower stopped.

That was interesting.

She hadn't realized it was on.

Cessy was too hungover to do anything but pull a blanket over herself. She kept staring at SpongeBob until the door to her bedroom opened and Anthony stepped out.

"You look like shit," Anthony said cheerfully. He walked over to her, towel around his waist, collapsed on the couch next to her. He stretched his long black legs out, crossed his ankles over the coffee table. Anthony had played basketball for Baltimore Community College and, almost a decade later, still had an athlete's lanky grace, even if his muscles had lost their definition and he'd added a few pounds.

Cessy tried to think of a response. Her sleep- and alcohol-infused mouth felt like a dirty bird's nest had been shoved inside it.

"Things have been weird."

"Yeah?" Anthony was staring at SpongeBob argue with his pet snail.

Cessy scratched her scalp. Her hair was hopelessly tangled. "Hector's dead. He was shot twice. One in the head, one in the heart."

Anthony bounded to his feet.

"What? By who?"

"They don't know."

"Last night you said he was out of town!"

"He sort of was. Where are you going?"

Anthony had been inching over to the bedroom. "I should probably go."

Cessy watched him. "You okay?"

"I can't believe your husband was killed and you're acting this way about it."

"We weren't married that long. And come on, Anthony, you got what you wanted."

"Well, okay, maybe, yeah. But after all these years of trying at the bar, and you finally giving me the green light . . . still, though, this doesn't feel right. See you, Cess. Sorry about what happened. But thanks for letting me use your shower. And for, um, last night."

Anthony dressed quickly in front of Cessy—stumbling as he pulled on pants, accidentally pushing his head into a sleeve—and hurried off.

Cessy dragged herself to the shower after he left, let warm water run down her back, rested her forehead against the tiles.

The same thoughts she'd been having since Hector's murder days earlier started rolling through her mind, like music from a player piano, a song she desperately wanted to ignore. Thoughts of how life had been before Hector was killed, when he was at his most depressed and withdrawn.

When things were awful.

When the beatings were regular.

At the end of their relationship, Cessy had been trapped by its beginning, the memories of when everything was magical and possible, love overwhelming. When Hector had been different, discharged from Baltimore's PD because of a lower back injury that kept him sidelined, rueful but not yet dejected. She'd met him at the bar, and they'd talked all night, gone to breakfast at three in the morning, finally left each other at noon without even a kiss . . . just the desire for one. He stopped by the next night and the same thing happened, but they left on a brief kiss that second time, a shy touching of lips.

His old-fashioned approach charmed her, his past as a cop and thoughts about what he would do next (private security, maybe something else entirely) intrigued her. It fit Cessy nicely given that she also considered herself to be in a transitional state—she was eventually planning to return to school and finish college. And she hadn't dated another Latino for a while, even if Hector couldn't speak Spanish. She teased him about that, and he struggled to comprehend what she was saying, responded back with high school skills: "*¿Por que . . . tu habla?*"

Cessy was only half Latina. Her mother was from Panama, and she'd never met her white American father, so she and her brother had been raised speaking Spanish, watching telenovelas, eating an indecent amount of rice with every meal. But her mother had been absent so frequently that she and her brother couldn't help becoming Americanized—by television, by their friends, by the stores and restaurants and adults around them. And so, as an adult, Cessy was able to slip into either culture.

And she and Hector slipped into love with the enthusiasm of children chasing each other. He moved in after a few short months. One bright Saturday morning, they spontaneously married, happily lost in love, aching to be as close to each other as possible. That was when, to Cessy, everything about Hector was endearing, even the playful annoyances. The way he loudly ate, his snores, the shirts he wore too often without washing. Those rough edges fit into her smoothly, like the natural flow of an easy conversation. Cessy had never been in love, and it was more than she'd expected. More than she'd hoped for.

It was only after the first year that she noticed Hector's moodiness, the irritation overtaking him about the lingering pain in his back, his inability to find consistent work. She started to learn more about him, about why he had really been discharged from the police, the scandal about the drugs he'd taken from dealers and sold on his own. The fact that his reluctance to find work was really his lack of interest in a regular job.

And when he first hit her, that's when she realized how corruption had stained his soul.

And she realized she'd made a horrible mistake.

Cessy tried to leave the day he died. Was almost out the door with a duffel bag of clothes, about to head back to her brother in Arizona, when Hector burst in, high and moody. Turned enraged when he saw her packed bag.

He fell on her, fists first.

Cessy was left stunned on the floor, taking slow pained breaths, her ribs and thighs on fire from his kicks. Cessy had sworn that was the end.

That night, he died.

And she almost wished that made her sadder.

It reminded her of another time in her life, when guilt and sadness should have overpowered her but didn't.

But that was a memory she couldn't let herself think about.

Something no one but Hector and her brother knew about.

Cessy turned off the water, wrapped a towel around herself. She stepped out of the shower and walked toward the living room, a trail of drops on the hardwood floor behind her like quivering eyes. She stared at the picture of Hector on the living room wall, the one he insisted be framed, an old one from back when he was a cop. Still thin, hair close cut, an intensity to his brown eyes as he gazed at the camera.

Cessy took the picture down.

She hated that picture. Seemed like such a lie.

The blank white wall was better.

Cessy couldn't stop staring at the wall. Marred only by a single nail. Reminded her of when she'd first moved in and had the place to herself. Before she'd met Hector.

She wanted it back that way, back when everything was new.

Cessy got a trash bag from the kitchen and shook it open. Put Hector's cop picture inside, along with a pair of his old fraying sneakers that had been sitting against the wall. She went to the bedroom, dried herself and dressed, and then viciously ripped his clothes out of the closet. Thought about sorting them to give some away to Goodwill, but figured nothing of Hector's should remain. Jeans and T-shirts and sweatshirts filled bags, along with boxers and socks and shoes.

The rush to throw everything away slowed, and Cessy found herself examining the clothing. Partially out of a sense of nostalgia.

And she hated herself for it. Hated herself for the confusion of feelings.

She stood. Dressed in jeans, a sweater, a jean jacket, boots. Headed out.

Cessy lived in Fells Point, a picturesque Baltimore neighborhood of cobblestone streets, eccentric shops, and running chains of row houses.

At its prettiest, Fells was a living oil painting; at its worst, it was drunk college kids throwing up on the street on a late Friday night.

Cessy's apartment was west of the tourist trappings, tucked between the stores and the homes. She walked to the water and the crowds of the business district, slipped into a little coffee shop. She stood in line for a few minutes, the men and women in front and behind her on their phones. She'd forgotten hers at the apartment and debated going back to get it. Not that she was expecting any important calls, but she didn't like waiting without anything to do. It made her nervous.

And Cessy always felt like she stood out in Baltimore, a small city that didn't include a large number of Latinos. When men stared at her, she had to wonder why. Was it because she was a woman? How she was dressed? Had she been looking at him? Was it her race? Was the gaze unfriendly? Threatening?

Was she safe?

She hated having to ask herself those questions.

"Can I help you?" a kid behind the counter asked.

Cessy blinked, realized the man in front of her had already ordered and left.

Ever since Hector's death, time had slipped by Cessy without her noticing.

"Yeah, coffee. Nothing special."

The kid stared at the register like he'd never seen it before, then slowly entered the order. "Three thirty-five."

A girl gave Cessy her drink. She heard the line shifting behind her. Pulled out a five and gave it to the cashier.

"Keep it."

She found an empty stool near the window and sat, facing the restaurant. Stared at a mix of older couples talking and young professionals texting. Reminded her of what she'd heard about the past and present of this neighborhood. Fells Point used to be one of the most *Bawlmore* of all the city's neighborhoods, deeply and proudly representative of Baltimore's unique personality, touches of Tyler and Simon and Poe and Holiday and Calloway and Lippman and Coates and Waters mixed together, beehive hairdos and Elvis figurines and marble steps. Softly slurred consonants.

Now it was transients and hipsters and tourists.

Cessy sipped coffee and frowned at the taste. She could have made something just as good at home, wondered if they had the same coffee maker she did. Could have, although she liked to think an actual shop wouldn't be that cheap.

She drank half, left the rest. The liquid splashed into her stomach, landing next to the vodka from the night before.

Not the best sensation.

She realized a man had been watching her the entire time. Cessy wanted to tell him to look somewhere else, but decided against it. She'd already made a bad decision by calling Anthony last night, even if she'd been drunk when she dialed. She didn't want to make another. No reason to be combative.

Cessy headed home.

She went through the rest of Hector's clothes when she got back to the apartment. Went through his nightstand and took out his guns, a pair of surprisingly heavy Glocks. Found a set of knives. Wondered if she should just throw the whole nightstand away and tried to lift it.

Something rustled inside.

Cessy frowned at the nightstand and opened the two drawers again. Empty. She pulled the nightstand toward her and pushed it back. Again, that sound.

She took the drawers out, looked behind them. Turned the nightstand on its side, wincing because she expected to find a dead mouse underneath. Nothing.

Cessy jostled the nightstand again. Pinpointed the sound and kept the nightstand on its side. She tapped the bottom, pressed it. Realized a small square of soft wood was stapled to the bottom. The thin board indented under her fingers, eventually snapped.

A blank, business-sized envelope fell to the floor.

She opened the envelope, pulled out a flash drive.

"Hector," Cessy said to herself, "what kind of disturbing shit is on this?"

She plugged it into her laptop, apprehensively opened a folder containing a group of photos.

Cessy cringed again, assuming she'd see some bizarre, probably illegal, pornography.

Or truth about the affair she'd originally suspected but hadn't wanted to pursue. Hadn't wanted to chance a complication of her feelings.

The first picture was blurry, taken at an odd angle, showed a group of shadowed people milling about. Looked like they might be on a street at night, or maybe a theater stage. Cessy couldn't quite tell. But they were all gathered around something.

She opened another picture and saw more of the same. More shadowed figures, all staring down at something she couldn't make out.

Cessy scrolled through the thirty or so thumbnails, trying to find one that was clear.

She stopped scrolling.

Stopped on a picture that showed two things clearly.

The first was a man holding what appeared to be a gun. For some reason, the camera had decided to make the gun its focus, and the weapon came in clearly. But that wasn't what drew Cessy to the photo.

It was the color red, the blood under a man lying on a bed. His hands were over his chest, his lower body halfway off the bed, eyes open.

Cessy had seen dead bodies before, but it took her a few moments to understand what she was looking at.

A group of men standing around a corpse.

Why would Hector have a photograph of an execution?

Cessy went through the rest of the photos.

Make that six executions.

"What can you tell us about Hector's associates?" the cops had asked the night he'd been killed.

"He hasn't worked for a while," Cessy had told them. "He doesn't have associates."

At least, not that she knew.

Cessy blinked, stood, held on to the sides of the desk. The world was moving too fast, like it was a story told in a language she could barely decipher.

Now, Cessy realized, as she hurried to the bathroom, was the right time to finally throw up.

CHAPTER

5

Aғᴛᴇʀ ʜᴇʀ ʜᴜsʙᴀɴᴅ's funeral, Deb went with Kim to a friend's house, a colleague of Grant's who owned a multimillion-dollar home in Ashburn, a small town on the manicured edges of Northern Virginia. Sandwiches and fruits and vegetables lined a long buffet table, and guests shuffled along, filling their plates. The guests made normal conversation now, in contrast to the service at the church, when their voices were lowered to whispers.

At least, the conversations were normal until people saw Deb. And then their faces and voices dropped, as if ashamed that anything other than her dead husband was on their minds.

"It's a good thing Kim's in college," a man told Deb, speaking with a grimace. "It'd have been awful if this had happened when she was younger."

"Why?"

"You having to raise a child after this happened. All on your own. It'd be so much harder."

You're right. Why didn't I look at the bright side? Dumb fucking me.

But Deb didn't say that. She couldn't say that. She just nodded and walked away.

"When I heard what happened with Grant," a woman told Deb, her eyes wet, "I was so scared. I'd been in an argument with Jeff, and I called him that same day and said I was sorry. You never know what's going to happen. Life's too short to waste arguing."

I'm so glad that my husband's murder helped your marriage.

Again, Deb didn't say that. She merely nodded.

"I'm so sorry for what happened."

"I'm so sorry for what happened."

"I'm so sorry for what happened."

To all of them, Deb said, "Thank you."

She wondered how Kim was doing, saw her daughter sitting on a couch by herself in the corner, staring down at her phone. No one bothered her, and she suspected that's why Kim was doing it.

Smart girl. Deb envied her.

Deb was tired of pity, tired of support. And just *tired*. This type of exhaustion had hit over the past couple of days, particularly as the funeral approached, like a blanket of sleep rising from her feet to her legs, to her waist, to her eyes. When Deb slept, it seemed like she could sleep endlessly.

She didn't want to be awake, remembering Grant was gone. In sleep, he was with her.

"Let's get out of here," someone told her.

Deb turned and saw Nicole Boxer, her best friend, holding her coat.

"Can we?" Deb asked.

Nicole gave her a weird look. "Of course we can. When's the last time you ate?"

Deb wiped her eyes. "I'm not sure."

"I'm going to buy you some food," Nicole decided. "Lots of food. Unhealthy shit. It's important that you learn how to eat your feelings."

"Can I come with you?" Kim asked.

Deb hadn't realized her daughter was standing next to her. "You don't want to go back home?" she asked.

"I don't think so," Kim replied hesitantly. "Not yet."

Twenty minutes later, Deb could tell that the staff at Wegmans grocery wasn't thrilled that she and Kim and Nicole were standing at the front of the grocery store, solemnly dressed in their funeral black while a clerk filled Nicole's order. It wasn't the kind of thing they usually did—having a clerk fetch their food—but after barely leaving their house for a week, the bright lights and busy crowds were overwhelming.

Still, Deb felt better being somewhere completely different. Somewhere with life, with people who had other concerns. Somewhere not filled with memories of Grant.

Deb hadn't realized how desperately she needed a break.

"Have you started online dating yet?" Nicole asked.

"I thought it might be a little soon," Deb replied. "You know, since we just left the service."

"Well, obviously you should change out of the funeral outfit for your profile picture. I've always said you look better in light colors."

Deb smiled. She couldn't help it.

"You're so weird," Kim told her, but kindly. Deb saw the humor in her eyes.

"We'd be a really good dating team," Nicole added. "No issues here, fellows!" That last line was said loudly. Customers turned toward them.

Nicole's husband, Marcus, had died during his military service in Afghanistan, the victim of a helicopter crash. Deb had known Nicole since their first year in college, when they had been randomly assigned as each other's roommate, and had known Marcus nearly as long. His death had shaken everyone, especially since it happened when they were all in their twenties, a time when death was unusual. Deb remembered how tough it had been for Nicole, remembered coming home to Grant and privately feeling grateful (and guilty because she was grateful) that she wasn't going through that same brutal grief.

Over the years since Marcus's death, Nicole had developed a caustic and resilient, if not ill-timed, sense of humor. It could be jarring, even upsetting, for those who didn't know her. But Deb loved it.

That said, she was far from ready to make jokes about her life without Grant. After her small laugh, sadness shadowed her eyes.

Nicole noticed.

"It's like an avalanche inside you, right?" Nicole asked, her voice lowered. "The sadness?"

Both Deb and Kim nodded.

"I remember that feeling. And I remember a lot of guilt. Just a shitload of guilt. I still have it sometimes."

"Why?" Kim asked.

Nicole shrugged loosely, as if guilt was bothering her even now. "Making jokes like I just did about dating. Actually dating. When I started doing anything, really, that felt like I was leaving Marcus behind, like moving to a new apartment." Her eyes turned distant. "Watching an old movie I suddenly remembered he'd wanted to see; you know he loved those. The first year I forgot our anniversary."

Nicole allowed herself a faint, sad smile.

"You're grieving and healing," she said quietly. "It's like running with sore legs. You think it'll feel better to just stop, but you have to learn how. The more you run, the less you eventually notice."

She paused.

"I'm assuming here," Nicole said, her voice back to normal. "I don't run. Or exercise. Obviously."

"Stop," Kim told her.

"I hated every moment of the service," Deb said. "Every moment. I feel shitty about that."

"Me too," Kim agreed, surprise coloring her voice. "I thought it was just me."

"Everyone looks at you the same way," Nicole put in. "Like they can only look you in the eyes for a few seconds."

"And you hear people having normal conversations," Deb said. "Even laughing. Which is okay, I know. But it feels weird."

"Excuse me, but who died?"

The three women had been so wrapped up in their conversation that they hadn't noticed the elderly lady standing off to their side.

"I'm sorry?" Deb asked. The question was so direct that she was taken aback.

"Who died?" the woman asked again. "You just came from a funeral, right?"

"That's really none of your—" Nicole started.

Deb interrupted her. "My husband."

"Oh, I'm so sorry. That must be awful."

She wore glasses and a sweater with a Christmas tree on it. Something about her seemed familiar, but Deb couldn't place her.

"I'm sorry," Deb said. "Do I know you?"

"I don't think so. How was he taken?"

Someone, maybe Kim, inhaled sharply.

"He was shot. It was a robbery."

The woman frowned. "In *this* neighborhood? Was it in the paper?"

"We really don't want to talk about this," Nicole said, assuming the role of family spokesperson.

"It was in the news," Deb said. The police had told Deb they had no idea who had shot Grant. There were no street monitors nearby, no visual witnesses, and the murderer had stayed beyond the reach of the ATM's cameras. Traffic cameras in the area revealed nothing suspicious. A witness heard but didn't see the two shots. The bullets and shells were being studied but were unlikely to reveal anything useful.

And, as she'd told Kim, there had been a rash of similar murders recently, but no clue as to who was committing them.

The elderly woman loudly sighed. "So awful."

"It was. It is."

"I'll pray for you."

Deb nodded.

Once the older woman left, Kim exploded. "What the hell was that?"

"She was just curious," Deb said.

"She was rude. Who does that shit?"

"Language," Deb told her mildly.

"Seriously, Mom. What. The. Hell."

"You're a lot more patient than I am," Nicole put in.

"Maybe. I need to pee," Deb announced tiredly.

That was true, but Deb really just wanted a moment to herself. She headed to the restroom, leaving Kim and Nicole still complaining, and passed small tables near Wegmans restaurant, displays of flowers and meat and snack food. She briefly stopped to stare at some cupcakes. She wasn't hungry, but thought they would make a nice thank you for Nicole.

And then Deb remembered what Grant's accountant had told her the other day, something about an issue with Grant's finances: the payments from his life insurance were going to be delayed. Deb had been too distracted to fully comprehend anything, a distraction the accountant seemed to understand.

"We can talk about this later," he'd said. "For now, though, keep an eye on your spending."

The restroom at Wegmans was for individuals—a single toilet and sink. Deb locked the door behind her and leaned against the wall, arms crossed tightly over her chest. Sadness had been crawling inside of her all day, hoarsening her voice, making the sun too bright. Now it broke loose.

Deb cried helplessly into her hands.

Jesus Christ, those tears. Like all the water in her body was being wrung out.

But of all the tears Deb had ever wept, none felt like this.

None left her so gutted and empty and scared.

It took Deb a few minutes to pull herself together, check herself in the mirror, leave the bathroom. She walked through the crowded grocery store to her daughter and her best friend, and found Kim crying on Nicole's shoulder.

She touched Kim, pulling her close.

"We'll be okay," Deb whispered to her daughter. "We'll be okay."

Deb didn't believe herself, but she was surprised at how honest the words sounded.

CHAPTER

6

THE KNOCKING WOULDN'T stop.

Annoyed, Cessy muted the television, downed the rest of her Guinness, and pulled herself off the couch. Opened her apartment door.

A sudden hand on her chest shoved her inside.

A man walked into her apartment, closed and locked the door behind him.

"What . . . ?" Cessy started, thinking about Hector's heavy guns, wishing she hadn't sold them to a pawn shop. "Who are you?"

The man walked past her, calmly sat on her couch. He was medium height, with short, thin blond hair. Muscles pushed through his long-sleeved shirt, as if his shirt was too tight, as if any shirt would be too tight. Tight line of a mouth, squinted blue eyes.

"Cessy Castillo?"

"Yeah?"

Cessy was trying to appear less worried than she was, but her mind raced. She had no idea who this man was, what he wanted, why he was here. She stood uncertainly, legs tensed, ready to dart to the door.

"Don't run," he told her. "I don't want to hurt you, but I will."

The sentence hung in the air.

"Who are you?" Cessy asked.

"I worked with Hector."

She folded her arms over her chest. Tried to put some strength in her voice. "Hector didn't work."

"Oh, he worked. You just don't know about it."

She wasn't sure what he meant, but had an idea.

Cessy thought about the pictures she'd found the day before, the photos of the executions.

"But he also borrowed," the man continued. "Especially from the people he worked for."

Cessy felt cold inside.

"What was he doing?"

The man just regarded her. Didn't respond.

She tried again. "How much was he in for?"

"Fifteen grand."

Dammit, Hector.

The man glanced around her small apartment. "Doesn't seem like he shared the money with you, so you probably didn't know about it. But he owed it. Still does."

"I don't know what to tell you. Hector's dead."

"You're not."

Cessy kept acting like she didn't know better. As if there was a chance this man had only come into her home to tell her about, and then excuse, Hector's debt. "I'm just a bartender. I don't have that kind of money."

He draped his left arm out over the couch, as if over an invisible girlfriend sitting next to him.

"I have an idea on how you can pay it back," he said.

Cessy looked warily at him.

"You could do what your mom did," he went on.

Cessy's left hand tightened into a fist.

The two of them stared at each other.

"I know all about you, Cessy Castillo," he said. "Hector told me everything. I even know why you're here, what brought you to Baltimore. What you're running from. What's in your blood to do."

Her eyes burned. "Fuck you."

"Exactly." He stood up from the couch, walked over to her. "Come up with the money soon, or you'd better take that idea seriously. And don't try the cops. We have the cops. Hector's not the only one who kept a foot in each lane."

"I can't pay you."

He looked her up and down, the gaze as violent as hands clawing her.

"You can."

Cessy locked the door after he left.

Her phone was in her hand before she realized it. She glanced down at her brother's number, thought about calling.

This was the first time Cessy had felt afraid since Hector's death.

But she wasn't ready to run.

Especially not to her brother.

Moments of sadness had hit her, occasionally stopped her cold, motionless, lost in some conflict of memories of when Hector had been loving . . . and then his face contorted in rage, his fists fast and everywhere. Cessy would be lost in those thoughts until a stranger's concerned voice woke her, in a store, on the street, at the bar, and she'd come back to the realization that Hector was gone, that those parts of her life were over.

That she was safe.

She'd escaped, freed herself from his violence and unpredictable anger. Walked away from his corpse without looking back.

But it turned out Hector could still hurt her. The visit from that blond man was like Hector's cold hand breaking through the earth, grabbing her wrist, forcing her to stay with him. Hector still making sure Cessy stayed in the shadows, keeping their darkness stretched over her.

* * *

Cessy spent the next few days looking over her shoulder, dreading a knock on the door, wondering how she could possibly pay the debt Hector had left. She took inventory of everything she owned, found it hard to see how anything in her apartment would come to more than a few hundred dollars.

She went back to work, still worried, hoping the bar was a good place to distract herself from these concerns. And, fortunately, regulars at the Fells Gate Tavern had realized they didn't need to tiptoe around Cessy about Hector's death. She was grateful for that. She'd hated the pitying looks that first week, the way voices softened when they talked to her.

Especially because no one had been nearly that concerned when Hector was alive and bruising her.

Not that they knew, Cessy reminded herself as she strained a whiskey sour, set it down next to a seven and seven. She picked up a twenty.

At least, probably not.

"Keep it," a regular named Michael Thompson, a former St. Francis high school football star, said.

Cessy looked at the twenty, surprised. "You sure?"

"All you," he said, and turned toward his girlfriend, Stacy Griffith, a cute short blonde. "Watch my drinks."

He headed to the restroom.

"I need to get him to be that generous with me," Stacy said.

Cessy could tell Michael felt sorry for her, which explained the large tip. It lingered in men, that sadness. The women felt it too, but they paid attention to Cessy, could tell she didn't want condolences.

"Is that new?" Stacy asked, and pointed at Cessy's shoulder.

It was a Japanese-style tattoo, showed an old man staring at a lake and a small rowboat docked on the shore.

"Couple of months? I might have been wearing something that covered it when you were in here."

Stacy leaned over the bar to get a closer look. "I like it," she announced. "Lot of nice detail for a small space."

"What about you?" Cessy asked. "Any new ones?"

Stacy didn't have any visible tattoos, but Cessy knew her back was inked. "Another dragon on my right leg. The tail curves around my thigh."

"Sexy lady."

"Mike likes it." She drank from her seven and seven, set it down, pulled out her phone, and glanced into it. "You okay, hon?"

Cessy reached down, scratched her knee. "Did you guys know about Hector?"

Stacy was using her phone to check herself out. She adjusted her shirt. "What about him?"

"That he—that he had a temper."

"Really?"

"Yeah."

Silence between them, the pause pregnant.

"I mean," Stacy said uneasily, "all guys have tempers."

Michael walked back, took his whiskey. "Thanks again, Cess."

He and Stacy went back to their table. She didn't talk to Cessy again.

Cessy walked home after work, fall and twilight in the city. She'd worked the afternoon shift and it wasn't quite dark yet, and the city held a pinkish-purple glow. It was nice, not enough to distract her, but nice. Cessy's favorite time of the year was late afternoon summers, when she'd leave work and walk among people happy about ending the day, excited about their evenings. The way apartment windows stayed up without concern for weather, high enough not to be worried about rats or robberies. That was when she'd first come here from Arizona, when she lost herself in Fells Point's cheerful embrace.

Three years had passed since then.

It felt like lifetimes.

Cessy walked into her apartment, pulled a beer out of the fridge, collapsed on the couch. Turned on the television and stared dully at the violence on the evening news.

She went to the bedroom, opened a drawer in the nightstand, pulled out the photos she'd printed.

She stared at the pictures, the blurry shots of masked men standing around bodies.

Cessy thought again about the money she owed, wondered what she'd have to do to get it.

Wondered what would happen if she didn't have it.

And she felt Hector's pull, like his hand was once again yanking her wrist, pulling her to pain, to fear.

To someone she desperately didn't want to be.

7

"Why don't you take some more time?"

Clark Carlson's voice was kind.

Deb held the phone tight, tried one last time.

"Look, Clark, I know you don't think I'm ready. But that's not the case. Yeah, I'm not fully recovered, but I don't know if I ever will be. I just know that I need to start working again. And I know you're gearing up for your next health-care push."

"You know about that?"

"There's always a next health-care push."

Clark laughed abruptly. "You're right."

Silence.

Deb looked around her backyard, the unkempt grass and ragged bushes. It was too late in the year to do anything about it, but she still felt the urge to garden. She liked kneeling in the dirt, layering mulch, pulling plants from their pots, giving new life to soil.

Grief had distracted her from so many things she used to enjoy.

And when she remembered them, it was like they were activities someone else had done. Hobbies that entertained a different person, long ago.

"The thing is," Clark was telling her, "we really don't have anything right now. You're right, we're working on a couple of big PR campaigns, but we staffed them weeks ago. And I would have called you, but I heard what happened and . . ."

His voice trailed away.

Deb stared at a small withered tree. She couldn't remember what kind it was. Normally, she could name all the plants in the backyard, but this one escaped her. It was a young tree, planted less than a year ago, thin and winding, like a person hugging herself.

"But if things change," she said, "you'll keep me in mind?"

"Definitely." Clark paused. "Is this . . . can I ask you, is this because you need money? Are you hurting? I mean, financially."

"I'm okay."

Another pause. "I wouldn't ask if we weren't friends. Oh, side note. Speaking of friends, you know Susan Myers? I'm meeting her for dinner tonight."

Deb hadn't really considered Clark a friend; she always kept her clients—especially her male clients—on a different tier. But she wasn't going to disabuse him of that notion. "Tell Sue I said hi. And really, I'm fine. I just want to get back to work. Give myself something to do."

"Are you sure?" he pressed. "With what happened with Grant, it must be a lot to deal with."

Deb wasn't sure where Clark was going with this. "It is. But like I said, I just want to work. And I really liked working with CPP in the past and would be happy to do so again."

"So how are you doing?" he persisted.

This was how the men reacted. An odd mix of wanting to be helpful and, underneath that surface, naked curiosity. Like violence was a fire to which they were drawn.

"I'm getting there."

"How's Kim? She's at Maryland, right?"

"Washington College, over in the Eastern Shore."

"Right, right," Clark said. "But she's doing okay?"

"She dropped her classes this semester. But she'll be okay."

"Have the police found any leads?"

"No."

"Are they still investigating? Have you thought about hiring a private investigator?"

"I'm not sure one could turn up anything the police couldn't."

"You never know. Might be something to consider."

"It might," Deb said wearily. *Deciduous* tree? Was that the term?

"And money's okay?"

Well, Deb thought, *you asked.*

"No. It's not. And I'm not sure what we're going to do."

Hesitancy returned to Clark's voice. "Yeah?"

"Our finance guy came by yesterday, and he went over Grant's accounts. We don't have as much as I thought we did."

"Well, that sounds . . ."

"Grant used his four-oh-one," Deb went on. "I never knew that. I mean, I wasn't one of those women who doesn't know anything about our finances . . . but I feel, like, maybe I was? And it just makes me feel so irresponsible. Like, how could I not know that he'd borrowed against his four-oh-one?"

"Didn't you have to sign for that?"

"He forged my signature. He forged it." Deb touched her eyes, let the tears come. "I found all this out yesterday."

"Do you know what he used the money for?"

"No, I never knew about any of this. I just feel so stupid."

"You shouldn't feel that way."

"But our lives are . . . I mean, Kim's college."

"Oh, right," Clark said uneasily. The tenor of his voice had changed. Deb could tell he wanted to get off the phone. This was more than he'd bargained for.

But Clark had pressed and pressed and, *dammit*, now he was going to deal with her.

"We can get loans, but they don't cover everything. There's a chance Kim may have to move schools. Go in-state so we can afford the tuition. And I don't know how to tell her that. She loves Washington College."

"Well, I think she'll understand . . ."

Deb was crying now. "She has some boyfriend there. I don't know. If I can find a way to keep her there, I will. It's just, I feel so stupid. I've been so out of touch with all this, and I wasn't that kind of wife. We didn't have that kind of marriage. I just stopped paying attention after a while. I mean, Grant worked in finance. Everything was covered. Money wasn't even something I thought about."

"One second," she heard Clark tell someone.

"We weren't rich," Deb told him. "And we didn't have much when we first got married. We lived in this tiny, one-bedroom apartment in Arlington until Kim was four. It was so small we could barely fit a couch inside. But things got better, and we got comfortable, and it was nice not to pay attention to anything like that. I should have."

"Deb, I hate to do this, but I really need to get going."

"I just don't know what he used the money for."

Silence.

"So . . ." Clark said. "I really have to go."

Deb wiped her eyes. "You'll let me know if anything comes up?"

"I will," Clark said. "I definitely will."

Deb hung up the phone, tapped it against her chin.

"Wow," Nicole said, sitting on a small stone bench across from her. "Talk about unloading."

"He thinks I'm a mess," Deb told her friend. "And he'll tell everyone he talks to about this conversation. Clark's a gossip."

Nicole recrossed her legs, briskly rubbed the cold from her thighs. "So why'd you go both barrels on him?"

Deb dabbed her eyes. "He said he's seeing Susan Myers tonight. He's going to tell her I was a wreck. She and I are supposed to talk tomorrow about a job, and she'll be sympathetic. She lost her husband a few years ago to cancer."

Nicole stared at her. "You devious little bitch. I like you a little more now."

"All that was waiting to come out. I just let it." Deb paused. "He kept pressing me."

"Do you really need money? I don't have any, but I'll help you rob a bank or something."

"I might."

"Were you serious about Grant's accounts?"

"It's even worse. Everything's gone. He drained his retirement. Cancelled his life insurance. We have what's left in our checking account, and that's it after a few months."

Deb walked over to her friend, sat down next to her, leaned against her shoulder.

"Are you trying to go through my purse?" Nicole asked.

"Shut up and hold me." Deb felt Nicole's arm over her.

The two women sat silently for a few moments.

"What are you going to do?" Nicole asked.

"Sell the house. Kim doesn't live here anymore, and I don't need a place this big. I can get an apartment or a townhouse. Something smaller, with enough room for Kim when she comes back to visit. And this house is full of memories of Grant; it makes me sad. It'll be good to leave."

"What about Kim's college?"

"This year is paid for. We'll have to take out loans for the next two, but I'll help her pay those back. I don't want her to have to change her life any more than she already has."

"What do you think Grant did with the money?" Nicole asked hesitantly.

"Honestly, I have no idea."

The two women watched a bird land on a branch, tiptoe awkwardly, then fly away.

Nicole left just before dinner. Kim had plans with friends and wasn't expected back until late. Deb didn't feel like cooking, so she heated a Lean Cuisine, paired it with a glass of wine, ate on the couch in front of the television. The DVR was full of shows she and Grant used to watch, programs they enjoyed together but she would probably never watch on her own—courtroom dramas, cop shows titled after prominent American cities, one or two popular sitcoms.

She turned on the news. Saw a teaser for a story about a murdered man, shot twice, the police confirming it was in similar fashion to other recent murders.

Deb quickly changed channels until she landed on a competition show about woodworking, forced herself to get sucked in. The contestants had been placed in teams and were designing and crafting gazebos. The camera lingered over the process of wood being selected, measured, a circular saw sinking its teeth into a board.

Deb woke on the couch, confused. Hours had passed. The television was off, a blanket pulled over her.

"Mom, are you drunk?"

Deb blinked, saw Kim holding her wine glass. She rubbed her eyes, sat up.

"Just tired. What time is it?"

"Almost two."

"You were out late."

The comment was a combination of observation and complaint, but Kim didn't take offense to it. She sat on the chair adjacent to the couch, picked up Deb's wine glass, swirled the drops of red wine pooled in the bottom.

Deb could tell something was bothering her. "Do you need to talk?"

Kim set the glass down, kept staring at it as she spoke. "I need to tell you something."

"Oh boy." Deb sat up, tried to calm the nerves rustling her stomach.

"It's not the end of the world or anything."

"You don't want to go back to school."

"What? No, I do."

"You're pregnant."

"Mom, stop guessing."

Those nerves refused to settle. "It's okay. You can tell me anything. You know that, right?"

Kim was rubbing her hands together. "It's about someone I'm dating."

Deb couldn't help guessing again, her words coming out fast. "Did he hurt you?"

"No. And he's not a *he.*"

Kim watched her mother, let that sink in.

Deb blinked.

"Oh!" She paused. "Really?"

"She lives down the hall from me. We've been together almost half a year." Kim looked helplessly, hopelessly worried. "Are you mad?"

As often happened when something momentous happened with Kim, Deb remembered when her daughter was just a little girl. When she was three or four and loved being held, and it seemed like Deb and Grant would never let her feet touch the ground. When she first learned to walk and ran unsteadily back and forth between them. When she first laughed.

Kim embraced drama as she grew older. Deb vividly remembered the fights, the stomped feet, sharp intakes of breath. Slammed doors.

And then, later, there was a time when everything was hell, when Kim seemed uncontrollable and inconsiderate, attracted to something dark that was foreign to Deb and Grant. They'd both grown up with their own share of wild times and regretted nights, and assumed they'd be prepared for anything a teenage daughter could throw at them. But they weren't ready for the terrifying insouciance that came with the attitude, like Kim was standing at the entrance of a dark alley. But not just standing. She was beckoning. Smiling.

That was high school.

In college, their daughter returned.

Maybe it was loneliness or not living in the same house or Grant's exhortations to treat Kim as an adult, but Deb noticed that much of her daughter's difficulty had left. Kim would visit them on weekends; sit at the small, sunny breakfast table in the kitchen, huddled over a cup of coffee; ask them about their jobs and friends. Like any kid, Kim still liked talking more than listening, but the fact that she listened at all was a welcome change.

"Mom?"

"What did your friends say?"

"They're all cool with it. What's wrong?"

Deb stayed silent, trying to determine the best way to say what was on her mind.

"Mom?"

"I don't care who you love," Deb said. "I just want you to be safe. It's a hard world for anyone who's different." That fear Deb had felt back when Kim started college returned, the worries about drinking, rape, bullying, peer pressure, drug use, death.

"I'm not going to hide who I am," Kim said impatiently. "I shouldn't have to do that."

"No, I know . . ."

"This is who I am. I'm attracted to men and women."

Kim was defiant, her thin arms crossed over her chest, narrowed eyes daring Deb to disagree.

"This is who I am," Kim repeated.

"I'm just worried about you."

"Can't you be happy for me?"

"I'm always going to worry about you. Even when I'm happy for you."

Kim's face darkened. "Rebecca said you wouldn't be on board."

"Rebecca is . . ."

"She's my girlfriend."

That defiance in Kim, burning. She wanted to fight.

"Was it scary?" Deb asked.

Something in Kim faltered. "Was what scary?"

"To discover this about yourself. Was it scary?"

Kim and Deb looked at each other.

"A little bit," Kim finally said. "Like, I'd always thought other women were pretty, but I didn't, like, *feel* anything for them. You know? Not attraction. And I didn't want to tell anyone. I wanted to figure this out for myself."

"You didn't want to tell me?"

"I didn't know how you and Dad would react." Uncertainty clouded Kim's face.

You and Dad.

Deb was relieved that Grant wasn't with her.

Deb had always found that men took this kind of news differently than women. Men needed to accept it, to first rationalize what it meant to *them.* Almost as if they worried that by accepting this change, their own sexuality would be threatened.

"You're not mad at me?" Kim asked.

"For not telling me?"

"For who I am."

"Of course not."

But Deb didn't tell her daughter the worries racing through her mind.

That identifying as bisexual or lesbian would push Kim even further to society's margins, far beyond where her mixed race already had.

There was more acceptance nowadays of cultures outside of straight and white, but those steps had been hard-fought and reluctantly granted, and could easily be walked back. The DMV (the intersection of DC, Maryland, and Virginia) was wonderfully diverse, but bigotry existed. Maybe it wasn't overtly shown in marches or demonstrations, but Deb had felt it in subtler ways.

Like the time Grant's father had asked Deb if it bothered her that she was "basically white. Not like other Asians."

Deb had heard variations of this statement her entire life, as if there was some general Asian stereotype she didn't fit. To some, her adoption by a white woman disqualified her. To others, she was too educated compared to other Asians, and still others complained that she wasn't educated enough. She didn't speak Vietnamese, and people felt that was ostracizing, and even her studied knowledge of the history and culture of Vietnam wasn't enough to satisfy them.

When you were a minority, Deb had learned, you had to fit into a certain definable context. A satisfying context.

You simply couldn't just *be*.

And there was the time a man had muttered, as she walked past him, "Slope." Deb, a college freshman at the time, had never heard the term and asked a friend what it meant. She remembered her instinct, upon learning the insult, was to wonder what she had done wrong, to replay her walk down that street over and over in her mind. It took Deb a while to realize she didn't deserve his stupidity or hate. It took longer for her to disregard that instinct for self-examination.

And there was the time a white girlfriend had confessed to her that she'd never let her children date someone from another race. "Not because I'm racist," her friend had explained, "but it'd just be so hard for them." As if Deb was supposed to sympathize. As if Deb was supposed to realize the problems she presented. As if racism was her burden, her fault.

There was something about the casualness in all of Deb's experiences with bigotry that was so ingrained, so deep-seated, that it didn't seem possible to dislodge, like a stone sunk into the earth. And it didn't seem fair to Deb that she should be expected to dislodge that stone, to stain her hands with someone else's dirt.

Kim's race hadn't been the kind of pained thorn Deb had experienced, as far as Deb knew anyway. But she was desperately determined to give Kim somewhere safe, a place she could run to. Race and sexuality weren't the same, but bigotry was bigotry, and Deb was fucking tired of it.

She and Kim had lost so much. It was nice to have something gained, to hear the hope and love beneath Kim's words.

"What's Rebecca like?" Deb asked.

"She's really nice."

Deb waited.

"Like, really nice, but maybe a little edgier than I am? Like, she wears a lot of black and listens to so much music. You'd be so impressed at how much she knows about music and musicians. And she's really smart. *So* smart. We have the best talks. She's not really into fashion, but she always looks good. Like it's just part of her, you know? And . . ."

Her daughter kept talking.

Deb listened, tired but happy that her daughter wanted to talk to her. They talked as light broke through the windows. They talked as a new day began.

Cessy wanted a distraction, and so she was happier than usual for her monthly trip to Baltimore's Halfway House for Victims of Sex Trafficking, Domestic Violence, and Other Forms of Modern Human Slavery. She loved volunteering at the Federal Hill home, even if the halfway house needed, in addition to a shorter name, a new everything else. The bars over the windows were rusted, the marble steps cracked, graffiti still visible under the white paint meant to cover it.

"How's it going, Rose?" Cessy asked as she pulled the stubborn front door closed.

Rose seemed smaller to Cessy, the way she did every visit. Not only in height; her face, hands, everything about her seemed to be turning into a miniaturized version of herself. Cessy knew it wasn't just because Rose had recently hit seventy. It was the victims, the escapees, their PTSD, often their desperate fight to stave off drugs. The pressures of running the house were crippling.

And Rose ran a strict program, a mix of counseling and community service, tasking the residents with projects ranging from picking up trash to cooking and serving food, to repairing donated clothing.

"It's going fine," Rose told her. "All four rooms taken."

"That a good thing?"

"Eh."

"Anyone new?"

"One. Want to go up and say hi? That what the bag's for?" Rose pointed to the plastic shopping bag Cessy carried.

Cessy opened it, showed Rose the contents. "Nothing exciting," she said. "Just some snacks. The new girl okay with visitors?"

"It's you, so yes." Rose studied her, then asked Cessy the same question Rose had asked for the past three months, ever since she'd accidentally seen bruises on Cessy's shoulder. "Did you leave that asshole son of a bitch?"

"Well, that asshole son of a bitch is dead. So yes."

Years of working with battered women had hardened Rose. "Good. Cheaper than a divorce."

"That's one way to look at it."

"Did someone kill him? Figured Hector was getting into stupid shit with stupid people."

"That's exactly what happened."

Rose grunted. "You should have told me what he was doing a lot earlier."

"Probably." Something in the conversation bothered Cessy; Rose's satisfaction with Hector's death. That attitude didn't feel right to Cessy, regardless of what Hector had done. Regardless of how Cessy had grown to hate him.

And it reminded her of the text she'd received an hour earlier. The message waiting for her response.

"I'm going up," she said. "What's the new girl's name? And what room?"

"Dana. Second room on the left."

Cessy walked up the creaky narrow stairs, holding on to a loose banister with chipped white paint. The stairs led to a narrow hall with faded, flat brown carpet. Two doorways were on her right, two on her left, the halls bookended by small, outdated bathrooms. Baltimore's Halfway House for Victims of Sex Trafficking, Domestic Violence, and Other Forms of Modern Human Slavery did many good things, but no one would call it luxurious.

Cessy walked to Dana's room, heard the whispers of televisions from the three other rooms in the hall. This was one of the few hours the residents had to themselves.

She knocked. A mattress creaked. Footsteps approached the door. "Who is it?"

The voice was deeper than Cessy would have guessed.

"Cessy Castillo. I'm a friend of Rose."

The door opened. A tall, thin young black man peered at Cessy from behind square-framed glasses.

Cessy glanced past him, confused.

"Looking for a woman?" he asked.

"Well, yeah. Rose didn't tell me." Cessy thought back to their conversation. "Or correct me."

His caution broke into a smile. "What's in the bag?"

"Chips, Coke."

"When you say Coke, you mean . . . ?"

"Nice try."

"Eh, come in anyway." He stepped back and let Cessy in his room. "Sorry, I haven't done much with the place."

A bed in the corner, a narrow writing desk under a window on the other side, a small closet, an outdated television mounted on a stand. A poster on the wall dictated the house rules:

No drinking, no drugs.
No fighting or stealing.
Think: Would an asshole do this? Then don't.

Cessy pulled out the chair from the writing desk. "You could 'guy' it up. Put up some posters of topless chicks on motorcycles, that sort of thing."

Dana made a face. "Yeah, that sort of thing isn't really my sort of thing."

Cessy grinned. She reached into the shopping bag, pulled out a Coke, handed him one, opened one for herself. They both drank deeply. She savored how the soda sizzled down her throat.

Cessy opened the chips. "How do you like the place?"

"I mean, it's okay," Dana reached for a handful. "Better than where I was. Rose seems cool. Maybe a little strict."

"Maybe?"

"I can't complain, right? Got free food, a free bed, so she can make whatever rules she wants." He stuffed the potato chips in his mouth.

"You been in a place like this before?"

"Not a house like this. But I just got out of rehab."

She glanced at his arms. "You don't have tracks."

"Alcohol. Mainly." Dana didn't elaborate. Cessy could sense him retreating back into his shell.

"The food here sucks though, right?" Cessy asked. "Rose is a shitty cook."

Dana nodded.

"Sorry I asked about your past." Cessy offered a smile. "I'm not a trained counselor or doc, so I don't really know what I'm doing with these conversations."

"Then why are you here?"

"My mom was on the streets."

"Working?"

"That's right." Cessy paused, thought again about the text message waiting for her response. "It really messed me and my brother up."

Cessy leaned over her crossed legs, paused.

She had to speak carefully here. This always affected her, and Cessy had learned that whatever she said needed to be like a pebble skipping over a lake.

If she lingered, she risked slipping under the surface.

Cessy couldn't risk remembering what she and her brother had done. If she did, she'd drown.

"My brother and I went separate ways after our mom died," she said. "I moved here, ended up in group counseling. That's where I met Rose. She asked me to start coming here about a year ago."

"To what, check up on everyone? See who she'll have trouble with?"

Cessy touched her throat as if she could smooth away the lump, the memory of her mother. "I don't know how to tell who she'll have trouble with. Most of the people who come here are scared. Desperate. The only trouble they cause is when they sneak out and leave. Rose doesn't let them back."

"That's what I mean. Strict." Dana ate a chip, and his face softened. "How's Rose afford this place anyway?"

"She made a ton of money in the nineties dot-com boom. Got out before it went bust, invested it, and those investments paid off. Now she runs this place."

"The nineties?"

"She's not exactly young. Anyway, that's my story. What's yours?"

"My grandfather wouldn't stop sleeping with me. Never ended until I ran away."

Cessy wanted to ask more but didn't. Just ate some chips and waited.

"I ended up dating different men. A couple of them put me on the street."

"Said they needed money, right?"

"Exactly." Dana munched for a moment. "Didn't take long for them to turn from boyfriends to pimps."

They ate in silence, both lost in their past, each wondering how much to share. Cessy hadn't lied about anything she'd said, including being new at this. She didn't have formal training or instructions. Rose just wanted her to talk to new arrivals.

Cessy had never been sure why Rose had singled her out, why she had taken her aside after one of the meetings in the basement of that church on Light Street, asked her to come by her house. And Cessy wasn't sure why she'd gone, how she'd ended up sitting at a table with Rose and a young newcomer to the home. The newcomer had come to the house recalcitrant, reluctant, but ended up talking with Cessy, the two of them soon laughing.

Cessy often felt like everything she did was still with the hope of escaping what she'd left when she first came to Baltimore. And maybe that was why new residents of the house opened up to her. They sensed a fellow runaway.

Or maybe they sensed that Cessy was still running, and they needed that. The comfort of knowing everything was temporary, because permanence had been a nightmare.

Her phone buzzed. She pulled it out of her jacket pocket, glanced down at the screen.

"I need to take this."

Cessy left the bedroom, headed down one of the halls to a communal bathroom. Closed and locked the door behind her.

Read the text again. It was the same one she'd received earlier.

You decided what to do?

She didn't recognize the number, but knew who the message was from.

The blond man who'd come to her apartment about the money Hector owed.

He was done waiting.

CHAPTER

9

Deb gave up on reading, set the Anne Tyler novel on her garden bench. Fault didn't lie with the author; it was hard for Deb to concentrate on anything without grief slipping through like cold air through a window crack.

Deb ran her hands through her hair, briefly massaged the back of her neck. And heard the distant sound of her doorbell.

Deb left the garden, walked through the house, assuming it was a delivery man with another gift from sympathizing friends or family.

Grant's family, anyway. Her mother had passed away years ago.

A man stood on her porch. He wore a dark suit, the jacket unbuttoned, a thin black tie.

"Mrs. Thomas?"

"Yes?"

"My name is Levi Price." He pronounced *Levi* the opposite of the jeans: "leh-vee." "I'm with the Federal Bureau of Investigation. And I need to talk to you."

He handed her an ID.

"Why?" Deb looked down at the badge in her hand. Stared into the stern photo, gold shield, embossed lettering. She couldn't help but be suspicious. Nicole had warned her about people who took advantage of widowers, cons who sought victims at their most troubled. Damaged people who formed some sort of attachment to a news story, like strangers calling the police to confess to a crime they hadn't committed.

"It's about your husband," Levi said after she gave the billfold back. "But we really shouldn't talk here. May I come inside?"

Deb ignored his request. "What about my husband?"

Still the present tense of the phrase—*my husband*. Like Deb was still connected to Grant, to a body, not just a soul.

Deb wondered if that would ever change.

She wondered if she would let it.

"He wasn't killed in a robbery."

Something in Deb stiffened.

"What do you mean?"

Her own voice sounded unfamiliar to her. Rough.

"Your husband was under investigation by the FBI," Levi said patiently, his blue eyes soft. "I'm sorry you had to find out this way. The investigation didn't extend to his family."

"Why?"

That small word was a big question, could refer to hundreds of different questions Deb had asked herself over the past weeks.

Levi glanced around again. "I really think we should talk someplace more private."

She didn't offer him a drink when they sat down at her kitchen table, in the window nook overlooking her backyard.

Levi leaned forward in his chair, one elbow on the table.

Deb sat across from him.

"There have been a number of recent deaths in the area," he began. "All men, all shot in the same way as your husband."

"I know, I keep seeing it on the news." Deb's voice was scraping, coarsening sadness. "The police told me that too. But they said they don't know who's doing it."

Levi was cautious when he spoke again.

"Did your husband ever mention a woman named Maria Vasquez?"

Deb shook her head. "Who is she?"

"Maria was a prostitute. Grant was one of her clients."

Deb stood, walked over to the sink, leaned over it.

She didn't feel the metal under her hands, couldn't even see straight. Her legs felt like they were threatening to float away.

When had she started crying?

"We don't believe Vasquez killed him," Levi went on, his voice patient and persistent. "But we have reason to believe these murders are being committed by a different prostitute. That this is some sort of revenge against clients."

Clients.

Deb's hands tightened over the edge of the sink.

"Grant was a client?"

"I'm sorry," Levi said.

Deb searched her memories. She tried to remember the late nights Grant worked, the trips he'd taken, any guilt or distraction. There were some oddities—days or weeks when he was distant to her—but Deb had always ascribed those times to the normalcies of any marriage. The rough spots, raising Kim when her relationship with Grant was strained. The small arguments she and Grant had—about money, about the house—that spiraled into heated fights.

But nothing to warrant this.

Nothing to deserve this.

"Were there other women your husband mentioned in a way that seemed unusual?" Levi was asking.

"What?"

"Did your husband ever mention other women in a way that seemed unusual?"

"I don't know."

Deb's own voice was faint to her ears.

Grant had always had female friends, a fact that bothered Deb early in their relationship. It was never something she got used to or fully accepted, and although she trusted him, she rarely trusted any of the women he knew. Not completely. He was a natural flirt but claimed to be a harmless one and, to be fair, Deb never had reason to doubt him. Even in tough times during their marriage, Grant had never strayed.

At least, not that she had known.

Deb had always felt like *she'd* be the one to wander. She'd experienced passing or lingering attractions to other men, coworkers, a neighbor or two, once a friend's husband. But none of those had moved beyond a playful flirtation, at least on her part. Occasionally the men seemed to want more, and then she'd guiltily retreat, ashamed, worried she'd led them on.

But Deb had pondered her resilience, wondered what would happen if the perfect opportunity presented itself. It wasn't hard for her to imagine having an affair.

Even if it was more a case of teasing herself.

"I didn't think he'd been with anyone else," she said. "Ever."

Levi watched her.

Except for this prostitute he'd paid.

All this time she'd doubted Grant had the willingness to cheat on her, that he'd never take any of those relationships beyond a friendship.

A prostitute.

The idea of Grant having sex with a woman on the streets, the money and the disease, felt like it would sicken her.

"Did Grant ever mention men's names you didn't recognize?"

"Men?"

"It's possible they could be other clients or pimps. We need to find them. Before she does." Levi rubbed the back of his neck. "The other similarity these victims shared is the amount of money they spent. It was beyond the normal cost of solicitation. Enough to warrant our involvement. In some cases, these men embezzled from their companies."

Another knife in Deb.

"How much did Grant give her?"

A pause.

"Tens of thousands."

The world kept falling away from Deb. She turned from the sink and faced Levi.

"That much?"

He nodded. "It's not uncommon for men to form an attachment, to give money for groceries, rent, clothes, bills. Especially if the professional relationship lasts and becomes personal." Levi paused again, seemed to weigh his words. "But I can keep you informed of anything I find, once we have information privy to share."

"I don't want to know . . . I don't want to know any of this."

Levi pulled a card and pen out of his pocket, turned it over, scribbled on the back. "This is my cell phone. You can contact me whenever you'd like. I'll be in touch, but know that these investigations can take a while."

"Is there danger?"

"Sorry?"

"Is there any danger? From the woman killing these men?"

"We don't believe so. But keep an eye out for anything unusual."

Anything unusual.

Nothing would ever be usual.

Nothing would ever be the same. Grant had changed the world and left Deb behind to stagger through unbalanced. With nothing to grasp.

"Please," Levi finished, "feel free to contact me if anything comes up."

He left.

Deb stayed in the kitchen, looking at the table and chairs and drawers and sink and cabinets as if she'd never seen them before.

10

THE KILLER WAS there as Agent Levi Price left Deb's home. Price stopped like he wanted to say something, then kept walking to his car.

The killer wanted to go inside, wanted to rush into Deb's house, but had already been inside her home.

Many times.

Deb had never known. The killer was quiet about it. Even standing next to Deb while she slept, her face in pain. Like she was dreaming about Grant.

Had stood over Kim too. That was harder because Kim closed the bedroom door; Deb left hers open. Kim's doorknob had to be held tight, slowly twisted, pushed open without letting the door creak or catch. Just to make sure the girl was home and wouldn't show up while the killer was staring down at her mother.

Kim slept naked, but the killer barely looked at her.

Didn't care about Kim, only Deb.

The killer could watch Deb endlessly, lost in love and beauty, but had other things to do in the house.

Two nights ago the killer spent hours in the basement, until morning's pale winter sun. It didn't seem like Kim or Deb had been down here since Grant died. Grant must have been the only one who used this storage space, the only one who had ever placed anything in the file cabinets. But nothing incriminating was here. Grant had been smart enough to burn his paper trail of payments.

The killer went through files all night, accidentally fell asleep, ended up trapped all day in the basement, unable to leave while Deb cried relentlessly for her dead husband above. Desperate to eat, forced to piss in an empty clay flower pot. Finally slipped away when the sun slipped out of sight.

Like any seduction, there was a point beyond return, a chance to be caught down here, murder as the only escape.

The killer had a gun but didn't want to use it.

And never against Deb.

But love unrequited is a powerful, unquenchable thing. Soon the killer would have to show Deb the depth of those feelings, how they clung like an anchor in the seabed floor.

And hope that anchor stayed firmly in place.

Unmoored, everything would be lost.

Everything, including Deb and her daughter, would be swiftly, violently destroyed.

CHAPTER

11

CESSY PAID THE Uber driver, stared at that man's house across the street. The man who had texted her.

This was too much like her mom's life, the bad life. Sitting in a car outside of someone's apartment or house. Entering a strange home owned by a threatening man, a man on his own property.

And men are dangerous when they feel powerful and secure. When they feel ownership.

Hector hadn't hurt her until she was his wife.

Cessy stepped out into the cold gray evening. The house was in Silver Spring, a small suburban Maryland city just on the outskirts of DC, an hour from her apartment in Baltimore. The houses here were old, some close to a hundred years or more, and the business district wasn't more than a block away from the residences. To Cessy, the close proximity between residential and professional neighborhoods added a schizophrenic quality to the community. Cities were meant to be confusingly combined. Not suburbs.

Cessy walked up his porch, knocked on the door as the Uber driver drove off.

It only took a few moments for him to answer.

"About time."

He was still the same beefy blond guy who'd come to her apartment a week ago, but now he was wearing a T-shirt and jean shorts and looked slightly ridiculous.

Cessy couldn't recall a man wearing jean shorts who wasn't a toddler.

It helped settle her nerves.

"What's your name?" she asked.

He looked surprised. "I never told you?"

Cessy waited.

"It's Barry."

"Barry?"

"What's wrong with that?"

"I don't think I've ever met someone named Barry."

And Barry, she didn't add, was about as nonthreatening a name as you could get.

He smiled. Instinctively, Cessy smiled back. The shared moment dispelled more of the tension. Not completely, but Cessy welcomed any sign of warmth.

"Shut up," Barry said playfully, "and get in here."

Cessy was hesitant to go into his house, but she had come to talk to him.

She followed Barry inside.

He closed the door behind her, his arm brushing her body.

"You live here?" Cessy asked. The house was big, but bereft of furnishings. Large, empty rooms with hardwood floors and white walls.

"I got a couple of houses," Barry said loftily. He paused at the base of a small staircase leading upstairs. The house was a split level, and each stairway only consisted of a handful of steps. "You coming up?"

Cessy crossed her arms over her chest. "I want to talk about what Hector owed."

Barry sighed. Cessy glanced into the kitchen, saw a table and a chair. So the house wasn't completely empty.

"You suddenly came up with fifteen thousand?" Barry asked.

"Not exactly."

Cessy thought about her answer.

"Not even close."

She thought about it a little more.

"Actually, just no. I didn't."

"So we do my other arrangement," Barry said, and he climbed a stair. "Pay it off in sweat."

"You were serious about that?"

He eyed her. "Absolutely."

"What happens if I don't break a sweat?"

"Still counts. Besides, I've never been with a Mexican chick. I'm curious."

"I'm Panamanian."

He shrugged. "Like it matters."

"Give me another way."

Barry cracked a knuckle. "This is the other way." He turned, ascended the rest of the stairs.

Cessy followed him, tried to keep calm. Tried to make sure nothing was between her and the front door if she had to run, relieved that the first and second floors were only separated by a small jump of stairs.

Had it been a traditional lengthy staircase, she wouldn't have followed him.

At least, she realized, that's what she was telling herself. Rather than admit that she was already under his control, already acquiescing to his demands.

That she was scared of what would happen if she didn't.

The second floor was a row of closed doors and an open bathroom at the far end. Cessy followed Barry to the closest room, a large master bedroom, empty except for a mattress in the middle.

"You're kind of a minimalist, huh?"

"I told you, I got a couple of houses. Haven't decorated this one yet." Barry rubbed his hands together.

And suddenly Cessy realized how careless she'd been. She'd been so caught up in thoughts about Barry and the money that she hadn't considered other men might be here.

Cessy stepped back into the hall.

"Hey!"

She ignored Barry. Walked down the hallway, opening doors and glancing inside. The rooms were empty.

"What are you doing?" he called out.

Cessy headed back toward the master bedroom, talked as she walked, trying to establish some control over the situation. Over herself. "I don't exactly feel comfortable. You know, in a house I've never been in with a man who threatened me?"

"It's just me here, Cessy," Barry said a little sadly.

At his tone, Cessy wondered if she was judging him too harshly.

And then Cessy dismissed that notion, wondered why she always did that. Why she was still willing to give men—particularly damned, damaged men—the benefit of doubt. Willing to make excuses for them.

She remembered the times Hector had asked for her forgiveness, especially when the abuse first started, and she gave it.

And the times he didn't ask. And she gave it anyway.

Cessy wondered if all women felt that way as she walked into the bedroom. Or if she was just projecting after Hector

Barry had his shirt off, his pants were around his ankles, and he was holding fuzzy blue handcuffs.

Cessy stopped in the doorway and stared.

It was a lot to process.

Barry grinned.

"You ready?"

Cessy stayed in the doorway.

"What . . . what's happening here?"

"Time to start working off your debt."

Barry stepped out of his pants. All he was wearing were black socks and tight white underwear. His chest was hairy, surprisingly so to Cessy. For some reason, it was natural to imagine someone muscular as hairless.

"I told you," Cessy said after a long moment, "I want a different way. I shouldn't have to pay Hector's debt. I shouldn't have to . . . I'm sorry, why do you have handcuffs?" She stared at the blue fuzz. "And what did you do to Grover?"

Barry ignored the *Sesame Street* reference. "I like to be in charge," he said. "Especially with whores."

"I'm not a whore."

Barry grinned. "Afraid you'll like it too much? Turn out like your mom?"

She didn't let the jab affect her. "Yeah, that's it. Come on, Barry. There has to be another way."

"The men I work with don't negotiate. Hector tried. You saw how that turned out for him."

"The people Hector worked for killed him?"

Barry didn't reply.

"Who are they?"

Barry absent-mindedly played with the handcuffs as he spoke. "They're killers. And they're everywhere."

Cessy didn't know what to say.

"Fuck me once and what you owe is cut in half. Seven five. I'll cover the rest."

She blinked. "Really?"

Slowly swinging the cuffs. "Promise."

It wasn't a bad offer, Cessy had to admit. Even if she couldn't afford seventy-five hundred.

But something deep inside Cessy thoroughly rejected Barry's sug-gestion, refused to even entertain it. Revulsion that came from some-where Cessy had never realized—sharp memories of her mother; the sorrowful women she and Rose worked with; the brutal names Hector had called her. She'd never accept those identities, never walk that bro-ken glass path, never again be what someone else wanted.

She'd find another way.

"Nah," she said. "Hard pass."

Cessy had seen quite a few different expressions on men's faces over the years, but the darkness and hate that crossed Barry's face startled her.

His rage was so palpable that her will nearly wavered.

"One time," he said, gesturing at Cessy in his underwear and socks, the handcuffs like excited open mouths flying through the air. "One time and you're basically free. And you won't do it."

"I'm sorry. But there must be—"

Barry lunged forward and smacked her across the face with the handcuffs.

Cessy took a step back, stunned, her face stinging.

She hadn't realized there was metal under the blue fuzz.

Barry brought his fist down on Cessy's head. She fell to the floor and sat, her hand touching something wet. She squinted up, saw Barry's twisted face, saw the metal handcuffs rushing toward her head.

Cessy lifted her hands, felt the steel slam into her fingers. Her foot shot out and caught Barry just under the knee. He yelped and fell.

Cessy pulled herself to her feet, lunged to the door.

The chain connecting the handcuffs wrapped around her neck.

Her fingers scrabbled at it, trying to find some space between her throat and the chain. She reared up, still on her knees, felt Barry behind her. Heard him grunting, her own tortured inhales.

Cessy pushed back, drove him into the wall. He didn't let go. The exertion only forced the chain tighter around her throat. She struggled until she couldn't breathe. Panic set in.

Her legs kicked and her arms flailed but Cessy couldn't get away. Her body flopped and she felt his head against hers, and she leaned forward and snapped her head back. Hard.

Cessy felt Barry's nose break. The chain loosened. She pulled it away, threw it, and ran from the room.

She ran, holding her neck, wondering if it was damaged, if she'd ever be able to breathe regularly. Barry was shouting, swearing.

She reached the stairs, grasped the bannister, and was suddenly in the air. It took Cessy a moment to realize she was falling. Her knees landed on the first floor and her hands reached out and braced her before her face could smack into the hardwood. She stood slowly, knees in pain, trying to figure out what had happened. Looked up, saw Barry watching her from the second floor. Realized she'd been pushed.

He cursed again and raced down the steps, the handcuffs back in his hand, waving back and forth. Blood from his nose masked his face.

Cessy limped into the kitchen, saw the chair. She picked it up. Swung it into Barry as he ran through the door.

The impact shook her arms, her entire upper body.

But Barry fell.

Cessy lifted the chair and brought it down on him. He raised a hand weakly and she brought it down again.

And again.

And again.

Cessy finally dropped the chair, sank to the floor. She couldn't look at Barry's body, or the blood on her hands and shirt and face. She put her elbows on her knees, her head in her palms. Stared down into the kitchen tiles.

Cessy didn't know what had happened. Everything was blurry.

She had no idea if Barry was still alive.

The only thing Cessy knew was that she was in more trouble than she'd ever been.

They're killers, Barry had told her.

And they're everywhere.

PART TWO

EVERYWHERE KILLERS

12

C ESSY WAS ABOUT a block from Barry's house, walking fast, when she realized she needed to go back.

She couldn't remember anything about the state of the house or the condition her fight with Barry had left it in.

Or what evidence of hers remained behind.

And, like the last time she'd been in this type of situation, Cessy knew the importance of clearing evidence.

She bit her lip, turned, started walking back. Kept her head down. Wished she had a baseball cap, sunglasses, a hooded sweatshirt, anything to hide her identity.

And anything to hide his blood.

From anyone who saw her, and from herself.

She walked up the sidewalk to the porch, saw that she'd left the front door open.

Or had she closed it?

Was someone else inside?

Had Barry woken and come out?

Cessy really wanted to turn around, head back down the sidewalk, call an Uber and go far, far away. Leave this night behind and never think about it again. Push everything away. But she'd run away once before, and it hadn't worked.

The past is your shadow, and it never truly leaves. You can never run away from yourself.

Cessy walked inside. Closed the front door behind her.

"Hello?" she asked.

Cessy waited for an answer, didn't receive one.

The house was quiet.

Cessy took a step toward the kitchen, then another.

Another.

She peeked around the wall and saw Barry lying in the corner.

She walked over to his body, nudged it with her foot.

Nothing.

Cessy knelt and pressed the back of her index and middle fingers against the side of his neck.

And felt a pulse.

*   *   *

It took an hour after she called, but Anthony Jenkins finally rang the doorbell.

Cessy was sitting in the empty living room. She stayed sitting as Anthony walked in.

"Whose house is this?" he asked. "It's nice!"

"The kitchen."

"Huh?"

"Go see the kitchen."

Anthony looked puzzled but did as she asked. Cessy looked back down at her hands, at the blood caked over the side of her thumb. She listened to Anthony's footsteps recede, stop for several minutes, then slowly return.

"Cessy?"

"Yeah."

"There's a dead guy in the kitchen. You know that, right?"

"He's not dead. I keep checking."

Anthony glanced back into the kitchen. "He looks dead. Who is he? And why's he holding fuzzy blue handcuffs?"

"His name's Barry."

"Barry what?"

"I don't remember." Cessy bit her lip. "I don't know if he told me."

"What happened to him?"

"I hit him with a chair."

"You . . . what? Why?"

Cessy's memory was spotty, just flashes of her running down the stairs and lifting the chair. "He tried to hurt me."

"So it was self-defense?"

"Yeah."

Anthony exhaled.

"Then it's not your fault."

"What do you mean?"

"When the cops come. It won't be your fault."

"I can't go to the cops."

"Why not?"

Cessy told Anthony about the money Hector owed, the demands that she pay it back. The warning about telling the police.

Anthony rubbed his chin. "Well, shit."

"I think we need to get him to the hospital. Fast. Everything's worse if he dies."

Anthony looked worriedly to the front door.

"You thinking about running?" she asked.

"Honestly? Yeah."

She reached out and held his hand. It was limp in hers.

"I need your help, Anthony. I don't know who else to turn to."

He grimaced.

"Please."

He withdrew his hand. "Let's get him to my car."

Anthony lifted Barry's shoulders, Cessy took his feet. They dragged him through the living room and outside toward Anthony's car, an old Nissan Maxima.

"Trunk's closed," Cessy said. "Where are your keys?"

Anthony dropped his half of Barry's body. Barry's shoulders and head landed hard on the driveway. Cessy winced. She could see Anthony digging in his pocket, and then he pulled his keys out and they flew into the night. "Oh shit!"

"Keep your voice down!" Cessy hissed, just as she heard someone say, "Hello?"

Cessy dropped Barry's legs and walked around the car. An older white woman, walking a small terrier, was standing on the sidewalk, shining the flashlight from her phone on the front of Anthony's car. The woman turned the flashlight toward Cessy.

"Oh, hi," Cessy said, squinting in the light. She lifted a hand to shield her eyes, grateful the woman wasn't in a position to see Barry's body behind the car. "Can I help you?"

"I don't recognize you," the woman said, her voice flat and serious. "Or him."

She pointed her phone to the yard, and Cessy saw Anthony, butt high in the air, searching through the grass.

"Hi!" Anthony said, his voice extra friendly, as nonthreatening as possible to white people. "Just looking for my keys."

"What are your names?" the woman asked.

"I'm sorry?"

"Tell me or tell the cops. We get a little worried when we see . . . strangers in this neighborhood."

Cessy was pretty sure she knew exactly what this lady meant by "strangers."

"Sure," Anthony said, still using his friendly tone. "I get that. Completely. My name's Anthony Jenkins."

"And you?" The flashlight's beam traveled up and down Cessy's body.

"Cessy Castillo." She immediately wished they hadn't given their real names. "We're friends with Barry."

"Barry's not here that often," the lady said. "Seems like a nice fellow, though. Needs to work on his yard."

"You're right!" Anthony called out, then went back to searching through the tall grass.

"He's really so nice," Cessy confirmed.

"Is he here now?" The older lady started up the driveway.

Cessy stepped in front of her, trying to appear as casual as possible. "He had a headache, which is why we're leaving. Probably already in bed."

"Oh, that's too bad."

"Yup." Cessy wondered if there was any part of Barry's body that the lady could see. Fortunately, she didn't seem to be looking in that direction. She kept glancing between Cessy and Anthony as he went through the yard.

"And we were leaving," Cessy added. "My friend Anthony there just lost his keys."

"Where are you two from?"

Cessy was growing impatient with this line of questioning, but Anthony said, "Baltimore!"

"Baltimore?" The lady said the word like she hated having it in her mouth. Cessy wasn't surprised. It hadn't taken her long, after moving here, to learn that everyone picked on the little city. They never bothered to see past the problems and find Baltimore's beauty—the brightly painted row houses, the long lovely parks, the dramatic mix of people.

"That's right," Cessy replied. "Baltimore."

"Where's Trip?" the lady asked.

"What?"

"Trip, my terrier. He was standing right behind me."

Cessy took a step back, looked around. "You didn't have him on a leash?"

"Trip doesn't need a leash," the lady said defiantly. "He stays right with me."

She walked toward Anthony's car, flashlight aimed at the ground.

Cessy stopped her with a hand on the lady's shoulder.

"I'll check here," Cessy said. "You check the street. Make sure he didn't run out there."

The lady inhaled sharply. "You're right." She turned and hurried to the sidewalk, calling out, "Trip! Trip!"

"Found them!" Anthony cried out.

"My Trip?"

"Sorry, no. My keys." He walked toward Cessy, asked in a low voice, "Should we move him now?"

"While this *puta's* twenty feet away?" Cessy whispered back. "No!" She walked toward the back of the car and Anthony followed her. She turned on her phone's flashlight, pointed it down.

"Oh shit," Anthony said.

The lady's terrier was crouched next to Barry's body and chewing on the handcuffs, his mouth covered in blue fur.

Cessy slowly walked toward the dog. "Hey, Trip, it's okay. Just drop that and come here. I'll give you a treat."

Trip glared at her and growled, like he knew Cessy was lying about the treat. He kept chewing and kept a watchful eye on her.

"Is he over there?" the lady called, her voice fortunately far away.

"I don't see him," Cessy called back, her eyes locked with Trip's. She took another step and he rose to his haunches, the handcuffs still in his mouth.

She saw Anthony behind the dog and took another step. Trip turned and ran and Anthony scooped him up in his arms. Trip dropped the handcuffs and his teeth latched onto Anthony's arm. Anthony yelped.

"Is that him?" the lady cried out.

"We got him," Cessy said, and she pushed Anthony toward the sidewalk. He whimpered and walked.

"Oh, Trip!" the lady said gratefully, then shined the light on Anthony's strained face. "Is he biting you?"

"It's fine," Anthony replied, his voice cracking.

"Come here, sweetie," the lady said, and she took Trip from Anthony's arms. He stepped back, rubbing his left bicep.

"Thanks to both of you," she went on. "He never runs off. Must have been . . ."

She took a step back. The flashlight's beam had lowered to the ground.

"What's that?" she asked.

Cessy and Anthony slowly turned.

Saw the furry blue handcuffs illuminated on the driveway.

They looked at each other, turned back toward the lady.

"Like I said, Barry's really nice," Cessy told her.

*   *   *

The lady didn't stick around long after that. Cessy and Anthony quickly loaded Barry's body inside and closed the trunk.

"Don't drive crazy," Cessy said when they climbed into the car. "Last thing we need is to get pulled over."

"What's going to happen at the hospital?" Anthony asked.

"We drop him by the door or down the street. Wherever's less crowded."

They drove in silence.

"And after that?" Anthony asked, eventually. "What are you going to do? What's going to happen next?"

Cessy wished she knew.

13

THE DOOR TO the motel room swung open.

Chris Castillo walked in from the South Carolina night, a plastic bag from Subway swinging from one hand, a half-eaten club sub sandwich in the other. He tossed the bag on the bed, closed the door with his foot. Took his Sig out from his jacket pocket, set it on the nightstand.

Lay down on the bed, swallowed the hard bread.

"This tastes like a sheep's fart," Chris said to no one. He laughed. "I don't even know what that means."

He ate more, stared at an episode of *M*A*S*H* on the muted television set.

When Chris finished his sandwich, he rolled off the bed, picked up the plastic bag. Pushed open the bathroom door and walked inside.

Like the rest of the motel room, the bathroom was small, as if originally sized to be a closet. A chipped sink, small toilet, and tiny tub filled it and barely allowed for anything else. Even the towel rack seemed cramped.

Chris pulled open the shower curtain. Removed the ball gag and blindfold from the older man chained to the pipes.

The older man didn't say anything. Didn't glare or even open his eyes. He kept his face down.

"Looks like we got to clean this," Chris said. He unhooked the nozzle, turned on the water, washed away the blood threatening to stain the shower floor.

"I'm going to do your back now, okay?"

The older man's eyes opened. He grimaced as water washed over the knife cuts crisscrossing his back.

Chris was impressed.

He'd seen men scream when water touched their wounds.

He finished, hung the nozzle, sat on the toilet.

"You want a sandwich?" he asked.

A nod.

Chris gave him the sandwich. The man took a bite, then spit the sandwich down to the wet floor.

"You trying to poison me?"

"That was from Subway."

"That explains it," the man said and coughed. "You going to let me out of here?"

"Maybe," Chris lied.

The older man frowned. "You'd better think about that. Like I told you, you kill me and the cops will never stop looking for you. People know me."

Chris shrugged. "Good thing I'm not staying." He reached down into his ankle sheathe, pulled out a long knife.

"Who are you?" the man asked, desperately.

"I'm just some guy passing through Charleston. Heading north to see my sis."

"Please let me go. I won't do anything like this again."

Chris wagged the knife at him. "Now see, I think you've done this before. I could tell by the way I heard you talking to her through the door. And I could tell, after I broke that door down, that she wasn't your daughter like you tried to say she was. She was working for you! In the motel room next to mine. What are the odds?" Chris reflected for a moment. "Actually, pretty good, in this motel. I should stay in nicer places."

"You had no right . . ."

"And I have the biggest problem with men buying women. You have no idea."

"I won't do it anymore. Please!"

Chris always hated it when they started to beg.

"Listen," Chris said. "You can just go."

He undid the handcuffs and the man's arms dropped to his sides, flopped down like broken chicken wings.

"What are you doing?"

Chris shrugged. "I told you that you can go." He handed him his shirt. "But you'll probably screw this up instead."

The man took the shirt, tried to put it on, grimaced as he lifted his arms, gasped when the shirt touched his bleeding back.

"Here's your gun," Chris said.

Chris admired how the man's face didn't change, didn't register surprise. He took the gun, ejected and examined the clip, shoved it back in.

"Ready?" Chris asked.

The man's gun swung upward, but Chris was faster. He slashed the man's forearm with his knife. The man cried out and his hand dropped, but he didn't let go of the weapon. Chris grabbed the man's hand, pointed the pistol away from him.

And dragged his knife across the man's throat.

The man let go of the gun.

He stepped back into the shower, his body pressed against the tiles. Sank to the floor, breathing wetly. His hands pushed against his neck, as if helplessly trying to stuff the blood back in.

"You see, you did that," Chris told the dying man.

Blood was pooling in the small tub. Chris washed his hands, cleaned off his phone. Pulled up an app for driving directions to Baltimore as the man's harsh gasps slowed.

CHAPTER

14

Deb wanted to drive Kim back to Washington College to clear out her dorm room for winter break, and potentially the spring semester, but Kim thought it best she take the trip alone. "Trust me, Mom," she said. "It's going to be a lot of goodbyes and friends stopping by. You don't want to see that."

"That sounds exactly like what I want to see. I want to meet your friends and watch the goodbyes. Don't you know me?"

They did the two-hour drive early one weekday morning, sitting in silence as they crawled through traffic. Deb could tell her daughter was upset, but couldn't figure out why.

"Are you sure you're all right?" she asked Kim, after about an hour. They hadn't said a word since the drive began. Instead, they'd been listening dourly to the radio play a tribute of Billy Joel songs. Which, Deb figured, could be a good enough reason for Kim to be angry.

Kim stayed slouched in her chair, hands jammed in the pockets of her hoodie. "I'm fine."

"Is it because of "Uptown Girl"?"

That brought a small smile. It didn't last long. "No."

They reached the Bay Bridge, a rising curved structure that stretched high above the Chesapeake, comprised of four thin lanes that pushed cars close to the long drop to the water below. Driving over the bridge had always terrified Deb. She would sit in the passenger seat as Grant drove, close her eyes, count silently to herself. Squeeze her fists. In the course of driving back and forth to Washington College, they'd crossed the Bay Bridge dozens of times, and every time Deb felt panic build in her, almost overtake her. Grant would tease her, take his hands off the wheel or close his eyes, and Deb had fucking hated him for it.

She wondered if Grant had thought about Maria Vasquez during these drives. Deb remembered their easy conversations, the laughing, the months—sometimes years—when nothing seemed wrong in their relationship. And she wondered how naïve she'd been.

What else had Grant hidden?

Had he been with even more women?

And given all of that, he'd still had the audacity to try to scare her when they drove on this bridge?

She turned her thoughts away from Grant and toward the drive, worried about getting distracted. It wasn't just the height of the bridge that scared her; it was that bizarre, instinctual pull to the edge. The suddenness of the plummet, how close and easy it was. Not that Deb had notions toward suicide, but there was something about the immediacy of death that was both terrifying and magnetic.

"You okay?" Kim asked.

Deb stared hard out the windshield as their Grand Cherokee climbed over the water. "This bridge always makes me nervous."

"I can tell."

"How?"

"Because your fingers are making indents in the steering wheel."

Deb didn't relax her grip.

The campus was quiet when they arrived at Washington College. Students were immersed in studying this close to finals, and only a few wandered through the brisk November chill, hurrying from one building to the next or walking with dazed, exhausted expressions. The diversity of the students warmed Deb. She hadn't been sure if Maryland's Eastern Shore held the same varied mix of races Northern Virginia offered, but the college had students from multiple ethnicities and nationalities. Kim wasn't alone.

They walked into Kim's dorm room, a plain square room with white brick walls and two thin beds. Deb had gone to college and lived in a similar environment, and couldn't imagine now how she'd done it. Everything was so cramped and communal. After years of living in houses, she needed her space.

That thought reminded Deb of her finances.

My God, she thought as Kim went through her closet, *I hope I don't have to move in here.*

"I think I'll just take my clothes," Kim was saying. "I don't need my books or the TV or anything."

"That's your TV?" Deb asked. She walked over and examined the wall-mounted plasma.

"Yeah, you don't remember? Dad bought it for me."

Deb honestly didn't, but the mention of "Dad" tightened her stomach and face.

The door to the dorm opened. "Hey, Tasha," a girl said, calling out for Kim's roommate as she strolled inside. "Do you have . . . ?"

The girl, a blonde wearing a gray Washington College sweatshirt and black tights, stopped just inside the doorway.

"Hey, Mary Beth," Kim said.

"Hi, Kim! I didn't know you were coming back."

"I'm just here to get my stuff."

Silence.

"This is my mom," Kim said, gesturing at Deb.

"Hi," Deb offered. "Mary Beth, right?"

"Right," the girl said uneasily. She pulled at the bottom of her sweatshirt. "I'm sorry for what happened to your husband."

"Thank you."

Mary Beth still seemed uneasy, as if she didn't know what to say.

Deb didn't either. She gazed at Mary Beth, her pretty face and young body, and wondered if that's what Grant had seen in Maria Vasquez. Was she young? Deb hadn't asked Agent Levi Price for information about her, but wished she had.

Ever since her meeting with Levi, Deb felt like she was staring into a dark room.

And she wanted to turn on the light.

She wanted to see Maria.

The other prostitute, the one who had killed Grant, who had killed other men . . . that woman meant nothing to her. Grant was a casualty in her war, had maybe never even known who she was. But Maria was planted in Deb's mind, like weeds or vines, growing and stretching and blotting out everything she could see.

"Tasha's probably at her boyfriend's place," Kim was saying. "At his townhouse."

"Okay," Mary Beth said. "I need to get going. I'm sorry again, Kim."

After she left, Kim looked at Deb. "Is everyone going to be like that?"

"That awkward? Yes."

"I guess it's hard to know what to say."

They packed up Kim's clothes, makeup, and a few books Kim decided she wanted to take home. Other students stopped by, and the awkward conversations were nearly identical. Usually a surprised "hello," followed by an "I'm sorry," maybe a hug, and then listlessness until they left.

"I'm not going to meet Rebecca?" Deb asked.

"She's off campus," Kim said.

Deb wondered if Kim wanted to live off campus next semester and if that would be cheaper or more expensive than the dorm. She checked her e-mail on her phone. No job leads.

They drove back that same day, arrived at night, had a quiet dinner. Deb wondered when she would get used to Grant not returning home, stop being jolted by the idea that she would hear him opening the front door, padding through the kitchen, opening the fridge to grab an apple. And, even as mad as she was, Deb wondered if she really wanted to stop remembering those sounds. To accept the silence.

The next morning she left Kim lying on the couch, staring at *Family Feud*. She drove into Alexandria, pulled up to a small medical clinic she'd made an appointment at a couple of days prior. Commuters to DC and a surplus of high-paying jobs kept Northern Virginia routinely ranked as one of the richest communities in the nation, but this section of Alexandria had been ignored. Strip malls filled with quiet stores, run-down restaurants, a few people holding signs begging for money or food.

Deb put her name on the patient log and sat in a corner of the waiting room. A Latino family with a red-eyed little girl was on the other side. An overweight white man slept sprawled on a chair.

"Ms. Linh?"

Deb followed the nurse practitioner to a small room, was weighed, had her blood temperature taken. She waited another twenty minutes for a doctor to show up.

When the doctor finally knocked on the door and entered, Deb was nervously tapping a tongue depressor against her knee. She was relieved to see a woman.

"I'm Dr. Suzette Franklin. Ms. Linh, right?"

Dr. Franklin pronounced *Linh* like "lint," but without the "t," rather than the correct pronunciation, closer to "lean." The same way Deb used to, before a Vietnamese friend in college corrected her.

"Right."

Dr. Franklin glanced down at her clipboard. "I see that you'd like to get tested. For HIV?"

"Yes," Deb said, "and everything else."

"Sorry?"

Deb uncrossed her arms from over her chest. She hadn't realized how tightly she was holding herself. Her shoulders ached from stress.

"I'd like to get tested for STDs," she said. "As many as possible."

Dr. Franklin sat in a chair next to a computer. "Have you been having different symptoms?"

"Like what?"

"Painful urination, nausea, a rash, vaginal discomfort?"

"No, no, and no. And no."

Dr. Franklin looked confused. "Then why do you need to get tested?"

"I . . . I had unprotected sex."

"Well, we can certainly test you for HIV. How long ago did that encounter happen?"

Deb bit her lip.

Dr. Franklin waited.

"My husband cheated on me. A while back."

Dr. Franklin's expression dissolved into sympathy. "I understand. You're not the first woman I've seen with similar concerns."

For some reason, that thought brought tears to Deb's eyes.

"Really?"

"Really."

The empathy was nice, but only for a moment. Now that she had admitted what happened to a stranger, Deb felt, more acutely than she had before, that her life was permanently something else. That she was someone else. She was one of those wives who have lost their husbands to another woman.

And even worse, to a prostitute.

Deb wished the woman had been a neighbor or friend or coworker of Grant's, someone with whom the transgression could be explained by love. Someone who would have offered Grant a level of complexity, of understanding. A prostitute lessened him.

And lessened her. Lessened her for believing in him, for being the type of wife who could be replaced by a hooker.

"Do you know if he used a condom?" Dr. Franklin asked.

"I don't know. He died."

Dr. Franklin started. "From a sexually transmitted disease?"

"Oh! No, sorry. He died because of something else. Not a disease. I only found out afterward about his affair." Deb put her head in her hands, tried to blink back tears. "This is all so hard. He passed away almost a month ago, and I just found out about this. I don't know how much else there is to learn. We had such a good relationship. I know you must hear that all the time, but it's true. I really never knew anything was wrong. I keep thinking it can't be true."

Dr. Franklin handed Deb a Kleenex. Deb pressed it against her eyes, let tears soak the tissue.

"Shit," Deb said. "Do other women unload on you like this?"

Dr. Franklin smiled. "All the time."

Deb took another Kleenex.

"You're going through a lot."

Deb nodded.

"We can certainly do the HIV test today, but I think it'd be best if you saw your regular doctor for any other concerns. Or I can give you a referral for some good doctors in the area. Would that be okay?"

Deb kept nodding.

*　*　*

Deb sat in her car in the parking lot, fingered the Band-Aid on her forearm.

She took her phone and a business card out of her purse.

He answered after two rings.

"This is Price."

"Agent Price? This is Deb Thomas."

"Deb?" She heard something on the other end of the line, a muffled thump.

"Hello?"

"Sorry!" Levi exclaimed. "Dropped the phone. How can I help you, Ms. Thomas?"

"Are you okay?" she asked.

"I was running on the treadmill. If you hear me gasping, that's why."

"I want to know the truth about my husband. About Grant. I want to know what happened with him. What he did. I feel like there's more to the story. I know there's more."

"Are you sure you're not trying to learn *why* he did it?" Levi asked.

"I think I'm trying to find out both."

Levi was silent for a moment. "I hate to say this, but it's been my experience that you may not find out either. Motive is often circumstantial with the deceased."

"I know," Deb conceded. "But I can't just stay here. Emotionally. Does that make sense?"

"It does."

"I'm desperate." Deb held the phone tight. "Please."

A few more moments of silence.

"What do you want?"

"I want to meet Maria."

15

C ESSY HAD JUST bitten into her hamburger when two men sat down at her table.

She chewed quick, swallowed hard.

The men were oddly similar. Both white, tall, thin, and bald, with small dark eyes and impassive expressions. One had a beard's early shadow; the other was clean-shaven. Both wore long-sleeved shirts—one, a black shirt; the other, a white one—with dark blue jeans. Brown work boots.

"Did you put Barry in the hospital?" one of them asked.

Over the past two days since she and Anthony had left Barry in an unconscious heap outside the hospital's doors, Cessy had expected to be questioned. But she still hadn't figured out how to answer.

Fear grew inside her like a swarm of roused bees.

She casually glanced around for help, avoided looking toward the restroom. The place, 203 Restaurant and Bar in Federal Hill, was nearly deserted. The only other people in the restaurant were an old guy reading a newspaper at the bar and a bored teenage waiter checking his phone in the corner. Not a lot of options.

"He's in the hospital?" Cessy asked, playing dumb. A phone call to the hospital had revealed Barry was still there, and alive, but that was it. The staff person she'd spoken with had warily refused to give her any more information.

Cessy had been relieved he was alive.

And then wondered if he deserved death.

Maybe he did, and her relief was because his death wouldn't come from her.

"You already know where he is," the other man said, "because you saw him last."

"How do you know that?"

"Two days ago, Barry texted he was going to see you. No one's heard from him since."

"What are your names?" she asked, trying to change the subject.

"Smith," the clean-shaven man said.

"Harris," the other added.

Cessy looked back and forth between them. "Those aren't really your names, are they? Harris and Smith sound like an eighties cop show. Also, how are you not related?"

"We're not cops," Smith said.

"You don't say."

"Or brothers."

Harris grinned. "I like her. She's sarcastic."

"I don't," Smith replied.

"Look," Cessy said, fear edging her voice, "I don't know what to tell you. I don't know where Barry is. I did see him that night. I was trying to work out a deal for the money Hector owed."

Smith reached across the table, started eating her fries.

"What'd he tell you?" Harris asked.

"He said he had to think about it."

"We can force you to tell us what really happened," Harris told her. "You understand that, right?"

That swarm of bees in Cessy's gut grew loud.

"I don't have anything else to tell you."

"That answer's not good enough. Or honest enough."

A sudden thought slammed into Cessy. Had there been cameras in Barry's house? Hidden cameras she hadn't seen, recording their fight?

Did these two men know the truth?

Were they just toying with her?

Shit.

"He didn't say anything about where he was going afterward?" she asked.

Neither man replied. Smith kept eating her French fries.

"What about the money Hector owed?" Cessy went on, thinking fast as she spoke. "I told Barry I couldn't pay and asked him if there was any way it can be less. Is there?"

"That's not our decision to make," Harris said.

"But maybe something can be worked out," Smith added.

Cessy kept thinking quickly. They still expected her to pay. That meant they didn't plan on killing her.

"I don't have that kind of money."

"We'll do installments," Smith said. "Five hundred a week, and you got a week for that first payment."

"One week," Harris put in, "and there's only one way you get out of paying it."

"What's that?" Cessy asked, wondering if they wanted what Barry had asked for.

"We find out that you ended up putting our friend in the hospital," Smith told her, "then we won't just take the money."

Harris pushed back his chair and stood. "We'll take everything else."

"I thought you liked me, Harris," Cessy said hollowly.

Harris smiled again. He and Smith walked out.

Cessy sat at the table, stared at her food. Her fries were gone, but so was her appetite.

It took almost a minute for Dana to return to the table from the bathroom.

He sat down nervously, eyes on the door.

"How do you know those guys?" he asked. "I saw you talking to them. No way I was coming out until they left."

Cessy picked up her water, took a drink. She hadn't realized how dry her throat was.

"My husband used to work with them. Well, ex-husband, I guess. The guy I was married to."

"He worked with Smith and Harris?"

Cessy almost spit out her water. "How do you know their names?"

Dana stared back at Cessy. "Your husband was a pimp?"

A moment passed.

"I think we need to start over," Cessy said. "How do you know those guys?"

Dana ran his hands over his head. His T-shirt seemed big on him, as if his body had shriveled from simply seeing those two men.

"They ran me when I was working. They . . . they weren't the nicest men."

"What do you mean, they ran you?"

"Like I said, pimps. I didn't work for anyone but me when I started. Kept the money to myself. Then they showed up one day, one day when I met this guy at his house, this politician. He and I were in his bedroom when we saw them standing in the door. He was just as surprised as I was."

"What'd they do?"

"They told me I was working for them now. Said they'd tell his wife if he said anything. Made him pay to keep it quiet."

"And he did, right?"

"Right. Then they offered me protection if I gave them a cut. I said I didn't need protection. They said I needed it from them."

"How'd they even find you?"

"There were rumors about this politician, some state senator. They were watching him. When they busted us, they asked me about my other clients. Started going after them. And I wasn't the only one. A bunch of us—men and women—got taken over by them. All in the same way." He paused. "You said your husband was working with them?"

"Yeah. You ever run into a guy named Hector?"

"I don't think so."

Cessy fished out her phone, pulled up a picture. "Him?"

Dana squinted at the photo. "No."

Cessy felt relief, and the sensation surprised her. She reminded herself that Hector was far from innocent, but at least she hadn't been married to a pimp.

It was a low bar.

"I don't know what he was doing with them," Cessy said. "But they worked with him. Until they killed him."

"They did?" Dana didn't wait for her to answer. "So why'd they come see you?"

"Hector owed them money. They want me to pay it."

Dana's eyes widened. "How much?"

"Fifteen thousand. By the way, do you have fifteen thousand dollars I can borrow?"

Dana's face was drawn, thin, almost skeletal. "Cessy, this is serious. Those guys, you can't mess with them."

"I know."

"I'm serious!"

Dana's fear was starting to push something in Cessy, bring that panic in her to the surface. She remembered those pictures she'd found, those men standing around corpses.

And she remembered her reluctant phone call to her brother, Chris, days earlier:

I need help.

I'm on my way.

"I'll be okay," Cessy said, trying to keep her voice calm, wishing she believed it. "I'll think of something."

"I don't mean to scare you. I just heard a lot about those guys when I was working for them. They always have blood on their hands."

16

THE SILVER AUDI pulled up in front of Deb's house at three in the afternoon. She was waiting for it, watching from the bay window in the living room.

"I'll be back," Deb called out to Kim.

"Don't forget about dinner tonight!" Kim called back, sprawled on the couch in the family room, staring at an episode of the *Real Housewives* of some city. Deb knew she'd probably be in the same spot when she returned. But she was too preoccupied to care.

She hurried outside through a misty rain, yanked opened the passenger door, climbed inside.

Agent Levi Price grimly looked at her from the driver's seat.

"You have no idea how much trouble I could get in for this," he said. "No idea."

"I want to meet Maria," Deb said resolutely.

She buckled her seat belt as his car pulled away from the curb.

"Like I told you," Levi said, "you can't say anything about me. You can't tell her I put you in touch or even that I met with you."

"I got it. Tell her that I found her name and address hidden in some of Grant's old files."

"Right." Levi squinted through the windshield, turned on the wipers. "I could be fired for this, maybe even prosecuted."

"I'll tell the same story I'm telling Maria to anyone else who asks. Your name will never come up."

"Good. And you can't say anything about the suspect I mentioned, the vigilante prostitute. It's an ongoing, classified investigation. Until we know more, please keep that to yourself."

"Do you have any leads?"

"I can't say."

The car headed onto I-66, the often-crowded interstate that ran past Northern Virginia's confused mix of tangled small towns and suburbs, and straight to DC. Deb's thoughts were rushing everywhere, but she couldn't help noticing how miserable Levi seemed, despondently driving through the light rain, his mood matching the dreary gray day.

"Really," Deb said, "I won't tell anyone what you're doing for me."

He didn't relax his posture. They drove for a few minutes in silence. It didn't take long for traffic to slow. Taillights around them gleamed red.

Deb felt like she needed to start a conversation.

"How'd you end up in the FBI?"

"Started there after college. And I haven't left yet."

"That's it?"

Levi shrugged. "My brother was killed when I was in college. He was hanging with the wrong crowd, some really bad people, and they took him out. Those guys were arrested, but I ended up going into law enforcement after that. Wanted to see if I could help other people from ever feeling that way."

Levi spoke easily, matter-of-factly, as if this was a story he'd told many times before. The words "they took him out" were nonchalant. And his body seemed relaxed, his posture looser, hand no longer tight on the wheel.

"How old was he?"

"Same age as me. We were twins."

"How did your parents take it?" Like most parents, the thought of losing her child left Deb raw. There had even been times since Grant's death when Deb thought—and she hated herself for this thought—that at least it hadn't been Kim. But it did help, gave her a touch of perspective, something to grasp. Something to live for.

"My parents didn't take it well," Levi said. Deb didn't follow up.

The cars started moving again.

"How'd you end up working in PR?" Levi asked her.

"You know I do PR?"

Levi allowed himself a slight smile. Deb thought it was nice, in the surprising way it often is with men since they rarely smile. "I'm FBI. It's what we do. Find out things."

That didn't bother Deb. "It's not that exciting a story."

"You didn't have a twin sister who did PR and was killed by criminals?"

That made her laugh. "Not exactly. I studied communications at GMU and then got a job after college. Switched to part-time freelance after Kim was born."

"Do you like it?"

"I do. But I haven't been able to find work since Grant passed, so I don't like that."

Levi shifted into the far-left lane as they started to hit the Arlington exits. "How have you been feeling lately?"

"About Grant?"

"About everything."

"I keep thinking I'm out of the hardest part, and then a day passes and it feels like I'm right back in."

They crossed the bridge from Virginia to DC. Aside from work or occasional dinners, Deb didn't often head into the district and, like outsiders do in all cities, she immediately felt a little lost. It wasn't like she was in New York City, with its clustered buildings and pushy crowds. The wide roads and monuments of Washington, DC, provided a sense of space most cities lacked, but Deb still found the city impenetrable.

"Are your parents close to you and Kim?" Levi asked.

Deb didn't know if Levi meant geographically or emotionally, but the same response answered both. "It was just my mom."

"Oh."

He didn't ask, but Deb knew she had to explain further. "My mom was single when she adopted me. And she never married."

"You're adopted?"

"Yeah." Deb could hear the change in his tone, a change she was so used to that it didn't bother her anymore. As if he suddenly felt that her life had been remarkably different from his, harder. Less filled with love.

Sometimes it annoyed her.

Now she just let it go.

"And it was just you and your mother?"

Deb nodded. "She always wanted a child, but not necessarily a husband. So she raised me on her own."

"Is she still around?"

"She passed away years ago. Cancer."

Levin grimaced. "I'm sorry. Cancer's awful."

"It was." Deb didn't elaborate, didn't want to revisit that long year, in her late twenties, when she'd traveled back and forth every weekend to Roanoke until, months before the end, her mother came up north to live with her and Grant and Kim. The countless trips to doctors, the pained weariness of chemotherapy, her mother's slow disintegration of strength and will until she begged to die.

"You don't hear about many single women adopting kids," Levi said.

"I was the only adopted kid in my town," Deb replied.

"How was that?"

"Lonely."

They passed from the long streets and tourists and historic buildings to a crowded residential neighborhood.

"You said she lives in Capitol Hill?" Deb asked, hoping to change the subject. "Here?"

Levi frowned, nodded. "Strange, right? Not really the neighborhood you'd expect."

"What do you mean?"

"It's kind of a nice area. You'd assume her clients live here. Not her."

"I see your point," Deb said as she looked at a street lined with row houses and postage-stamp yards. The houses were large and colonial and, in the gray mist of the overcast afternoon, had an intimate feel.

"A lot of the people who live here work on Capitol Hill," Levi told her. "And then you have some people who like the idea of living in DC but staying on the outskirts."

"Do you live in the city?"

"No, I'm in Arlington."

"Why not in DC?" Deb was only mildly curious, but she wanted the conversation. Wanted a distraction from her nerves, from what she was about to do.

From what she might find out.

"The city's just never done it for me," Levi said. "I mean, I like cities, just not this one." He paused. "It doesn't feel real to me. Too many transients, too many tourists. Other cities have their own culture, their own accents. You can tell when someone's from Boston or Philly or New York or Jersey just by their voice. I never get that with DC. It has no personality. Like it's too guarded to reveal one."

"So you like suburban culture?"

A sharp laugh. "Not exactly. But I do like how close I am to work."

Deb nodded, trying to concentrate on the conversation, trying to tamp down her rising nerves.

Levi slowed to a stop near a squarish, brown brick building.

"This is where Maria lives."

They stared at an apartment building called Capitol Hill Lofts. A young white couple, legs and arms covered in tattoos, pushed a stroller past the car.

"Remember what I told you," Levi said. "She's in apartment three-oh-four, and you can't tell her anything about me. All she can know is that you're Grant's wife, and you have some questions about their relationship."

"So, the truth, basically?"

"Basically."

"Got it." Deb pushed open the door, stepped outside, wrapped her arms tight around herself. Colder than she expected. She looked up the building, counted six stories.

The passenger window slid down, and she turned back toward the sedan. Levi was leaning over from the driver's seat.

"Be careful."

Deb nodded.

The passenger window rose.

Deb headed up the sidewalk to the door. It was locked. A buzzer was next to it, and Deb had a sinking feeling when she realized she'd need to buzz Maria's apartment.

She'd been so focused on the questions she was going to ask about Grant that Deb hadn't even thought what she'd say as an introduction.

Fortunately, the front door opened. A man emerged. He smiled briefly at Deb, said a quick "Hey," and held the door open.

Deb walked up a dark, narrow staircase with brick walls on either side, saw room 304 directly off the third-floor landing. Heard loud music and female voices inside.

Deb knocked on the door. The voices stopped. The music didn't.

The door opened a crack. A woman with short, boyishly cut blonde hair glanced out, eyed Deb up and down disdainfully.

"Yeah?"

"I'm—I'm looking for Maria."

The woman rolled her eyes. "Is this about your husband?"

It took Deb a moment to recover. "Well, yeah. I was—"

The door slammed shut. The conversation inside resumed.

Deb glanced up and down the hallway and knocked again.

An audible sigh from inside, even over the voices and the music.

No response.

Deb tried the knob and then knocked harder.

The door flew open. The same woman stood in front of her. "Listen, eggroll, you're not the first chick to come here asking about your husband. Whoever he is, he's not here and never was."

"Eggroll?" Deb replied, confused. "Because I'm Asian?"

The woman smiled wickedly. *Woman*, Deb realized, might be stretching it. If she was twenty-one, then she'd just turned. Her face was young.

"Yes," the woman said. "Because you're Asian."

The door started to close again, but Deb caught it with her hand. Surprise took over the woman's insouciance.

The music stopped.

Deb was also a little surprised that she'd caught the door. "Listen," she said, "is Maria here or not?"

"It's okay," another female voice said from inside, "let her in."

The woman at the door grabbed Deb's hand and yanked her inside. Slammed the door behind her.

The small apartment reminded Deb of Kim's dorm. Three girls sat on a twin-sized bed against the far wall, catty-corner from a tall dresser. A thin hall to her right showed glimpses of a bathroom and kitchen.

The other thing Deb immediately noticed was that there were five women in the room—potentially women, she checked herself, but probably girls. Any of them could have been in their late teens. Their bodies and clothes were youthful, but there was a hardness to them, a sadness that aged them. They were dyed blondes and one brunette, wearing sweats and yoga pants and loose T-shirts. Deb could see that their clothes were casual, but their hair and makeup was done. It wouldn't take much for any of them to be ready to go out. Almost like they were waiting for a call.

Deb wondered if that was how their lives worked.

And then she worried they could tell how intensely she was studying them.

"Eggroll," one of them repeated, and laughed.

The others didn't join in. They just stared at Deb, their expressions guarded.

Deb felt like she was back in high school, a time when she'd once walked into the bathroom and saw a pair of popular girls getting high and laughing together in an open stall. The laughter stopped when they'd seen her, and the two girls had each given her the same look, an unwelcome look.

It wasn't just that Deb hadn't been as popular as those girls; it was that she wasn't white. Her defining element, to everyone back then, had been her ethnicity. When those two girls stared at her from that open stall, she could feel the contempt in their gaze. The stretching sense of difference.

And in this room with these five girls, she felt it again.

But then she remembered that she was nearly twice as old as any of these girls.

And she had a federal agent parked outside.

And she needed answers.

And fuck them.

"So who's Maria?" she asked.

"She's definitely one of us," a girl said.

"But which one?" the girl who'd answered the door asked. "Ooh, we're tricky."

"I don't know this for sure," Deb said, "but this Maria may have been sleeping with my husband."

"Shocking."

"And he died," Deb added.

A change in the room, a sense of fear.

"From what?" one of them asked. "He catch something?"

For a second, Deb realized she could trap them. Lie and say he'd died of some disease. Syphilis had driven him insane. AIDS had ravaged him. See which girl started to panic.

But something about that approach seemed too cruel.

"He was shot to death. An ATM robbery."

That fear disappeared.

"So why are you here?" one of them said. "Shouldn't you be wearing black and lighting candles or some shit?"

"You know us eggrolls," Deb said. "We multitask really well. I want to find out more about what he was doing."

"Thought you knew what he was doing."

"I want to know more."

One of the girls, Deb noticed, wasn't quite as unfazed as the others. The brunette sitting between two blondes on the bed. She was slowly rubbing her hands together, as if she was cold. Her mouth was a thin line, but her eyes were big.

And afraid.

"Grant Thomas," Deb said, watching the brunette. "His name was Grant Thomas."

The brunette's eyes flicked up at her, then back down. Not enough for Deb to figure out if it was a definitive tell.

"So here's what you think," the girl who'd opened the door said. "You think your husband was sleeping with a hooker, got killed, and you're digging around for more info. Like we might know something about it. Or about him."

"That's right."

"Seems like whoever did it gave you an answer."

Deb was confused. The confusion must have shown on her face.

One of the blondes sighed. "If someone really did kill your husband, then maybe you should just deal with it."

"I have to know the truth," Deb said.

The brunette finally spoke. "Not a good idea to chase bad people," she said, her voice low. "They get tired of running."

The rest of the girls stayed quiet.

* * *

Deb was at the bottom of the stairs, about to close the door to the stairwell, when she felt a hand on her shoulder.

She wasn't startled. It was almost as if she expected the brunette.

"You're Maria, aren't you?" Deb asked.

The brunette glanced up the stairs before she answered.

"Yeah."

"Did you know my husband?"

Maria nodded.

A deep sadness filled Deb, weighed her down.

"You slept with him?"

Another nod.

Deb leaned against the wall, rested the back of her head against it, closed her eyes. Her hands felt heavy.

Any shred of hope for Grant's innocence was gone.

"I'm sorry," Maria said uncomfortably. "But I have to ask, how'd you find me?"

Deb lifted her hands to her face, her eyes, pressed her fingers against them. Felt tears tumble down.

"Grant had your name and address in some old papers. With a note that he'd paid you."

"Oh." Maria paused. "It was just a couple of times."

"Just with you?"

"He said it was just me. And he felt really bad about it."

It didn't make Deb feel any better. She wondered if Maria had thought it would.

If anything, hearing the details made Deb sadder. And angrier.

Maria seemed like she was able to tell Deb's mood. "I'm sorry," she said. "I thought you came here because you wanted to know."

"When did you see him?"

"Last year. Around Christmas."

Last Christmas. Deb ran through her memories. Everything had been fine with their relationship. She thought they'd been happy.

Something else was building inside Deb besides anger. Disgust.

This girl was so young.

That almost pushed her over the edge. Deb felt bile rise up her throat, steadied herself.

It took her a moment to realize she was sitting on the cold stone stairs.

"Are you okay?" Maria asked.

Deb wanted to leave. She wanted to stand and rush down the stairs and out of this building and head home and pack and move. She wanted to move far away from this life. Run from the truth of what had happened, the undeniable truth, the embarrassing stain.

"Miss?" Maria asked.

"How old are you?"

"What?"

"How old are you?"

"I'm nineteen."

Christ, Grant.

"You look younger than nineteen."

"Men like that. Me looking young."

The two women were quiet. Deb still cried, but she'd stopped wiping the tears away. She let them run freely down her face.

Maria sat down on the same stair as Deb, but on the far end, pressed against the wall.

"How do you even remember him," Deb asked, "from a year ago?"

"I don't know how much to tell you," Maria said hesitantly. "I mean, like I said, we only did it a couple of times. But I also saw him after that."

"Why?"

Maria tugged a strand of her hair and stared at it. "He gave me more money."

"Why?" Deb asked again.

"The guys who run me . . . run us . . . they say I can stop working if I pay off what I owe them."

"What do you owe them for?"

"A place to live, food. Clothes. They take care of us."

"You and the other girls in there?"

"Yeah. But I don't think they ever meant it. I think we'll always owe them."

Deb stood. She didn't want to share the same space as Maria, didn't even want to do the same actions. If Maria was going to sit, she'd stand.

"Look," Maria said quietly, "I haven't been doing this that long, but Grant was the only one who ever came back to talk to me. He's the only one who ever cared about me. That's why I remember him."

"Awesome."

"I know you're not going to care about that. But he wasn't like the others. And he never stopped feeling bad for what happened."

"Why did it happen?"

Deb watched the girl shrug. "He never told me."

It wasn't a fair question to ask. Deb wanted to know if it was because Maria was younger. Or prettier. If Grant had been unhappy. If she was bad in bed. If he secretly hated their life together. If he wanted something she couldn't give.

If she'd done something wrong.

"Did he ever mention me?" Deb asked.

"No. But, honestly, they almost never do."

They.

Grant was part of *they.*

"Did he ask you to do something weird, or different, or did he say . . ." Deb let the questions die off.

"I don't really know why some of them come here," Maria told her. "I think it's the danger? But I don't know."

"The danger?"

"Yeah. Of being with someone like me."

That last line was said without sadness, but it still affected Deb. She tried not to think about it, tried to avoid any trace of empathy or pity.

She wanted to hate this woman, this girl. Wanted to hate her as much as she hated Grant. Even more.

Another woman should understand the pain of what she'd done.

"Grant told me he was sorry about what happened," Maria said. "I haven't been doing this for that long, but no one had ever done that; literally, no one. He said he couldn't stop thinking about what he'd done to his family."

Deb nodded, still trying not to let a crack in her anger. She hated that Maria had said his name, how it revealed a casualness to their relationship.

He didn't feel bad enough to stop seeing you and paying you, she thought.

"And then we started talking," Maria went on, "and he asked me about this stuff, what I do and why and stuff like that. And I told him the deal, how I'm on the hook for a bunch of money, and he told me he wanted to get me out of it. That's when he started paying me, just giving me money to give them."

"He felt guilty."

"I guess."

Deb closed her eyes and breathed slowly.

It really sounded like the kind of thing Grant would fucking do. Like the time he found a snapping turtle crossing the street and brought it home in a box. And it had almost bit Deb's finger off when she tried to feed it a piece of lettuce.

"The thing is," Maria was saying. "You need to be careful. Like, I don't know what happened with Grant, but I know he met with the guys who run me. And then I didn't hear anything from him until today. Until you showed up."

"Who runs you?" Deb wasn't sure why she asked. She just wanted to know more, needed to know what else Grant had hidden.

Maria glanced down the stairs. "You're going to have to pay me to learn anything else."

Deb was surprised, then suddenly felt foolish. "I didn't bring any money. I didn't think about it."

"You didn't bring any?"

"But I can come back. I will come back."

"Shit."

"Really, I promise, I'll pay you!" Deb felt like she was begging. And didn't care.

"How much?"

"I don't know. A hundred. Two hundred?"

Maria stood.

"Five hundred?"

That was a lot for her.

Deb remembered how, just months ago, five hundred seemed like a relatively small amount of money.

"I can't really talk about this," Maria said. "We're not supposed to. The others would kill me. They just think I'm asking you how you found me."

"Please. It's the only way I can find out what happened to him."

The door at the bottom of the stairs opened.

"I promise. Five hundred."

"Come back Friday with the money," Maria said, her voice low.

And then she left.

CHAPTER

17

Cessy dried off the last glass and set it in the drink tray. Two in the morning, and no customers were left in the Fells Gate Tavern. William, the bar's owner and manager, was in his office in the back. Otherwise, Cessy was alone.

Two in the morning. She'd woken at this exact time the last couple of nights, worried about Smith and Harris. Their grim seriousness. The unrelenting sense of duty. The money they wanted.

And she thought about Barry, her repeated phone calls to the hospital that had finally revealed he was locked inside a coma because of a brain hemorrhage, which was due to a fractured skull, which, she knew, was due to trauma from a chair.

Cessy wondered if Barry was going to die, wondered how she'd feel if he did. She didn't regret defending herself, and she didn't feel guilt for hitting him with that chair.

But she wondered if she should.

At two in the morning, those thoughts nagged her like a rush of insect bites.

William came out of the back office. He was in his late twenties and had the benefit of a young man's body and energy—naturally thin, bright eyes that didn't show the effects of late evenings, mussed black hair that always looked as if he'd given up brushing halfway through.

"You're here late," Cessy observed.

"Just going over stuff." He picked up a glass Cessy had cleaned, filled it with water. "How you been? Since Hector . . . are you doing okay?"

"I'm okay."

Weird about Hector.

Sometimes Cessy had to remind herself that she'd once loved him, been crazy about him. That romance seemed so distant to her, almost unimaginable. The hitting had pushed it further away, until his death had seemed more like the loss of an acquaintance than a husband. Sometimes, at two in the morning, to deflect her worries, Cessy thought about the early days of their relationship. How, that fall they first met, they would walk around Bolton Hill, the neighborhood Hector lived in, every night.

She remembered how the weather was cool but not cold, the fall young. An occasional mild wind waved down the street and wide side-walks, past white marble steps. They would pass F. Scott Fitzgerald's house—Cessy vaguely remembered the writer's name from school—a plaque demarcating where he had lived when Baltimore held him, a high purplish building with carved iron railings on the bottom win-dows and bordered on either side by homes of brick and stone. They would pass the residence of someone neither of them knew, named Edith Hamilton, another giant dwelling, but this one adorned with low-to-the-ground balconies. They would pass the statue of Billie Hol-liday, a green, surprised-looking statue of Lady Day singing. Cessy often felt, as they walked between the trees and the houses, that they had slipped into another world inside the city. The red brick was stout, the white marble sparkled; people congregated on porch steps to gossip and chat and commune. Sometimes she and Hector would just sit quietly on those steps, him sprawled above her, she leaning back between his knees.

"I only met him a couple of times," William said, "when he'd come here to the bar. But it's weird: I can't stop thinking about you guys."

"Really?"

"It was just so sudden." William glanced apologetically at her. "Sorry."

"It's okay."

"It's not like it's weird to have a killing in Baltimore, right? But when it happens to someone you know, or sort of know, things feel shaky."

As he spoke, William seemed to turn even younger to Cessy, chang-ing from his twenties to a teen. But she understood what he was describ-ing, remembered the first time violence had swarmed her emotions.

Back in Arizona.

With her brother.

Something else occurred to her, and she hated herself for seeing William's concern as an opportunity, but she was desperate.

"Hey, Will, ever since Hector died, money's been tight. And I was wondering, well, this is really hard to ask . . ."

It was hard. Cessy couldn't remember ever asking someone for money. Even when she had first moved here with almost nothing.

"Do you need a raise?"

"Kind of."

"I can't believe this," William said.

"What do you mean?"

"It's just . . . things aren't going that well with the bar. We haven't turned a profit for the past couple of months. The crime rate or something is keeping people out of the city, like Baltimore's going through another exodus. Like the ones the old-timers say happened in the seventies and eighties." He rubbed his eyes. "I think we need to do some advertising or something."

Cessy blinked. "Wait, do you want to borrow money from *me*?"

Will laughed a little. "No. Not really. I wanted to ask if you'd consider foregoing your pay for a month or two. Only working for tips. Just for a month or two."

Cessy looked him in the face. He didn't look into hers.

And she felt hope fading inside her, like a trail of smoke from a snuffed match.

"I mean, I don't make that much to begin with," Cessy said.

He kept staring at the floor. "I know."

"I can't give it all up," Cessy said. "But maybe a little."

Will nodded. "I'd appreciate that. It's just been so tough. I've been sleeping here lately. I got rid of my apartment, and all my stuff's at a friend's place. I can't afford it."

"I understand," Cessy said. "I'm going through some hard times too."

"Did you try getting a loan?" William asked. "I did that at the beginning. I can't go back to the bank now, but they gave me money."

"My credit's shit. Mainly because of Hector. It's okay." Cessy paused. "I have a plan B."

But the thought of plan B filled her with dread, a turn in the road leading somewhere dark.

A place from which she couldn't return.

18

Deb barely spoke while Levi drove her back home. Instead, she stared out the window, one knee pulled up under her chin, silently crying.

"Do you need to talk?" Levi asked her.

Deb wiped away tears. "I'm not going to tell anyone what happened."

She meant that she wouldn't tell anyone about the help he'd given her. Levi misunderstood. "Keeping this stuff to yourself is a big mistake," he said gravely. "Guys who work with me try that shit. It hurts in the long run. Better to talk about it."

Levi looked at her for so long that Deb told him, "Please watch the road."

Despite everything she'd learned, despite the urgency with which Maria had confided in her, Deb was back to square one.

She wished Levi had been wrong about Grant.

Deb had been desperately hoping for a different outcome. Hoped those girls would be baffled when she'd mentioned Grant, deny convincingly they'd ever come across his name. Wanted Levi to realize he had the wrong person.

Deb felt like she was standing on the deck of a sinking boat, grief like water lapping her ankles. And rising.

She and Levi spent the rest of the drive in silence, she staring out the window and crying. Once she felt Levi's hand on her shoulder, two quick pats and a brief squeeze. And then his hand left.

They slowed to a stop outside her house.

"Thanks," Deb said. She wiped her tears, pushed open her door, stepped out.

She heard Levi's door open and close as she walked up the sidewalk.

"Hey," he said, hurrying behind her. "Are you okay?"

It was the kind of annoying question Grant used to ask when she was obviously angry. It still annoyed her. Deb stopped and turned.

"No, Levi," she said. "I'm pretty fucking depressed."

"I think you should talk with me."

"Nothing to talk about. My husband slept with a prostitute."

The front door opened.

"You're late," Kim said sternly, standing in the entrance. She glanced behind Deb. "Who's that? Is he coming to dinner?"

"Dinner?" Deb was confused. "We're having dinner?"

Kim's voice turned into a high-pitched whine. "Mom, I told you we were! So you could meet Rebecca!"

It took Deb a moment.

"That's tonight?"

"Yes! Who are you?"

Levi seemed taken aback. "I'm—my name's Levi. Levi Price."

"And are you staying for dinner?"

"Am I what?"

Another woman emerged behind Kim, looked out the front door. "You didn't tell me your mom was bringing someone."

"I didn't know," Kim replied.

"I mean, I could eat," Levi said, and he looked questioningly at Deb. "If it isn't an imposition."

A third woman appeared behind Kim. "Well, well, well, who's this young man?"

"And Nicole showed up," Kim added.

And that was how Deb found herself at dinner with her daughter, her daughter's girlfriend, her best friend, and an FBI agent.

Kim had prepared dinner, but Deb wasn't hungry, which was a shame because Kim was a terrific cook. One of Deb's favorite memories was standing in the kitchen with her eleven-year-old daughter, Kim silently watching Deb prepare a meal, eager to learn how to do it on her own. Cooking, especially after Kim had been born and Deb had grown older and days turned tiring, had often been more burden than pleasure, but Kim's enthusiasm brought back Deb's excitement, reminded her of the pleasure that comes from preparation, the almost mathematical, artistic perfection of ingredients forming to produce a lovely meal.

Tonight Kim had prepared juicy roasted herb chicken, with sides of small boiled potatoes and green beans. Deb ate a little of her chicken and fiddled with the green beans, too lost in her thoughts about Grant and Maria to enjoy Kim's cooking. Next to her, Levi shoveled his food down.

Nicole sat on the other side of Deb, occasionally leaning forward to take a quick peek at Levi.

The two girls had barely touched their dinners. They sat across from Deb and Levi and Nicole, holding hands under the table.

"So where were you?" Kim asked. "Why were you late?"

Deb picked up a small piece of chicken with her fork, set it down. "I had to deal with some things about your dad."

Kim indicated Levi with a gesture. "And who's he?"

"Hmph?" Levi asked, his mouth stuffed with food.

"He's an attorney," Deb lied. "He's helping me go over some of your father's things."

"An attorney!" Nicole exclaimed.

"I'm sorry," Rebecca said unexpectedly, her face softening. "When you came late, Kim and I thought . . . we've had to deal with a great deal of pushback."

"I didn't mean to give you that impression," Deb replied. "I'm sorry too."

Rebecca smiled at her, and Deb wanly smiled back. Rebecca was pretty. Black with long braids, expressive eyes, and lips curved in a natural, delicate pout. Deb could see why her daughter was taken by her.

"Kim said you were cool with it, but she wasn't, like, sure," Rebecca said.

"I'm cool with it," Deb answered. It was nice, she reflected, to have control of her emotions in one situation. To feel happiness and have that feeling affect someone else in a good way. Everything she'd learned about Grant had pervaded too much. She needed honesty.

"I didn't know you'd hired another attorney." Nicole frowned.

Deb didn't know what to do with that. "Yes?"

She'd planned on telling Nicole everything, but not Kim. At least, not yet.

Kim and Rebecca brought their hands up to the table and set them down.

"You two are dating?" Levi asked, surprised.

The women all looked at him. Kim and Rebecca lifted their joined hands.

And Deb wondered exactly how perceptive an FBI agent Levi was.

"For months now," Kim said.

"I couldn't tell," he said.

Kim and Rebecca's eyes narrowed. Nicole shook her head. Deb inwardly groaned.

"What does that mean?" Kim asked. "Couldn't tell?"

"Oh boy," Nicole said.

Levi hard-swallowed whatever food was left in his mouth. "Nothing bad. I just meant you don't look, I mean . . ."

"We don't look all dykey to you?" Rebecca asked.

"You done screwed up now, Levi," Nicole put in.

Levi seemed unsure of himself. Deb might have felt sorry for him if she wasn't already annoyed about Grant. And men in general.

"It's this sense that people need to conform to a stereotype," Rebecca told him, "a stereotype that the privileged hold us to. That we need to act or look in accordance to a way that makes straight white men comfortable. And anything outside of that is unacceptable."

Levi frowned. "I don't think that's what I meant."

"It's what you implied," Nicole added.

"Well, look," Levi said, trying to recover, "I don't have anything against gay people. It's really no big deal to me. My old colleague was gay. Totally cool guy. Liked football, even."

Deb saw Kim bristle, and decided to jump in. "Listen," she said, "go easy on him. He's trying."

"Trying?" Rebecca asked.

"All I mean is," Deb said, "sometimes people try to do good, and mean well, but they're clumsy about it. Their hearts are in the right place, even if they're not as caught up as everyone else."

"Exactly," Nicole offered. "Just like . . . Canadians? No, that doesn't work. I can't think of a good analogy."

"But that's the thing," Rebecca countered to Deb. "Their hearts aren't always in the right place. They're fine with gay people being gay, black people being black, or poor people being poor, as long as it's in ways that don't bother them. Meaning we stay in our place, or our role. It's like Harriett Beecher Stowe."

Everyone at the table looked blankly at her.

"Harriett Beecher Stowe," Rebecca went on, "wrote *Uncle Tom's Cabin*. And it helped bring about the Civil War. The book showed slavery in a way that bothered people, got them to act. But it was also a reductive look at blacks and one that emphasized a path to resistance that many found destructive. It brought the sins of slavery to a personal level, but not an institutional one. And that allowed discrimination to evolve into different forms and flourish."

"What are you studying?" Nicole asked.

"English."

"That's where we met," Kim put in. "English class."

But now Deb was interested in the conversation. She liked what Rebecca had to say, found it engaging. Part of that, she realized, was the distraction from what she had learned that afternoon, but it also reminded her of the debates she'd had in college.

She hadn't been intellectually stimulated for a long time.

Grant used to take the lead in all debates, with family or friends, regardless of topic. He was overbearing when he argued, and Deb just listened quietly.

She hadn't realized how much she missed being part of a discussion.

"So you're saying," she asked Rebecca, "that people are shortsighted, and that's part of a system that placates them? Because they don't fully understand cultural norms. Right?"

Rebecca thought it over. "Kind of."

"Look at you, Deb!" Nicole marveled. "I'm so impressed, especially considering how much we all drank in college."

Kim laughed. Deb ignored her.

"But aren't they always shortsighted?" she asked Rebecca. "Aren't cultures always changing? When I was in school, we were learning the basics of racial understanding. I'm betting that twenty years from now, that approach will be different."

"That sounds like an excuse," Rebecca countered.

"It is, a little," Deb admitted. "Mainly because I don't think people are always secretly bad."

But Deb thought about Grant and wondered if she still believed that.

"Me neither," Rebecca replied. "I think they're unintentionally bad."

"You don't think someone will find what you're saying now unintentionally bad twenty or fifty years later?"

Rebecca smiled again. "I mean, I hope not."

Her smile warmed Deb. She did like Rebecca.

She wondered how Grant would have reacted to Rebecca, and to Kim's changing identity. Politically and culturally, Grant had been liberal, but a relatively untested one. He championed stances—pro-choice, anti-capital punishment—that had yet to affect him. But Deb had noticed his views had a tendency to narrow, to traffic largely in self-interest, when something directly impacted him. Like taxes or proposed city ordinances. Under scrutiny or application, Deb had often thought Grant's views would drop like leaves from December trees.

She doubted he'd be able to easily accept his daughter was bisexual or that she was dating a black woman.

That thought annoyed her more.

"Sorry," Rebecca said. "I'm in your house, and I'm getting all political and feisty."

"That's okay," Deb said. "I like it."

"I yell at her all the time," Nicole confided to Rebecca. "It's cool."

"Do you, um, want me to go or stay?" Levi asked.

Deb was relieved when Kim and Rebecca laughed.

"No, but let's talk about something else," Kim said.

They finished dinner without Levi annoying anyone again, and instead talked about college life, how Kim and Rebecca were enjoying it, where Rebecca was from. Deb learned that Rebecca had been born in Annapolis; her father taught at the Naval Academy, and her mother was a lawyer. She hoped to become a professor like her dad.

And she noticed how Kim watched her as Rebecca spoke, with admiration, adoration.

Her daughter was smitten.

"Well," Levi said as they finished their food, and the conversation drew to a close, "this ended up better than it started, but I need to go."

"Me too," Rebecca said, glancing at her watch, then at Deb. "But it was really nice meeting you."

"Lovely meeting you too. Make sure my daughter treats you well."

"Cripes, mom," Kim said, but with humor.

The small group walked to the front door, and sadness started creeping through Deb. It was the sadness she'd felt when Kim first left for college, that sense of abandonment, the empty feeling a once-crowded house brings.

She was happy Nicole was with her.

"We have a *lot* to talk about," Deb whispered to Nicole.

"I'm not going anywhere," Nicole whispered back, and she headed into the living room.

Kim and Rebecca were talking by Rebecca's car, a small Prius. Levi glanced at Deb, and his expression turned troubled.

"You okay?"

Deb nodded.

"Kind of forgot about everything during dinner, right? And now it's all back?"

Deb nodded again, surprised at Levi's prescience.

"Yeah," he went on. "I thought that might happen. You go through a tragedy, and your mind wants you to forget. Your body wants to heal. Like any bruise or injury. It's just your body trying to scab over."

"I guess so," Deb said.

"I'm not a shrink or anything," Levi added, "but you ever need to talk, I'm here."

Deb still had her eyes fixed on her daughter and her daughter's girl-friend. She was watching them, but her mind was elsewhere. Back in that Capitol Hill apartment building, on the staircase with Maria Vasquez.

"Thanks for being so nice to me," she told Levi distantly.

"What are you thinking about?" he asked.

"I'm wondering what Maria's going to tell me on Friday."

19

CESSY BLEW INTO her cupped hands. It was cold inside Scoops Ice Cream Shop, but it wasn't just the temperature making her tense. She picked up her coffee, took a sip.

She was already nervous, so it didn't seem like a good idea to add caffeine to her fraying nerves, but Cessy wanted warmth. And she had an addiction to caffeine. Cessy often downed extravagant coffees from Starbucks during work breaks, let energy drinks fuel her mornings. She glanced at the other customers in the shop—a young couple with two kids, a group of talkative high school kids in the corner—and wondered if this was enough of a crowd to stop anything bad from happening. If anyone here would actually jump up to help her if she needed it.

A hand fell on her shoulder.

Cessy almost screamed.

Smith and Harris walked around her, took the opposite two seats at her table.

"How'd you get behind me?" Cessy asked. She turned, saw a door for staff. "You guys work here?"

Harris smiled. Smith didn't. Once again, they were wearing nearly identical outfits—blue jeans and black T-shirts. Harris's arms were heavily tattooed, so much so that she couldn't actually tell what the designs were. Smith's arms were bare.

"We don't work here," Harris said. "We just know a lot of people."

"Even the people at Scoops?"

"Every business has a boss," Harris said. "And every boss has a boss."

Cessy thought about that, about the warning Barry had given her.
They're killers.
And they're everywhere.

"Do you have our money?" Smith asked, his voice soft but menacing.

Cessy took a breath. "Not even a little of it."

"Then why are we here?" Harris asked.

"Because I wanted to tell you that you're right. I did put Barry in the hospital. After he attacked me."

Neither of the men allowed themselves much of a response. Harris rubbed the stubble on his chin.

"He's still there," Harris said. "Hasn't woken up."

"I know. I've been checking."

"Why'd you tell us?" Smith asked.

"Because you should know what I'm capable of," Cessy told them, and immediately realized how hollow the words sounded. But it was the truth.

She wanted them to know she'd fight back.

At least, that's what Cessy had planned ahead of time. She'd had no idea how unconvincing her threat would sound.

Or how little they'd care.

"Where's our money?" Smith asked.

"I told you, I don't have it."

Their expressions didn't change.

"But I have something else," Cessy went on, and bent down to reach into her handbag.

"Ah," one of the men said. Cessy looked up. From her bent position, she could see under the table, and she saw a gun in each man's lap, pointed at her.

"Sit back up," Harris said.

Cessy did, slowly, leaving her handbag on the floor

"You don't want to move too fast around us," Smith told her. "We get nervous."

Cessy inhaled. It felt like she hadn't taken a breath in hours. "How'd you get your guns out so quickly?"

"Keep your voice down," Smith said.

"And what's in the purse?" Harris asked. "Is it our money?"

"You have a one-track mind," Cessy joked, but she couldn't keep her voice steady or strong. She'd grown up around guns in Arizona, but never had one pointed at her. Knowing that any slip of the finger, any increase in tension, could end her life brought a panic she could barely keep at bay.

"It's not the money?" Smith asked.

"It's something else in my purse. Can I show you?"

Smith reached down and picked up her handbag. He opened it up and glanced inside.

"It's in the envelope," Cessy told him.

Smith handed her the envelope, and his hands disappeared back under the table.

Cessy paused before opening the envelope.

"Please put your guns away. They make me really nervous."

Neither man moved.

"Seriously, it's hard to concentrate or do anything," Cessy continued, her voice low. "Could you at least point them somewhere else?"

"Open the envelope," Harris told her.

Cessy was so shaky that she felt like the envelope might drop to the floor, but she managed to tear it open. She pulled out copies of the photos she'd found in Hector's nightstand. Placed them on the table.

Harris flipped through them with one hand.

Smith looked at her, and she didn't like his look. It felt invasive and angry, like he was staring at something that had been stolen from him.

It took Harris a few minutes to finish leafing through the photos. But he finally set them down, pushed them toward his partner.

Smith glanced through them.

Cessy watched him carefully.

"What are these?" he asked.

"You know what they are."

"Awfully blurry," he said. "Hard to see anything. Harder to prove anything."

"Really? Because I think it proves Hector was working with some disreputable shit. Including a bald guy with tattoos who probably wishes he was out of the frame."

"You're looking at this like an execution, like we did it," Smith said. "This was taken after we found the bodies."

That hadn't occurred to Cessy.

"But what are you saying?" Smith asked, his expression still maddeningly blank. "You're threatening to take this to the cops?"

"I'm saying I can because, no matter what, I'm sure you don't want them to see this. So drop the money Hector owed and forget I ever knew you. Let me do my thing, you do yours, and we never see each other again."

"Well, see," Harris drawled, "you just made that kind of impossible."

Despair started filling Cessy, like it was being poured from a pitcher. "What do you mean?"

"You show us these pictures, and you think we can just let it go?"

"But . . . you don't have a choice."

"No?"

"I have a friend who has a copy of these, and she's ready to go to the cops if anything happens to me."

That was a lie, but Cessy hoped it was a good one.

The thumb drive with the pictures was at the bar, beneath a loose floorboard.

"You think you can blackmail us?" Smith asked.

"I think I can make a deal with you. You don't mess with me, and I don't mess with you. That's it. We go our separate ways."

"Why should we trust you?"

"Because I'd have already gone to the cops if you couldn't."

The two men regarded her, then abruptly stood. Their guns were hidden once again.

"We'll let you know," Harris told her.

"When?"

"You'll know when."

CHAPTER

20

THEY CAME TWICE a week to collect from Maria Vasquez, to take her money and divide it up, to ask her questions about her clients, to find out what she'd learned. To give her new questions to ask.

They would bring her food and clothes and bed sheets and towels. Check to see if there was anything she needed. Sometimes even bring her what she wanted. Most of the time they ignored her requests.

They came Wednesday and Sunday mornings between nine and eleven. They came after the men who fucked her in the morning; before the men who fucked her on their lunch breaks. And never in the evenings, when her schedule was full.

Long ago, Maria had stopped keeping track of how many men she'd been with, how many showed up at the apartment down the hall throughout the day. How often she had to smile, pretend that they were the first one she'd been with that day. How she'd learned to disguise the noises she made from pain, make them think it was pleasure.

That was the most important thing, the lesson ingrained in her forever.

Maria had learned that the men who liked hearing her in pain, and there were many, only wanted more. They wanted to push Maria to the point of begging, breaking, death. They yanked her hair so hard the roots were torn, callously smacked her, wrapped burly arms around her throat.

And Maria acted like nothing ever hurt or scared her, buried her grimace in their shoulders or chests or the pillow or bed sheets.

They'd already been by on Wednesday and brought her money and questions. But Maria wouldn't be there when they stopped by on Sunday.

Maria planned to be gone by then.

Grant's death and Deb's visit had shaken her. Set off an unease that refused to settle. Something wasn't right, and Maria didn't know what it was, but she knew she had to leave. Maybe head back to Michigan, get a job waiting tables, leave the past three years in DC behind. Pretend they never happened. It wouldn't be hard.

There was nothing here she wanted to remember.

And tonight was the perfect time to leave. The other girls were gone, called away to go to dinner or something. They'd return and she'd have disappeared. With luck, no one here would know she'd even existed.

Maria didn't have much money, but she had enough for a bus ticket that would take her a state or two away. Had a bag halfway packed.

She wondered about her mother, wondered if her mother would even want to talk with her again. It had been three years since Maria had run away from home, and she didn't know if her mother's worry and concern had turned to resentment. Maria had been cruel to leave and never contact her, and didn't know if that cruelty was reparable.

But she wanted to try. Wanted to return to that little house outside Detroit, knock on the door, the way someone was knocking on her apartment door.

She wanted to see her mother's face again, even if it was angry.

Maria walked to the door, pulled it open mid-knock.

Something smashed into the side of her head.

It took Maria a few moments to realize she was on her hands and knees. To feel blood. To understand that gasping sound was coming from her.

The brass knuckles sank into her forehead again, tearing skin, cracking bone.

The killer hit Maria twice more until she was lying down, until her hands trembled beside her.

Until blood poured from her skull like wine from a spilled goblet.

That's when the killer took off the knuckles, pulled on gloves, and searched the apartment.

Searched for any incriminating information Maria had collected about the men she worked for. Or anything about Grant Thomas.

And, like the killer's search through Deb Thomas's basement, nothing was found. Except for Maria's half-packed suitcase. The killer unpacked it, hung the clothes back up, returned the toiletries to the bathroom. Hid any signs Maria was distressed or running.

Last, the killer washed off the brass knuckles.

The DC night was dark, the way darkness descended on the city in winter, like the suddenness of a hand clamping down over someone's mouth. A man walking a dog stared down into his glowing phone. A woman hurried up the street, an oversized satchel slapping her side with each step, with the quick pace women assume when walking alone at night.

Something started gnawing in the killer's gut. Distress. Not about what the killer had just done. Distress because the killer knew the same thing would need to be done to Deb Thomas, soon.

She was getting closer.

CHAPTER

21

Dana laughed and bit down on a doughnut. "No way," he said to Cessy, wiping jelly off his chin. "You almost drowned in a kiddie pool?"

"Hey!" Cessy said, pretending to sound sharp, but only for Dana's amusement. She liked seeing him laugh. "Lots of people drown every year. It's not funny."

"Yes, but not in kiddie pools when they're seventeen."

"I never learned how to swim! We didn't have very many oceans or lakes in Arizona, you know."

"But you had pools, right?"

"Sorry I wasn't born into luxury, like you, so I could take swimming lessons. And horseback riding. And— I don't know—archery, probably."

Dana was still laughing. "I just can't get over the image of you splashing around in two feet of water."

"You know," Cessy said, "it's pretty terrifying for someone who doesn't know how to swim, thank you very much."

"But you know how to stand up, right? You could have done that."

"I never should have told you this."

"No kidding." Dana finished off his doughnut. "You definitely should have kept this to yourself."

"Well, I made the whole thing up to make you laugh. You're welcome."

He looked at her, his face wonderfully light and uncomplicated. "No, you didn't."

"No, I didn't," Cessy admitted.

Dana stretched back in his bedroom's chair, raised his hands to the ceiling. "I will say one nice perk of being here are the free doughnuts."

"Every Friday morning," Cessy said. "Rose really should put that in the brochure—if she had a brochure."

"No kidding," Dana said. "I'd bring dates here. You sure you don't want one?"

Cessy hadn't, but the Diablo Doughnuts box she'd passed on her way in, and seeing how ravenously Dana devoured his, changed her mind. "Yeah, okay. I'll be right back."

She headed into the hallway, listening to the televisions in the other bedrooms, decided to stop in the bathroom for a quick pee. One of the inexplicable things Cessy liked was the sounds of televisions behind closed doors. She wasn't sure why, but thought it might be because it reminded her of a trip she'd once taken with her brother and mother when she was six years old. They'd gone to a family-friendly hotel in Phoenix, one that had its own water park on the premises, and she remembered running with Chris down the outdoor hall smelling of chlorine, with flip-flops smacking against their soles, their mother, somewhere behind them, calling to them to slow down.

She and Chris had been so excited that day. They'd stopped at the end of the hallway, panting and waiting for their mother to catch up. The trip had been lovely—just the three of them, everyone happy— and Cessy and Chris had confided to each other countless times that neither of them wanted to go back home. They loved living in the hotel, loved the lighthearted nature of other guests, the intimacy of the environment, as if they were all on an adventure together. They waited for their mother as Cessy listened to the television coming from the room closest to her, the slow, soothing, low-tension music of some day-time soap opera's theme song. It was one of her best memories from childhood.

Cessy stepped into the bathroom, closed the door to the halfway house's restroom behind her. Pushed down her jeans, peed, pulled them up. Washed her hands in the cracked sink. Glanced at herself in the mirror.

It had never occurred to her, until that moment, that part of the reason she liked volunteering here was because it reminded her of that hotel in Phoenix, especially the temporary nature. Their mother had been so happy that trip; they all had, but especially their mother. Cheerful and silly and indulgent, a world away from their lives.

Cessy walked back into the hallway, listened to the television behind the closed bedroom door next to the bathroom. Heard the sound of cartoons.

Paused.

Odd that someone here would be watching cartoons. The residents of this house were occasionally younger, but not that much younger.

And then Cessy realized something else strange. The person staying in this room, a young woman named Holli, had moved out days ago.

Cessy knocked on the door. When no one answered, she walked in. The room was empty of anything but the base furnishings Rose supplied. And the television was on. The coyote from *Looney Tunes* lighting sticks of dynamite.

Cessy snapped off the television. Rose was a worrier about electricity, both its expense and environmental impact, and leaving the television on was an odd mistake. The kind Rose didn't often make.

Still, Cessy wasn't alarmed. Rose was in her late seventies. It wasn't a surprise something had finally slipped past her.

Cessy headed downstairs and was about to walk into the kitchen when she saw that Rose had fallen asleep. She stopped, afraid of waking her. Rose often fell asleep at the kitchen table and was moody upon waking.

Well, Cessy reflected, *Rose is normally moody.* But Cessy knew from prior experience not to rouse her.

Still, Cessy stared hard at the box of doughnuts sitting on the table in front of Rose's sleeping form, wondered if it was worth the effort.

She sighed quietly, headed back upstairs.

Walked back into Dana's room and stopped at the door.

He was sitting half-collapsed in his chair.

Cessy walked over to him.

"Dana?"

He didn't move.

Cessy touched his shoulder, grabbed it. Said his name again.

He was breathing, but Cessy couldn't wake him. She started saying his name louder, nearly shouting.

And that's when Cessy realized something was terribly wrong.

She ran out of the room, headed back to the stairs. Saw a gray and black cloud of smoke rising up, impossible to see past. Somewhere inside it, the rustling sound of fire.

"Shit!" Cessy raced back to Dana's room, screaming "Fire! Fire!" She hurried inside, closed the door behind her.

Cessy didn't see smoke but felt it closing in on her, circling her, pushing its way into her throat.

"Rose!" She remembered her suddenly, thought again of hurrying downstairs.

A rushing sound from downstairs, and Cessy remembered something else, a term that sprung into her memory from years ago. Something Hector had told her about when he was considering becoming a firefighter.

Flashover.

When a fire grows so intense that everything in a room—chairs, tables, curtains—bursts into flames. A room-sized ball of fire that instantly consumes everything inside of it.

Rose.

Cessy had to get downstairs, had to save Rose, had to save Dana and everyone in the house, had to escape—had to do something.

She ran to the window in Dana's room, opened it with the thought that the smoke would disperse. And the thought that this would be the easiest way to get outside.

And then she remembered the bars.

All the windows in the bedrooms had bars. She opened the bedroom door again, looked out. Smoke was spreading through the hall, turning everything hazy.

She glanced back at Dana.

"Stay here." Cessy said. It was unnecessary to say but made her feel better about leaving Dana behind. She ran coughing through the knee-high smoke to the shared bathroom, pushed open the door.

Bars on the window.

Cessy ripped off her shirt, ran it under the sink, loosely tied it into a makeshift bandana over her nose and mouth. She had no idea where she'd learned that technique—maybe from Hector? But it helped. She could still taste the smoke, but it wasn't as strong. She rushed back into the hall, pushing open the four bedroom doors. The other two residents, women whose names Cessy was too scared to remember, were lying on the floor.

That haziness had increased, turned the world gray, clouded her mind.

She ran to the staircase, remembering Ruth, thinking escape. Looked down the stairs.

Smoke was a black wall.

And then, through the panic, Cessy heard something.

Someone screaming.

Dana.

The smoke in Dana's bedroom was thick on the floor. And it wasn't just smoke. Fire had spread into the room, burning the walls, burning the bed, burning Dana as he sat slumped in the chair.

"Help me! I can't, I can't move!"

Cessy called his name, grabbed his hand, tried to pull him with all her force. She stumbled back and fell, stared at her hands.

Stared at his burnt and melted flesh.

The screaming was all she heard now, his screaming, more screaming, the women in the other rooms. She watched the fire eat Dana's body like starved ants.

A finger of smoke reached into Cessy's throat.

She coughed, climbed to her feet. Ran through the fire and smoke to the door.

The room had grown too dark to see a thing. Smoke blinded her, filled her mouth and nose and airways like a thick cluster of hair clogging a drain.

Nothing but darkness from the smoke and pain from the fire.

Cessy tried to stand and couldn't.

Couldn't even figure out where the door had gone or which direction it was in.

Smoke had so filled Cessy that she couldn't cough, couldn't throw up. She had to find Rose and Dana and the others, and she had to escape. Call someone. Do something before the flames reached her.

Cessy fell to her knees.

She couldn't do anything.

Like smoke in her lungs, terror and desperation filled Cessy's soul. And consumed her.

PART THREE

FOLLOWING DEATH

CHAPTER

22

"It just doesn't seem like Grant." Nicole frowned. "I can't imagine him cheating on you with some prostitute. And I still can't believe you actually went to her place."

"I had to find out for myself." Deb held herself tighter under her jacket. It was far too cold to be in her backyard, but Nicole wanted to smoke, and Deb refused to let her smoke inside the house.

"Jesus. I'm so sorry, sweetie." Nicole took a drag from her cigarette. "Are you going to tell Kim?"

"She doesn't need to know. She doesn't ever need to know."

Nicole nodded.

Deb gestured at Nicole's cigarette. "Are you done yet?"

Nicole took the cigarette out of her mouth, glanced at it. "Does it look done?"

"You're the only person I know who still smokes."

"What's your point?"

"Shouldn't you vape or something else?" Deb adjusted her coat. "And by something else, I mean, something you could do someplace warmer?"

"Vaping's for quitters."

"I'm really not looking forward to sitting next to you while you're going through chemo someday."

"But you will be there sitting next to me, right?"

"I guess."

Nicole took another puff, then ground the cigarette out on the brick walkway. "Happy, nerd? I wasn't even finished."

"Thank you. Can we go inside now?"

They walked into the kitchen, sat at the kitchen table. Nicole smelled her hair and frowned. "Do you still love Grant?"

Deb took a moment to answer. "I'm not sure," she said uncertainly. "If this had happened when he was alive, I couldn't have stayed with him. I would have left."

Nicole nodded. "I think you would have too." She paused. "And I don't think it was just a couple of times . . . or that she was the only one."

Nicole said that last part cautiously, but it still stung Deb.

"What do you mean?"

"I mean, just . . . isn't cheating usually a sign of something else wrong? Like something else was bothering him?"

"I don't know," Deb said defensively. "Maybe he just wanted to get laid."

"I'm sorry," Nicole said. "I didn't mean to hurt your feelings." She rubbed her arm. "I just, I knew him too."

Deb stared down at her thumb, the chipped polish at the edge of her nail. "Did anyone ever cheat on you? Marcus never did, right?"

"No. I mean, I don't know. I don't think so. But some of the guys I dated afterward did. But maybe you're right. Maybe they just wanted to get laid."

"Well, shit," Deb said, "so did we. What's wrong with them?"

Nicole smiled.

"I don't even know if the sex was the worst thing," Deb went on. "Honestly. I mean, that's the thing that just kills me, that hits me hard when I think about it. But it's more the money."

"What do you mean?"

"Grant gave her—or the people she worked for, I don't know—everything we had. His savings, his retirement. He didn't have as much as I thought he did, but still." Deb paused, continued moodily, "Nothing about him seems like what I thought it was."

"Yeah?"

"Who would leave their family like this? I need to find work, Nicole. Or I'm going to have to put this house on the market a lot sooner than I thought. And how am I supposed to pay for Kim's college? Thank God she's not going back next semester."

"Have you looked into loans?"

"I'm going to have to. For her school, for our lives, for everything."

"I don't think," Nicole said uncertainly, "that Grant expected to leave you like this."

"But he did, and now we're here." Deb cupped her hands over her mouth and nose, breathed into them slowly.

"I knew Grant. He'd hate to see you like this."

"Can't you just call him an asshole?"

"What an asshole!"

"Thank you."

Deb's phone buzzed. She took it out of her pocket, checked the number.

"What's wrong?" Nicole asked.

"I don't know who this is." Deb accepted the call. "Hello?"

"Deb? This is Levi. Agent Price."

"One second." She signaled to Nicole that she needed a minute, and walked to the living room. The room was tidier than it had been the first weeks following Grant's death; still disheveled, but in a lived-in fashion. Almost as if it echoed the slow repair of their emotional recovery.

"I was hoping to stop by," Levi said. "Do you have a few minutes?"

"Sure." Deb picked up a square white pillow, placed it in the corner of the couch. "When were you thinking?"

"I'm parked outside."

"What?"

"Sorry. This is important."

"Um, okay. I need a minute or two."

Deb hung up, walked back into the kitchen.

Nicole had been playing with her phone; she was the only adult Deb knew who still played Candy Crush. Nicole set the phone down and looked up. "Who was it?"

Deb had told Nicole everything about Levi. "The FBI guy. He's outside."

"He is?" Nicole asked, surprised. It took her a moment to recover. "And I get to talk to him about FBI stuff?"

"I was hoping you'd leave through the back."

Nicole placed her hands behind her head, leaned back in the chair. "No. I'm going to stay here and make things awkward."

"Awesome. Thank you."

The doorbell rang.

Deb left Nicole in the kitchen, absent-mindedly ran a hand through her hair. Kim was getting lunch with a friend, and Deb was glad she didn't have to try to explain why Levi was here.

And lie to her daughter again.

She opened the door.

Levi Price was standing on the porch, wearing jeans and a black Gorillaz T-shirt under a worn leather jacket.

Deb blinked.

"You look different," she said.

"It's the jeans. People always say that the first time they see me in jeans."

"Also the shirt. But I guess I've never seen you in anything but a suit."

He didn't smile. Just maintained a serious, almost mournful expression.

Nicole's head appeared over Deb's right shoulder. "Hi! Have you ever shot anyone?"

"Nicole!" Deb said, and she told Levi apologetically, "I told her who you are."

"Are aliens real?" Nicole asked. "Who killed JFK?"

Levi looked confused. "Um . . ."

"She has no self-awareness or understanding of boundaries," Deb explained.

"Can I hold your gun?" Nicole asked. "That's not a euphemism."

Levi had been looking at Nicole in confusion, then his gaze turned toward Deb. "Can we talk alone?"

Deb took Levi to the living room. Nicole flounced back to the kitchen.

"Nicole can be a bit much," Deb said. "She'll say anything and has no self-awareness. I don't know why I love her. Anyway, I hope you're not upset that I told her."

"Maria Vasquez was killed."

"What?"

Deb hadn't realized she was sitting on the couch. Hadn't realized Levi was next to her.

He nodded tersely. "One of her roommates discovered her body in their apartment. She'd been bludgeoned to death."

Deb's mind felt like a feather in a hurricane.

"Bludgeoned?"

"We don't know why."

"Is it because she talked to me?"

"I'm sorry. We truly don't know."

Deb's jaw, neck, body ached from tension.

"Are we in danger? Me and Kim?"

"I don't think so," Levi said. "I hope not."

23

CHRIS WATCHED HIS sister sleep.

An IV was in her arm, sensors adhered to her chest. A breathing tube stretched down her throat. Cessy's expression was contorted, even as she slept. She woke occasionally, looked around, and then her eyes fluttered and closed. She'd glance at Chris, but without recognition.

A nurse told Chris that Cessy was in shock.

"The smoke inhalation was extreme, but she's going to be okay. We're going to keep her here for forty-eight hours to make sure. She didn't receive any direct burns, which is fortunate. They got to her just in time." The nurse, an older woman with tired eyes, wearily rubbed the back of her neck. "I heard about the fire. Who would do that to all those people?"

"Whoever did it should be fired!"

The nurse looked at Chris with a puzzled expression—an expression he was used to receiving—and left.

Chris didn't know where to go, wasn't sure what to do. He'd missed Cessy more than he'd realized. Seeing her lying unconscious was like someone ripping open a scar.

And his memories bled.

* * *

Three years ago, Chris had been watching television in his room and he'd heard a gunshot. He'd rushed out of the double wide into a sudden blast of Arizona heat.

A car raced around the far corner. A hot breeze raked the world. A slim jackrabbit darted across the street. Hard yellow weeds snapped under his feet. Chris noticed all of this; in that moment, he noticed everything. He'd remember all of it forever.

He saw Cessy kneeling by their mother.

Cessy turned toward him, blood on her hands, her shirt, her face, her leg. Their mother was dead when he knelt next to her.

Chris peered into the hole where her face had been.

No one came outside. The housing park just outside of Phoenix might as well have been deserted. But Chris knew people were staring from behind curtains.

Eventually the police showed. Walked and stared hard at the ground, at the street, talked to neighbors. Tried and failed to identify the car. A social worker arrived by mistake, under the assumption Chris and Cessy were under eighteen. She left after giving the trailer a pitying glance.

* * *

"Rohypnol," a doctor was telling a nurse, in conversation outside Cessy's room. "Incredibly high dose. She must have not ingested any to make it out into the hall."

"Those poor people," the nurse said.

"And who would drug doughnuts?" the doctor said, his voice lighter. "What a waste of jelly doughnuts."

The nurse smiled, but it was a forced smile.

Chris mulled over the joke from his chair, down the hall from Cessy's room.

Not bad, he decided.

* * *

Zack came by later that night, knocked on their door.

Chris let him in. The day had been long, exhausting. Their mother's body had been taken away. Cessy had gone somewhere—Chris had no idea where. He was lost in an old episode of The A-Team.

Zack sat at their small kitchen table, his arms tightly crossed. "Where is she?"

"Ambulance took her," Chris said. "I don't know why. She has no face."

"Can I pay my respects?" Zack asked. He took an envelope out of his pocket and tossed it on the table.

Chris didn't pick up the envelope.

Zack clapped his hands to his knees and started to stand.

"Who did this to her?" Chris asked. "One of her regulars?"

"I'm not sure. But trust me, I'll find out."

Chris didn't trust him. "Some of those clients were bad."

"I always made sure those men were okay. Never wanted anything to happen to her. You know I always took care of her."

"Sure," Chris replied.

"Sad as hell, though," Zack went on. "Your mother worked her ass off for me. But at least you and your sister are of age to take care of yourselves now. Cessy's over eighteen, right?"

"She's a year older than me. Twenty-one." Chris stood and walked over to the front door.

"She working? Because I was thinking . . ."

"Couple of years ago," Chris said, "Mom brought home this guy. A lawyer."

Zack pulled his ring finger until a knuckle popped. "I don't remember him."

"I was supposed to be out," Chris went on. "Leave the house to her. But I got the times screwed up, showed up while they were still here. While the lawyer was hurting our mom."

"I never would have let that happen," Zack declared.

Chris ignored him. "I heard her begging. Heard him smacking her. I wanted to go in right away, but thought maybe this was just some kink they were doing. Mom always told us to wait outside. But then she screamed."

He could hear Zack breathing.

"What'd you do?" Zack asked, his voice small.

"Buried him out back."

Zack paled.

Chris walked behind Zack. "I don't think you ever cared about our mom. I don't think you were anything more than her pimp."

Zack's hand dove into his pocket, and he pulled out a folding knife. He tried to unfold it, but Chris ripped the knife out of his hand.

He shoved the knife up Zack's neck.

Then pulled it out and shoved it up deeper.

Walked around, stared into Zack's eyes. Listened to Zack gasp, hands around his own throat like he was strangling himself, blood running through his fingers.

Watched the light fade away.

"Aw, dang it," Chris said.

*　*　*

Chris wandered down the hospital hallway. Saw an open door, peered inside at an elderly woman breathing mechanically through a ventilator. No one was with her, no family, no medical staff.

Something about the machine's rhythm and the isolation made Chris want to turn the ventilator off.

Chris hadn't been inside a hospital for years, had forgotten how quiet and lonely they were at night. He'd gone as a child for standard kid injuries—chicken pox, a broken arm, a fall where a front tooth had been knocked out—but hadn't returned to a hospital as an adult until Cessy insisted.

After Zack.

*   *   *

When Cessy came home, eyes wide with grief, Chris was trying to wrap Zack in plastic garbage bags.

Cessy stared at the dead man on the floor, the knife handle still jutting out from under his chin.

"He pulled the knife first," Chris told Cessy.

"Did he?" she asked softly.

Chris nodded. "But who cares? You know what they did. They killed mom."

"They?"

Chris ignored her, went to work on the plastic bags and the masking tape.

"Who's 'they,' Chris?"

He cut open another bag, wrapped it around Zack's legs.

"Have there been others?" Cessy asked.

After a moment:

"Chris?"

Chris wouldn't look at her when he spoke.

"They were all guilty."

His voice sounded like it was coming from far away, from the inside of a deep cave.

"Oh," Cessy said.

Later that night, between three and four in the morning, Cessy helped her brother bury Zack's body behind the double wide.

He was careful to make sure they didn't accidentally dig up one of the other bodies. Best that Cessy not see them.

But she knew, even if she didn't want to know. The same way their mother didn't want to know.

Knowing, but not absorbing.
Hearing, but not acting.

*   *   *

Chris stood next to the sleeping elderly lady, stared down at her, tried to figure out why she was in the hospital. She had liver spots, but no visible bruises, no bandages or wraps that indicated why she was here. No chart hanging at the foot of her bed that described her illness, like in television shows.

Chris remembered the rabbit he'd found at work months ago. He'd been spreading rocks on some family's yard, scooping them out of the truck and laying them on plastic tarp. His shovel had hit something soft, something that sounded different than the rough shriek of metal scraping stone, even through his ear plugs.

He'd set the shovel aside, reached into the rocks, pulled out the body of a small jackrabbit.

Despite being buried under hundreds of pounds of stone, the rabbit's dead body was intact. Limp in his hand, eyes narrowed but open. One ear bent at an improbable angle, like an "L." But otherwise unharmed.

The old lady seemed the same to Chris. Her body unbroken.

Like him, after he and Cessy had buried Zack, when Cessy insisted Chris go to the hospital or a doctor, or find someone to talk to him.

Either that or she'd go to the cops.

So Chris had gone to see a doc a few days later, hung out in the parking lot for an hour, idly threw rocks at cacti. Did the bare minimum to make her happy, make himself honest.

Chris didn't need someone to tell him what everyone else told him—that he was just a little off. He could work and function and live just fine.

If anything bothered him, it was the memory of some man years ago, doing things Chris didn't want. Those flashes of memory—his small pants around his ankles, a giant hand over his own, leading him to a bedroom—sent him to a new space, a place inside his mind where Chris was safe; a funny, disjointed place inside him, where everything was detached. Where nothing was real.

After a while, he stayed there.

But when Cessy found out Chris hadn't actually gone inside the doctor's office, she was furious.

Even so, she hadn't gone to the cops.

She'd just left.

* * *

"Ay niño," *Octavia, Chris and Cessy's mother, said one rough morning as she emerged from her bedroom. She delicately lowered herself to the couch, picked up an open bottle of warm beer from the small end table. Drank deeply.*

"¿Puedes traer la bolsa de hielo?"

Chris barely spoke any Spanish, but he understood it. He walked over to their little freezer. Gave the blue ice pack to his mother.

Octavia rested it on her abdomen. "Gracias, mi amor."

"De nada."

Another long drink. Octavia set the empty bottle on the floor. "¿Dónde está Cassandra? ¿Escuela o trabajo?"

"She's going to school, then work."

"Ah." *Octavia grimaced as she shifted her weight.* "¿Y cómo están tus clases?"

"Good."

Octavia glanced at Chris, closed her eyes, and nodded.

He hadn't been back to Pima Community College for at least a year.

His mother knew but didn't want to know.

* * *

"Can I help you?"

A voice behind Chris. His hand moved away from the ventilator. He turned toward the hospital room door.

"I'm okay."

A nurse watched him. "Do you know her?"

"She reminds me of my mom."

"What?"

"She doesn't look like her. Just reminds me of her."

The nurse seemed like she wanted to say something but wasn't sure what. "You can't be here."

* * *

"¿Mi amor, me puedes conseguir otra?"

Chris pulled a cold beer from the fridge. Opened it and gave it to Octavia.

She drank, patted the couch next to her. "Siéntate conmigo."

Chris did. His mother leaned into him, rested her head on his shoulder.

"No vi a Cassandra esta mañana."

"Me neither."

Octavia started to say something, stopped. She and Cessy shared a strained relationship. Apart from formalities—helloes, goodbyes, how hot Phoenix was that day—they barely spoke.

"Dile que la ensalada de papas en el refrigerador es para ella."

"Okay."

Octavia finished her beer.

Silence.

"It's hot today," *Chris said.*

* * *

Chris woke, had no idea he'd been asleep, no idea how long he'd been slouched in this uncomfortable hospital chair. He was sweating, his forehead and chest and armpits slick.

He looked over at Cessy's room, saw it was empty of everyone but his sister. A cop stood at the other end of the hall, staring into a vending machine.

Cessy had sounded so worried over the phone, something about a group or gang after her. Chris couldn't quite understand the voice message, but he could tell she was scared.

Something moved out of the corner of the eye. He looked up, saw the cop reach into the machine, take a bag of chips and saunter around the corner.

When the cop was gone, Chris walked to her room.

Cessy was lying on her back, looking up at the ceiling, tears making a trail down the side of her face. The breathing tube was out, the sensors gone. The IV still attached to her arm.

"They all died," she said, her voice weak, an out-of-tune instrument. "Everybody in the house."

Chris nodded.

Cessy wiped her eyes, smeared tears. "I'm glad you're here."

CHAPTER

24

"THERE ARE THINGS I need to tell you about your father," Deb said.

Kim was slouched on the couch, wearing a T-shirt and yoga pants, staring at a cooking show on television.

"Like what?" Kim asked without looking away.

Deb sat next to her, her legs folded under herself. "He may not have always been honest with us."

"What do you mean?"

Deb hadn't planned what she was going to say. After what Levi Price had told her about Maria, Deb knew she had to tell Kim the truth, or at least some of it. But she hadn't decided how much to reveal.

"The man that we had dinner with the other night? Levi Price?"

"The kind of cute guy?"

"I guess." Deb paused. "The truth is, he works with the FBI. That's how we met. He's looking into what happened to your father."

Kim muted the television. Deb ruefully wondered what kind of news it would take for Kim to turn the television completely off.

"What did he tell you about Dad?"

Deb repositioned herself, rested her chin on her raised knee. "Someone was after men. A bunch of men were killed the same way. The ATM holdup may not have been random."

"This Levi guy thinks it was on purpose? Why? What did Dad do?"

Kim looked so worried that all of Deb's resolve wilted. The mother in her surged.

"Nothing, sweetie. I'm just telling you what I learned. It was probably mistaken identity."

Kim didn't seem to believe that. "Someone was killing men? Only men?"

Deb thought about Maria, remembered what Grant had told her. How Maria's murder had been different, less deliberate.

"Bludgeoned to death," he'd called it.

And it might not even be related to Grant.

"Looks like it," Deb said.

"Do they know why?"

Deb shook her head. "And I need to tell you something else. Your father lost some of our money."

"During the robbery? They made him take it from the ATM?"

"No. It's gone from his accounts—savings, retirement. A good deal of what we saved is missing."

Kim's expression was more serious than Deb had ever seen it. "What do you mean? Mom, are we broke?"

The maturity in Kim's face and voice broke something inside Deb; it was the type of maturity brought on by crisis. Deb knew she should be happy to see this reaction in Kim, but she didn't want to force her daughter to face it.

So again, Deb lied.

"We're not broke. Things will be okay. I promise."

Kim watched Deb carefully, as if she didn't trust what Deb had told her.

"Was Dad mixed up with something bad?" Kim asked.

"I don't think so." Deb hoped her voice sounded believable. "Like I said, it was mistaken identity. Wrong place, wrong time. Those other men were probably doing some pretty bad things. And we'll figure out what happened to his accounts soon. It'll all get straightened out."

"You sure?"

"I'm sure."

The hole was being dug deeper. And the lying was difficult; this wasn't a lie to her daughter, but to another woman. A grown woman who knew not to believe in fairy tales or fate or the innate safety of the world. And still, Deb was lying to her, desperately protecting her. Holding her daughter's hand and looking into her eyes and murmuring inaudible nothings as men emerged from the shadows all around them.

But she'd do anything to spare Kim this suffering.

Deb remembered when she'd woken this morning, her body tense, already primed for pain, her first thoughts about Grant as they were every morning. When would those relentless thoughts end, Deb wondered? And, despite everything, did she want them to?

And why couldn't she remember his face?

Deb had so many memories and emotions and circumstances all related to Grant to deal with . . . but, often, she couldn't remember what he looked like. As if her mind was protecting her from some sort of deepest grief, intentionally hiding his laugh or sorrow.

And then photos reminded her. Deb would stare at a photo of him somewhere in the house or buried in the thousands of pictures on her phone, and then she'd remember. Sometimes it was like looking at a stranger, seeing his face for the first time.

A man she'd never met.

No, Deb decided. *Kim doesn't need this.*

Even if it meant defending Grant.

"You should switch like I did," Kim said. "Guys are the worst."

Deb managed a smile despite everything. "Seems complicated."

"Men are complicated too."

"Not really. Men are like Occam's Razor. The answer to whatever question you have about them is usually the simplest answer."

Occam's Razor.

Grant fucked Maria to make himself happy.

Because he was unhappy.

"I guess. I just never felt really one hundred percent comfortable with guys, you know?" Kim asked. "I always felt like they were keeping something from me, like they were always holding back. No matter how close I got with them."

Kim seemed like she wanted to turn the conversation away from her father, toward something relatable, understandable.

Deb let her.

"I don't feel that way with Rebecca. If anything, it's nice to be with someone just as honest and intimate and vulnerable as I am. It's scary, and it's hard not to have your guard up. But it's nice."

Ever since Kim had told her about Rebecca, anything that came up in their lives, no matter what, somehow found its way back to her. Going out to eat? Rebecca liked that restaurant. Something on TV? Rebecca had thoughts about that show.

"Do you two fight?" Deb asked.

"Not that much. But, I mean, when we do, the arguments never end. They seem like they can go on for weeks. The whole semester, even."

"That's what I assumed. Sounds exhausting."

Kim smiled. "It is. In a good way."

"When your dad and I argued, he always assumed the end of the argument meant I wasn't angry anymore."

"That's such a guy thing."

"I know. He was always so angry and confused when I'd bring something back up."

Forcing herself to sound bemused. For Kim.

And, as much as Deb hated herself for it, for herself.

For some shred to cling to.

"One time," Deb went on, "your dad said he didn't like how I looked in a sweater, and every time I wore the sweater after, I felt mad. And since he'd forgotten about the argument, he had no idea why I was irritated."

"Which sweater?"

"The pink one. The turtleneck. It's like a cotton candy pink with a bunched neck?"

"It sounds like he might have had a point."

Deb and Kim laughed.

"I don't actually have it anymore," Deb said. "I threw out a bunch of stuff after he passed."

"See, when you're with a woman," Kim said, "there's so much bullshit you don't have to deal with. I hear about the guys my friends are dating, and it's so annoying. I don't have any of that with Rebecca. I mean, we have our problems and all, but you know what I mean."

Deb didn't know what her daughter meant, but she didn't pursue it.

"Anyway," Kim said, "I'm sorry that you have to deal with all of this."

"It'll be okay."

But Deb's mood darkened at Kim's words. Like the sun died inside her. Questions filled her with shadows.

Why would you lie to me, Grant? Why would you do this to me? How could you risk so much? How could you leave us like this?

CHAPTER

25

T HREE LONG DAYS after the fire, Cessy still had trouble breathing. Every inhale felt forced, like air drawn through jagged rocks. The doctor told her that smoke had done damage to her windpipe, and full recovery would take time. She had pain meds for her sore throat, but shock had left her body weak, unused. She stiffly walked out of the hospital.

Chris was gone when she left. But she knew he'd find her.

The Uber driver didn't ask her any questions. She didn't offer conversation.

Cessy closed the door to her apartment behind her, went to the bedroom. Lay down on the bed. Coughed hoarsely. Wept bitterly.

"Everybody in that house died," a cop had told her, one of those times in the hospital when she'd drifted back to consciousness. "Everybody but you."

There was nothing accusatory in his tone. He said the sentence plainly. No emotion in his voice.

In her apartment, Cessy rubbed her fists over her eyes, rolled to her stomach, moaned and cried.

Everybody but you.

Her chest exploded into dark clouds, and she coughed until she nearly vomited.

Everybody because of you.

For this kind of grief, there was no reprieve.

Cessy went to the kitchen, opened the fridge, drank greedily from a water bottle until the plastic crumpled. She grabbed another, went to the front door, coughing on the way, and sat down, her back against it.

Four people were dead.

Rose was dead.

Cessy thought about Rose's life, how she'd built her own business dedicated to caring for the less fortunate, the countless people she had helped . . . all to end up dying in a fire.

Because of me.

Cessy cried and coughed and vomited.

She cleaned the vomit, leaned back against the door like a broken doll flung against it. It wasn't just Rose, of course. Dana and the other residents of the house. Dana, with his soft eyes and thin body and hesitant smile.

A knock on the door echoed against her back.

Cessy scrambled to her feet, breathing hard. She faced the door, which seemed larger now, dominant, a drawbridge to some castle.

Another knock.

It could be Chris.

Or it could be the men who'd tried to burn her alive.

Cessy had known they'd come back for her. It was what she deserved, after all. Her penance was to bear the deaths of everyone in that house, and then her own.

She remembered reading somewhere that people who survived suicide had spoken of the regret they felt the moment they stopped off a bridge, fired a gun, swallowed pills, felt a noose tighten, or however else they'd decided to end their life. It didn't stop them from another attempt, because regret fades and is forgotten, but it did indicate some will to live.

And that regret flooded Cessy now. She didn't want to die, even if she felt she deserved it.

The door lock suddenly flipped. The knob turned.

Chris sauntered in, holding up a shiny gold key. "Hey, Cess. Had this made while you were in the hospital. Oh, I'm taking your bed while I'm in town. Also, I still snore and fart in my sleep." He studied her. "Your place smells like puke."

"Thanks."

"By the way, they didn't see me."

"Who didn't see you?"

"The guys watching your place. Two bald dudes sitting in a car across the street. Same guys who were outside the hospital."

"Shit." Cessy thought about Smith and Harris. Fear spread inside her like a web. "What do they look like?"

"I don't know. Kind of boring? Maybe both in their thirties. Wearing polos."

Her throat was scratchy when she spoke again. "Their names are Smith and Harris. I think they burned down the safe house."

Chris nodded. "Cool. This place have a back door?"

"There's a window in the bathroom that leads to a fire escape."

"A fire escape?" His face wrinkled. "How old is this building?"

"Very."

Chris walked to the bathroom and peered inside while Cessy coughed. "Nice bathroom, though. They work alone?"

"No, they work for someone—I don't know who." Cessy glanced at the door, expecting a knock at any moment. "Do you have a gun?"

"Oh yeah," Chris said cheerfully. He walked into the bathroom, and Cessy heard him slide the window open. He walked back out, holding a bottle of nail polish, toothpaste, and a toothbrush.

"What are you doing with my nail polish?"

Chris dropped the items on the floor. "People in a rush aren't going to take time to look at clues, just follow them."

Cessy heard footsteps down the hall.

Chris heard them too. The siblings glanced at each other, and he walked to the hall closet. "We know who's trying to find you. We know where they are. Which means they can't surprise us." He pulled open the closet door. "Let's keep it that way."

Cessy followed him into the closet. Chris took out his Sig and grinned. Cessy closed the closet just as someone pounded on the front door.

She had an overpowering urge to cough, as if that smoke was filling her again. She buried her mouth into her brother's shoulder and coughed once, softly.

He smelled of sweat, of the outdoors.

"Did you lock the front door?" Cessy whispered.

"Huh?"

They heard the front door open.

Shadows rushed past the thin line of light at the bottom of the closet.

Cessy waited, trying not to cough, staving off panic. Chris was a statue next to her, the gun pointed at the closet door, unwavering.

"Fire escape," a man said.

Footsteps rushed past the closet. The front door slammed.

Chris lowered his arms. He told Cessy, in the dark, "I need to follow them."

She thought about Rose.

About Dana.

About the screams throughout the house during the fire.

"Yeah," Cessy said, "we do."

CHAPTER

26

"DON'T YOU FEEL," Nicole asked Deb, "that we should be able to do what we want?"

"Definitely," Deb said. "I just don't think that's how life works."

Nicole drank from her coffee, set the cup back down on Deb's kitchen table. "I've been doing my job for twenty-five years. Working for someone else, busting my ass. Life feels like it should finally be paying off. Like I should be happier in my job. Find it fulfilling. Your husband used to tell me that."

Nicole headed public relations for a small museum in DC dedicated to the history of medical science. She'd complained about the job for as long as Deb had known her.

"He did?" Deb asked. "I didn't know you two talked about that."

Nicole looked uncertain for a moment. Nodded.

"Are you still thinking about going into business for yourself?" Deb went on.

Nicole frowned. "It's so risky. I don't know if I can do what you did."

"Right? And I still don't have any leads. Not that winter is a good time to find work, but still."

"Ugh. See? As much as I like the idea, I don't think I could. My job is like a bad marriage. Things may be better outside it, but do I really want to take that chance?"

Deb gazed at her friend.

Nicole stared into her coffee. "Yeah, I know. I should have the balls to do it. But I'd rather just complain about . . . I don't know, capitalism? Shut up."

The doorbell rang.

Deb pushed back from the kitchen table. "I'm with you," she told Nicole as she headed out of the kitchen. "Starting your own business will be a lot to handle. Especially at your age."

"We're the same age," Nicole called back. "And did you miss the part where I told you to shut up?"

Deb opened the front door.

It took her a moment to recognize the young woman outside.

"You were there with Maria," Deb said. "The other day at her apartment."

The young woman didn't respond. She just crossed her arms and looked around. She wore torn jeans and an oversized flannel over a hooded sweatshirt, and the hood covered her dirty blonde hair. Her face was thin. Knife-sharp cheeks.

"Can I come inside?" she asked.

"No," Deb said simply.

"It's cold out here."

"Not until I know why you're here. And how you found me."

The girl sighed impatiently. "Obviously, I found you through Google. And I came here to help you, to tell you something. But it's really cold and I'd like to come in."

Deb didn't budge. "What do you need to tell me?"

The girl grimaced, blew into her hands. Winter's warm days had passed, and now the region was gray and lifeless. And the descent of cold without snow exaggerated the effects, turned the world barren and harsh.

"Maria's dead."

"I know."

"You do?" The girl seemed confused.

Deb decided not to tell her about Levi. No need to disclose him to a stranger. "I saw it on the news."

"It was on the news?"

Deb changed the subject. "Did Maria tell you anything about my husband?"

The girl's expression turned hard. "Christ, lady. They killed my friend a couple of days ago, and all you can think about is your husband?"

"They killed him too." But her comment gave Deb pause. It did seem callous to ask for insight into Grant.

"Why did Maria die?" Deb asked instead.

The girl shrugged. "I don't know. Maybe it was some random dude. That happens. Or maybe it's because she talked to you."

Pricks on Deb's skin. "Do you really think that's why?"

"Depends on what she said." The girl held up her hand. "And I don't want to know what she said. You understand that?"

Deb nodded.

She and the girl stood quietly for a few moments. The girl shivered, and Deb couldn't help feeling a little sorry for her. She could see the girl's fear, just under the hard surface she was trying to project.

And she changed her mind about disclosing her contact with Levi.

"There's a guy I've been talking with," Deb said. "He's with the FBI. He can probably help you."

The girl made a dismissive sound. "Before or after he arrests me for what I do?"

"Hopefully, before."

A quick grin flashed across the girl's face at Deb's response, as if she couldn't help herself. "He did seem nice," the girl offered. "Your husband. I mean, from what Maria told me. He was sweet with her."

That wasn't *sweet* to Deb. And she felt it again, that change in the grief she felt for Grant, in the memories. The smile, the hugs, the kisses. The way he would touch Kim's hair.

Everything now held a sinister quality.

"Anyway," the girl was saying, "whoever killed Maria, and maybe your husband, isn't fucking around. That's what I came to tell you. You need to be really careful. I heard the cops were looking for some crazy whore or something, but the guys that ran us? Some dudes named Smith and Harris? They were for real."

"Their names were Smith and Harris?" Deb made a note of the names, so she'd remember to tell Levi.

"Yeah."

"What's going on?" Nicole called out.

"Nothing," Deb said, leaning back inside the house. She stepped outside and closed the door behind her.

The girl had been right. It was cold.

"You got someone here?" the girl asked. "That your daughter?"

"How do you know I have a daughter?"

"Maria told us."

Deb was stung at the idea of Grant telling some other woman about her, about their daughter, their lives.

The girl had the same thought. "That's probably why they went after Maria," she said. "All that talking." She glanced around again. "Listen, I got to go."

Deb wanted to ask her for more information, but she was conflicted. Too many emotions—betrayal, fear, anger—swirled inside for her to come up with anything clear.

"Do you have any money?" the girl asked. "That I could have?"

The request distracted Deb, clarified things. "Why?"

"I need a bus ticket or train ticket or something."

"You're leaving?" she asked.

The girl stared at her. "Wouldn't you? I'm not staying around here."

Deb went back to the kitchen for her purse, told Nicole to give her another minute.

Nicole barely glanced up from her phone. "Fine."

Deb gave the girl half the cash she had, a little less than seventy dollars. The girl took Deb's money, opened her duffel bag, stuffed it inside. Deb saw piles of clothes and a large blue bong in the bag before the girl zipped it shut.

"I'm sorry about Maria," Deb said. "I know she was your friend."

"I didn't know her like that." The girl paused. "And if anyone asks you about me, that's what you tell them. I didn't know her like that."

Deb watched her walk away, and something occurred to her. Something, Deb realized, she should have thought of right away.

I heard the cops were looking for some crazy whore or something.

You got someone here?

That your daughter?

What if that girl was the killer, and she was gathering information about Deb's house? Scoping it out, learning everything she could before she came back later?

Deb's fingernails dug into her palms in fear and frustration.

And she hadn't even gotten the girl's name.

Deb closed the door, stood inside the hall alcove.

Worry built relentlessly inside her. Deb tried to stop it, or at least slow it. She was happy that she'd mentioned the FBI. Knowing that she had some connection to federal law enforcement might give a killer pause.

Smith and Harris. She'd need to tell Levi those names, call him as soon as possible and tell him what had happened.

Levi.

She relaxed a little, remembering what he'd told her when he'd stopped by to tell her about Maria:

"Are we in danger?" Deb had asked. "Me and Kim?"

"I don't think so," Levi replied. "I hope not."

"You hope not?"

"I've studied people like this for a long time," Levi told her. "A long time. This is someone who works in a pattern, going after specific people for certain reasons. Your husband and the other men were all executed in the same fashion. Maria was killed differently. It could have been a client, it could have been one of her pimps. But it doesn't seem like the same killer, and the motives don't appear to bear any relation."

Deb thought about all that, fought the fear down. That fear, like a great black void rising up and threatening to swallow her whole. Threatening to divorce her from reason. Telling her to take Kim and run far away from the life they'd built here and hide in some distant city.

Like that girl was doing.

But she didn't need to run, not yet, even if there was that pressing voice inside, telling Deb to leave. The same voice that urged her to take Kim out of school whenever the nation was sent reeling from another school shooting. The same way she wondered why people lived in California, when a giant earthquake was guaranteed to someday wreak havoc on the state. The same fear of living just outside of Washington, DC, one of the obvious targets of terrorists worldwide, an area destined to be struck as the sophistication of weapons, and the heated desire for destruction, advanced.

And, as always happened, fear receded.

The worst might happen, but probably not to her. Or Kim.

Deb took a breath, steeled herself as best she could.

Walked back to her friend, one of the only people in the world she still trusted.

CHAPTER

27

Chris and Cessy sat in Chris's gray Honda Civic. A blue Acura idled a block away, parked on a quiet residential side street off Rockville's town center. Fortunately, even with the other parked cars and the darkly thick night, they could still see the shadows of the two men's heads.

Smith and Harris were sitting inside the Acura. And had been for the past thirty minutes.

"What the hell's taking so long?" Chris asked.

Cessy took a long drink from a bottle of water Chris had in the back seat. Her throat felt better, although now she had the pressing sensation that soon she'd need to pee. "They're probably trying to figure out where I went, what their next step is."

"Or they're dating, and saying goodbye is hard."

Cessy frowned. "I didn't get a relationship vibe when I talked to them."

"Either they're dating," Chris said, "or they know we're here. And they're watching us and waiting for backup."

Cessy thought about that. "Shit."

"Right? So let's just say they're dating."

Cessy couldn't figure out if her brother was serious. She was used to his humor, but he'd grown more deadpan over the years.

"You just have the one gun, right?" she asked.

"Yeah, but does it matter? When's the last time you went to a range? Has it been since you left Arizona?"

"Once," Cessy said. She coughed. "With Hector."

Cessy paused, thinking about the tone in her brother's voice when he'd asked, *"Since you left Arizona?"*

There was resentment buried under that question. And she wasn't sure if she should address it.

They hadn't talked much about their time apart, and it wasn't due to a lack of opportunity. Smith and Harris had driven for close to an hour, out of Baltimore and into Rockville, a small town near DC. Cessy had never been here before, given the city's exorbitant reputation, based on its proximity to Washington and concentration of high incomes. She'd always assumed she could barely afford to live, shop, or eat in Rockville, and pretty much figured her credit card company would suspend her account if she even drove within the city's limits.

She and Chris had spent the drive talking about Arizona, about people they knew, about traffic, the conversation as smooth as the surface of a lake. Nothing about how little they'd communicated, the distance between them, why she'd left him behind.

And Cessy hated it.

She hated the forced formality, the uneasiness.

She drummed her fingers on her thigh.

"I'm sorry I didn't do a better job of keeping in touch," Cessy said. "I should have."

"Maybe."

"No, I should have."

Chris shrugged. "I was lonely after you left."

Sorrow stirred in Cessy at Chris's words, at the way he pretended nonchalance despite pain. "Were you?"

"Well, you were gone. Mom was gone. And I was so angry about what happened to her." He paused. "I took my anger out on a lot of people."

Cessy didn't pursue that.

"But I get why you left," Chris continued. "That wasn't you."

And then Cessy admitted something she never had, something moored deep inside her.

"I left because maybe it was me."

She and Chris stared hard at Smith and Harris's shadowed heads, unwilling to look at each other.

She could hear Chris breathing.

"What's that mean?" he asked.

"I could never do what you did. I never could. But something in me understands why you did it. Even worse, something in me doesn't blame you for it."

"Really?"

"Yo también la amaba."

The front passenger door of the car they were watching opened; either Smith or Harris emerged; she couldn't be sure from this distance and darkness. Whoever it was leaned into the car, said something, closed the door. The man started walking away as the car's taillights briefly gleamed, and the car pulled out of the space and drove off.

Despite her earlier desire to talk, Cessy was happy with the chance to end the conversation. None of this was anything she felt comfortable discussing.

"Let's go," Cessy said.

28

THE MOMENT DEB walked into Ruth's Chris Steak House and saw Agent Levi Price waiting for her, wearing tan slacks and a white button-down under a navy sports jacket, she wondered:

Is this a date? Should I have dressed better?

Wait, is this a date?

Nicole had assumed it was.

"He's taking you out for steak?" she'd asked, earlier that day. "At Ruth's Chris? Of course it's a date. Are you ready for that?"

"Not even remotely." Deb frowned. "He has to know that, right?"

"I mean, he's a guy. So, no."

If there was a misinterpretation, Deb wondered if it came from her. The idea for dinner had come right after Maria's friend had left her house. In her confusion and concern, Deb had decided to call Levi.

"Yeah?"

His brusque tone had thrown her off. "Oh, hi. Levi?"

"Ms. Thomas. Is everything okay?"

"Yeah, I'm just . . ." Her words faltered. "Do you have time to talk?" Deb tried to clear her mind from the woman's visit and Levi's hurried tone.

"Not now," she added, assuming he was busy. "Maybe tonight?"

Now he sounded uncertain. "You mean in person?"

"Okay."

"Well, I have wanted a dinner out," Levi said. Deb wondered if he meant with her. "How about six? Do you like Ruth's Chris?"

Levi still sounded uncertain when he said goodbye, as did she. Their halting conversation would make the perfect meet-cute, Deb thought, if he wasn't an FBI agent investigating her husband's murder and if she had even the remotest interest in dating.

Levi walked up to Deb at the entrance, as if to embrace her or kiss her, then stopped awkwardly.

"You look nice," he said.

It's not a date, she reminded herself.

A host led them to their table. Deb wore black pants with a thin olive sweater and low, blocky heels, and noticed the other women in the restaurant all wore high heels and dresses or skirts. Men dressed as they always did—the older ones in suits, the young yuppies in a mix of business casual, the dads who were too tired to care in jeans.

"I love this place," Levi told her after they'd been seated. "Especially the view."

Deb wasn't sure if this was a clumsy flirt or if Levi actually meant the view, but decided on the latter.

"I like it too," she said. The restaurant was in Crystal City, a Northern Virginia city seemingly comprised only of office buildings and apartments, gray concrete and gray businesses. Ruth's Chris overlooked DC's monuments and Ronald Reagan National Airport, providing a look at the planes constantly gliding in and out of the city.

Then again, Deb remembered how it was years ago, right after the attacks on 9/11, when planes sailing overhead took on a dark new meaning. When everything seemed to hold a shade of something menacing—airplanes, traffic jams, people, the breaking news chyron on the bottom of the television. Until then, the news, regardless of its severity and reach, had always seemed to have a removed, sensational distance. Clinton and Lewinsky, O.J. Simpson, the unremarkable aftereffects of Y2K. Now, like those planes overhead, there was no distance anymore. The world had seemed to irreparably change. Deb couldn't imagine that ever happening again.

Grant had been at the Pentagon that day. A few years out of college, he was working for a government financial contractor and spent half his work week at the Pentagon. He and Deb were engaged, in the midst of planning their wedding for the following spring. She'd turned on the television prior to heading to her own job, a marketing assistant for a temp agency, and suddenly found herself sitting on the floor. The towers were falling, the Pentagon was reeling. There was potential, the panicked media reported, that thousands in DC were dead.

She called Grant's cell phone.

The call didn't go through.

"Do you want wine?" Levi asked.

"I'll just stick with water."

Levi gave the wine menu back to the waiter.

Deb had thought Grant was dead. It was easy to believe, easier than believing he'd somehow survived. Deb wanted that, of course, but automatically prepared for the worst, as if her heart was aware of something her mind had yet to process. She tried calling Grant repeatedly, called his friends, his family, but no one had heard from him. No one knew anything. She stayed in her Arlington apartment, stared at the news, avoided the window and the black smoke filling the sky in the near distance.

It was just after one when the phone rang. Grant told her he was safe. He hadn't been near the impacted area. He'd spent the morning helping victims, and cell phones were overwhelmed and not working. And she'd cried and laughed and never—not before and not after—felt such joy.

"Are you okay?" Levi asked.

"Not really," Deb admitted. "It's all so much. The truth about Grant. What happened to Maria. The idea that Kim or I could be in some danger." Deb rubbed her eyes. "She went out tonight with a friend, and I know you said we should be safe, but I'm still scared."

Levi was quiet for a few moments. "Here's the thing, though. You *are* safe. This is over for you."

The waiter returned. Deb hadn't looked at the menu, but she scanned it while Levi ordered. She picked an expensive filet mignon but privately decided to pay for her own meal. She hated spending that much money but, after everything over the past few weeks, wanted to treat herself. And she still held that old-fashioned belief that if a man paid, it was considered a date. Not just a friendly gesture.

Was it old-fashioned? Deb wasn't sure. It'd been so long since she'd been on a date.

Not a date, she reminded herself.

"One of Maria's friends came by my house today," she told Levi.

"What?"

Several nearby diners turned. Levi glanced around, lowered his voice.

"What?" he asked again.

Deb nodded. "I don't know what her name was, but—"

"What'd she say?" Levi interrupted her.

"She told me to watch out for her pimps. And that she was scared, and leaving tomorrow."

"That's it?"

"And she gave me some names. Smith and Harris? I don't know who they are."

"Smith and Harris." Levi stared at her intently, as if he was in the process of memorizing their names. "Did she say anything else?"

"No."

"How'd she find your address?"

"She said she used Google."

Levi made a quick face, and then Deb imagined how much more difficult technology had made his job. After a moment, he sighed.

"I'm sorry about that," he said. "I mean, sorry you had to go through that. Was Kim home?"

"No, thank God. Nicole was there. But she didn't see her."

"Are you sure you're okay?"

"Yeah."

"And you said Nicole was there? Your friend?"

"Right. She didn't see her, though. Nicole stayed in the kitchen."

"She did? That seems . . . unusual for her."

Deb thought about it. "Good point."

"How long have you known Nicole?" Levi asked.

"Since college. She was close to both me and Grant."

"She was? To him too?"

"Yeah. Hey, I wanted to say thank-you for talking with me about this, for keeping me informed about everything. I know you don't have to, but it helps."

He smiled uncertainly.

Deb wondered if all FBI agents were awkward when it came to receiving praise.

"Were you ever married?" she asked, and immediately regretted the question. It came out like a first-date question. What type of music do you like? What do you do on weekends? What's your favorite TV show?

"No," Levi said, and he seemed relieved for the subject change, the chance to talk about something other than work. "Never. I mean, not yet."

"Haven't met the right person?"

"Haven't really looked. The job makes it hard."

They talked for a few more minutes, staying on familiar topics to preserve the atmosphere. Their work. Where they had lived. Family.

"So you said you grew up down South?" Levi asked.

"Roanoke. About a four-hour drive from here."

"There's not a big Asian population in Roanoke, is there?"

Deb laughed. "Well, I moved away. So I think that's all of us."

He laughed with her. "Really?"

"It wasn't that bad. But there weren't many of us. It was definitely lonely."

Levi didn't press, and Deb appreciated that because she didn't want to elaborate. It was hard to explain that distance, the sense of closeness she felt to other people who weren't white. Grant had never understood that concept when she tried to explain it to him, and he even once told her that her attitude was offensive. Borderline racist.

But Kim understood.

There was an ostracizing element Deb had always felt growing up with her white friends, a sense that they were free to do and say whatever they wanted, and it played into a type of superiority. Deb never felt allowed to be that superior . . . or even that such a feeling was right. She was always coming across some stereotype or slur about Asians, in conversation, in books or television or movies, that seemed intended to put her in her place, to make sure she understood the distance between her and white people.

It hadn't been until she'd gone to college and met other Asian students that she'd realized she wasn't alone in feeling that way.

And that was a lovely, life-changing thing to realize. To know that you're not alone.

That your experiences are shared.

"How'd you end up in Virginia, from Vietnam?"

"My mom went through a Catholic adoption agency that worked in Vietnam. I was born there, and they brought me here."

"Have you ever tried to find your real parents?"

"My mom was my real parent," Deb responded sharply.

"Oh, sorry, I didn't mean . . ."

Deb exhaled. "It's okay. I just get that a lot, this idea that my mother wasn't a mom. She was."

"You're right. I shouldn't have said that."

Deb took a quick drink of water. "But, no, I've never looked into trying to find my biological parents. I know there are organizations dedicated to matching Vietnamese adoptees with their biological families, but I never contacted them. I think it would have bothered my mom if I had."

"But you wouldn't do it even now? Even just for medical information?"

Deb thought about it. "I kind of feel like if something was going to happen to me, it would have happened."

They talked on, and Deb kept having to remind herself that Grant wasn't alive, and not just in the sense that she kept feeling like she had to keep this dinner a secret. She wanted to share it with Grant, to tell him about Levi and his work, about the restaurant, the evening. As upset as the revelations about Grant and Maria made her, she still had those instinctual tugs to him, those reactions that had become as natural as breathing. A longing to tell him about her day.

The food arrived, long sizzling steaks on dangerously hot plates, side dishes spread out over the table.

"That's *a lot* of food," Levi remarked, staring at the layout.

"Grant used to eat everything I made," Deb said, "and then bitch that he was getting fat. But then, why eat it, Grant, right? Sorry, that's the most married thing I've ever said."

"Ha."

Deb wondered if she was talking about Grant too much.

The conversation quieted as they ate.

"Thanks again for talking to me," Deb said when she was halfway through her steak, debating on whether she should save or eat the rest. "I feel like I've been all over the place since Grant died. First it was nothing but grief; then I had this desperate urge to find out what happened, and then it was fear. And it seems like lately it's all sadness."

Levi ate his last piece of steak, dabbed his mouth with a napkin, swallowed. "Fear turns into despair. The more you're afraid, the more hopeless you feel."

Deb thought about that. "I guess that's true. It doesn't help with everything I'm learning. Finding out so much of what I thought was true was really a lie." She paused. "Sometimes I just want to grieve, not grieve and question."

"It doesn't sound," Levi replied cautiously, "like Grant was that bad a guy. I know he was with Maria, but it seems like he was good in many other ways."

But that one way invalidates all the others.

Deb didn't say her thought out loud.

Instead, she said, "Yeah."

Levi smiled a small smile. "I'm sorry. I'm doing that guy thing, where I try and solve problems or make you feel better instead of just trying to understand what you're saying, right?"

He was, but Deb kept that to herself. "I appreciate you listening. You've been nice through all this. And I know you put your job on the line just so I could get even more answers. It means the world to me."

He reached out and patted her hand.

His hand stayed on hers.

She watched her hand turn, her fingers slip between his.

Then she let go, and they both withdrew.

"Sorry," he said, and she said, "It's okay," nearly at the same time.

An awkward silence ensued. Deb tried not to let expression show on her face. She didn't want him to think she was entertaining anything.

Even if, briefly, his touch did feel nice.

"You really think Kim and I are safe?" Deb asked.

"Look, I'm not going to lie to you about anything in this investigation. Even when I knew something would be painful, I've shared it, right?"

"Yes."

"If I thought you and your daughter were in danger, I'd tell you. I wouldn't risk it."

"Okay."

But now Levi seemed uncomfortable. "There is one thing I need to tell you. And I'm not sure how to say it."

Deb's heart sank. "Is it about Grant? Did he actually sleep with other prostitutes?"

"I can't tell you here." He glanced around. "It's about the case. I normally wouldn't share this, but I don't want to see you worried. And this is something you need to know. About someone close to you."

"What is it?" Deb asked again.

"Like I said, I can't tell you here."

"Then let's go."

CHAPTER

29

JAMES SMITH PULLED into a parking space at the far end of his apartment building's lot, turned off the engine, closed his eyes. Rubbed his forehead. He'd been working long days and hadn't slept much at night, driving back and forth through the hellacious traffic between his apartment in Rockville and the hospital in Baltimore.

Waiting for Cessy Castillo to get out of the ER.

Just so he could put her in the morgue.

Everything felt heavy: the pull of sleep, the seatbelt crossed over his body, his worry like a giant's boot flattening him to the earth. He hadn't even set the fire at the safe house, but still felt nervous whenever he saw a story about it on TV.

And Cessy's pictures didn't help.

After all, James hadn't been raised as a criminal. Had grown up in Catonsville, outside Baltimore. Middle class. Went to a decent high school.

And then his dad was arrested for beating their mom, and he never saw him again.

The case was public—not national news or anything, but his father's position on the city council made him a statewide figure. Everyone knew what had happened. Other kids in James's high school started avoiding him, the way kids do when something happens that they can't handle or understand. Like James had done something wrong.

That's when he felt hate.

He hadn't felt it when his father hit his mother. Hadn't felt it when his father was taken away. But when those kids at high school made him feel that way, like he'd messed up and they needed to distance them-selves, that's when his anger first emerged.

When kids he knew started using in his third year of high school, James went a step past them. Contacted dealers, started selling his own stuff. Got kicked out of high school. Pity for him because of his father—something James realized could be weaponized—helped him get back in. He went back, got into a fight, and put a kid in the hospital. He loved fighting, felt like it was that hate given action, like a painting turned into a movie. He fought more. More kids ended up in the hospi-tal. James ended up expelled.

His mother barely hung onto him, seemed like she barely wanted to. A rush of cancer had ended her abusive husband's life while he was in prison, and she seemed determined to distance herself from every-thing related to him. James left her house the day he turned eighteen. She didn't try to stop him.

That bothered James more than he let on.

A traffic stop a year later revealed a glove compartment full of hard drugs and an unlicensed gun. He used that middle-class earnestness to plead his case, got a lenient sentence from the judge. Met someone in community service who was connected, who asked him if he wanted to make some money and didn't care how.

James did, and didn't.

For years afterward he skated by on that line, slipping over to what-ever side he needed, able to play each side against the other.

And now that nice middle-class disguise was threatened, had the potential to blow away like it was nothing but a pile of leaves awaiting a gust of wind. Those pictures Cessy had implicated him. Defined him.

James rubbed his eyes, looked up. Saw Cessy Castillo standing in front of his car.

The hell?

He blinked, undid his seatbelt, pushed open the door. And then someone grabbed him from behind.

*   *   *

Chris wrapped his arms tight around Smith's chest, pinning his arms to his sides.

"Don't fight," Chris said, "and we won't hurt you."

The back of Smith's head struck Chris's nose. Pain webbed his face. His arms loosened.

Smith's heel kicked Chris's shin.

His arms dropped.

"Shit," he heard his sister say.

"I'm okay," Chris said, holding his aching nose, moving slowly, like the ground was unsteady beneath him.

He looked up and saw Smith in front of him.

Chris felt Smith's fists on his face, his chest, his stomach. He dropped to his knees, covered his head with his hands.

"How about we come back another time?" he asked.

Then he peeked up, saw his sister disappear into the woods bordering the parking lot. Smith was following her.

Chris groaned, pulled himself to his feet, thought briefly about getting his gun out of his car. Decided against it. It was dark, the woods would be pitch black, and he couldn't risk losing sight of Smith.

Chris thought about the frantic sounds Smith had made when he was trying to hold him, the animal grunts, and the worry spreading over Cessy's face. And he felt that familiar distance inside him as he loped into the woods, that emotional and physical distance, like Chris was watching a TV show of himself. But not even watching it intently; more like he was glancing at the television over his shoulder while he hunted for something to eat in the fridge.

He followed the hazy faint blue coming from the shirt Smith had been wearing, watched it dart through trees about a hundred feet ahead of him. Chris pushed past branches and brambles, desperate to catch Smith before he caught Cessy. He ran through the dark, a stumbling bruising run of whipped branches and grasping roots. This was the first time he'd ever been in a forest. Arizona was dominated by mountains and dry land, unless you went north to the pines and ski lodges of Flagstaff. Chris never had. Until recently, he'd never even left Phoenix.

This was a hell of a first trip.

He saw the silhouette a few feet in front of him and dove forward.

Chris landed on the hard ground with his sister.

"What are you doing?" Cessy asked, beneath him.

Chris took out his phone, shined the light into her face. "Cessy?"

She pushed the phone down, pushed him away. "Why'd you tackle me? I thought you were him."

"I thought he was you! Is he wearing blue too?"

"This is . . . what? He's wearing black."

"He is?"

The siblings gazed at each other in the dark.

"So where is he?" Chris asked.

They stood together, hurried back to the parking lot, their steps slowing and quieting as they reached the edge of the woods.

Smith was pulling a shotgun from his trunk.

"Well . . ." Chris whispered. "Damn."

"He doubled back," Cessy said.

"Run over to my car." Chris pointed. "Distract him."

"What are you going to do?"

What Chris did, as Cessy exploded from the woods and raced to his car, was sneak behind Smith. Smith was watching Cessy run, frozen.

Chris used the distraction to grab Smith from behind a second time. The shotgun fell into the trunk.

"Let's try this again," Chris said.

And then Chris felt like he was trying to hold onto a hurricane of fists and kicks, a thrashing whirlwind of anger.

"Just hold on please," Chris asked, as his arms loosened.

There was a cracking sound and Smith's fight slowed.

Cessy was holding the shotgun by the barrel. She slammed the handle into Smith's head again. His body slumped.

The siblings piled his unconscious body into the trunk and slammed it closed.

Chris was breathing hard. "Glad you got a handle on things," he managed. "Get it? Handle?"

"I should leave you here just for that joke."

*   *   *

Cessy rubbed her hands together to stay warm. She walked over to the edge of the parking garage roof, where they had tied Smith to a chair with jumper cables.

"It's my arm," Smith said, his voice hoarsened from pain. "I think it's broken."

"It's not broken," Chris said.

"How do you know? You're not a doctor."

"No. But I know what a broken bone feels like. And I know what it can do."

"Whatever." Smith grimaced, leaned forward, eyes tightly closed.

Cessy didn't say anything, but if Smith's arm wasn't broken, it was still pretty damaged. Smith had tried to run when they opened the trunk, despite the fact that she was holding his shotgun. Chris had caught him, twisted his arm, forced Smith to the ground.

Stomped his elbow.

"You want to go to the hospital?" Chris asked. "We'll take you. Right after you tell us who your boss is."

"I tell you that, I'll never leave the hospital."

Cessy walked closer to Smith. "Who set fire to the safe house?"

Smith kept his head down.

Chris walked behind the chair, held Smith's shoulder, tipped him backward over the ledge. Rockville's city lights and the night and air were the only thing behind him.

"You'd better answer her," Chris told him.

Smith's right arm flailed, so much so that he almost lost balance. His left arm stayed tucked in his gut, like a bird's broken wing.

Chris set the chair back down.

"Feel like talking yet?"

Smith kept looking over his shoulder toward the ledge, at the twelve-story fall to the concrete below. It took him a few moments to turn his head around.

"Fuck you."

Chris kicked his hurt arm.

Smith's body convulsed. He bent completely over, hissing in air.

Chris reared his leg back for another kick.

"Wait, wait," Smith said. "Okay."

"What's it going to take for you to leave me alone?" Cessy asked. "Pay off what Hector owed? Because I told you, I can't."

Smith spoke through a grimace. "That's nothing now. You know too much. You have pictures and names. They're not going to stop. No matter what you do to me."

Cessy tried to keep her face calm, but her stomach felt like a paper bag being crumpled.

He was right.

There was no chance for compromise now. And she hadn't realized she still needed it as an option.

"Who's 'they'?" she asked. "Other pimps?"

"This isn't all about hookers," Smith said after a long moment.

"Then what's it about?"

"Information."

Chris and Cessy waited.

"They target married men, blackmail them dry," Smith said. "Easiest marks out there. Married men get too scared, show their ass the minute there's a chance we'll tell their families."

"What does this have to do with Hector?" Cessy asked.

"Hector was one of their killers."

"Come on," Cessy said. "Hector didn't have it in him."

"You saw the pictures. What'd you think? Hector was just the photographer?" Smith snorted. "He tried to leave. They didn't let him."

All along Cessy had assumed that, yes, Hector was just the photographer. He'd always been more of a lackey than anything else, a sidekick to other men.

She hadn't known what he was, or what he'd become.

And Cessy had assumed she was the only one who knew the depths of Hector's depravity.

"Was he going to the cops?" she asked. "Why was he killed?"

"We thought he was. And if we'd known Hector was taking pictures," Smith said, "he'd have been killed a lot earlier."

Again, a moment of emotion hit Cessy. She wondered if she should feel anger that Smith discussed Hector's death so cavalierly. But the moment passed. She felt it pass.

She was surprised at how distant from Hector she'd grown.

How distant in just weeks.

Maybe it wasn't only the men she knew who were damaged.

"Story time!" Chris suddenly exclaimed happily. "One of our mom's clients was a former Green Beret. Nice guy! Used to teach me and Cessy—I guess she was about fourteen and I was thirteen—all the cool stuff he knew. About guns, tactics, hunting, killing. He was convinced the government was going to turn on him someday, thought he might need to hide out with us. Remember him, Cessy?"

"I do. Cool guy until he shot himself."

"He teach the two of you how to torture someone?" Smith asked. "Break someone's arm?"

"Nah," Chris replied. "He always said torture doesn't work. That men and women will say whatever you want to hear to save themselves. Which is why you're staying with us."

Smith's eyes widened in surprise; maybe even, Cessy noted, fear. "What?"

"You stay with us, keep giving us information," Chris said. "Or off the deck you go. Your choice."

"Neither has to happen if you keep talking," Cessy said. She was tired of waiting. And she was tired of the cold. Tired of conflicting emotions. Tired of men and their violent recourses. "We just need a name—who you work for."

Smith bit his lip and refused, and Chris pushed the chair's back legs off the roof. But he was a bit too eager, and ended up struggling to keep Smith from falling. Cessy had to help him pull Smith back up.

That was enough for Smith. He gave them a name that Cessy had never heard.

"Who the hell is Levi Price?" she asked.

30

LEVI LIVED IN Arlington, in a long rambler on the outskirts of a residential neighborhood, separated from his neighbors by a ring of trees. He pulled his silver Audi into the driveway. Deb followed him, parked on the street.

They opened their car doors at the same time, stepped out into the quiet night.

"Would you like to come in?" he called to her. "I just need to find a few case files, but it might take me a minute."

"Sure." Deb tried to act nonchalant as she walked over to Levi. Not for any desire to impress him; more that she wasn't sure she wanted to know whatever he had to tell her.

"I like Arlington," Deb said. "It'd be nice to live somewhere closer to DC. I just can't afford it."

Levi nodded. "That's why I rent."

Deb wondered if Levi could sense her awkwardness as they walked to the door. She kept thinking about what he had to tell her and about that brief moment in the restaurant where his hand covered hers. It was just a quick touch, and it may only have been a nice gesture . . . but she worried he expected more.

She blamed Nicole for putting the idea in her head. There was no reason to believe Levi had anything other than a professional interest in her, maybe friendship, but nothing else. It had been so long since she'd been in the company of another man besides Grant. So of course she'd misread signals. His hand, the gesture, had been nothing more than a comforting touch.

Levi unlocked the door, walked in. She followed him but stayed by the door.

The rambler was nicely, if sparsely, decorated. An open floor plan revealed a stainless steel–filled kitchen to her left, a hall with closed doors—presumably bedrooms—to her right. Modern furniture with sharp edges. Bay windows on the other side of the living room showed trees lining the back of the house.

"It's really nice," she said, surprised. "You decorated it?"

"I did." Levi looked proud. "You like it?"

"It's lovely. Especially for a guy." She took a few steps in, peered into the kitchen. "Did anyone help you?"

He laughed. "Turns out I'm good at two things. Investigating and interior decorating."

"I guess so!"

A pause, and Deb couldn't put it off any longer. "Speaking of investigating—"

"Right!" Levi snapped his fingers. "Can I get you a drink?"

"I'm good."

He stood in front of her uncertainly. "Well, here's what I needed to tell you."

"What about the files?"

He ignored her question. "It's three things, actually."

She waited.

Levi smiled as if embarrassed. "I know who killed your husband."

A mix of emotions tornadoed through Deb. Relief. Fear. Anxiousness. "You do?"

"And second, I'm not with the FBI."

Deb felt like the ground was slipping away from her. She wanted to grab something.

"What?" Her voice, miles away.

His eyes burned. "Three, I fucking love you."

*   *   *

Deb didn't remember backing up, didn't realize what was happening until she touched the kitchen wall. Then the world seemed to swirl until it returned to her, and she saw Levi standing before her, his hands lifted to show a lack of threat.

"You okay?" he asked.

"I don't . . . I don't know."

"Is it because I lied about being in the FBI?" he asked. "Or because I said I loved you?"

Deb felt like she was standing on a round metal plate, and that plate was starting to spin and sway, and if she fell off she didn't know where she'd land. There was nothing for her to grasp, nothing to reach.

"Both," Deb said. "I think it's both. Everything. Who are you?"

"Look," Levi said, "don't freak out, okay?"

"Don't freak out?"

"It's really not that big a deal."

Deb kept moving along the wall, slowly coming closer to the kitchen door. "Did you kill Grant?"

"What? No! Of course not."

"You lied to me this whole time."

"Yeah," Levi said uncomfortably. "But I had to. You get that, right? You never would have talked to me if I'd told you the truth. That I'd been watching you—and falling in love. But I did tell you my real name. Not everything was a lie."

It was amazing how quickly he changed, turned excited, flushed, impetuous. Deb wondered if that side had always been there, and she'd been too distracted to see it.

Too trusting.

"How long were you watching me?"

"A few months." Levi's voice changed, almost turned sad. "You're easy to fall in love with."

Deb's hand reached out and touched the door frame. If Levi was aware that she was leaving the room, he didn't seem concerned.

"Did you kill Grant?" she asked again.

"I promise I didn't. I promise you. But I know who did."

"Okay." Deb ran out of the room.

She raced down the hall to her front door, thoughts rushing through her mind like bullets. She had to leave, she had to find Kim, she needed help. Deb had just touched the door handle when a hand on her shoulder firmly pulled her back.

She was spun around, ended up staring right into his eyes.

"Don't be mad," Levi said. His hands had moved down to her biceps, and he held each firmly. "I had to lie about who I was to get to know you."

Deb managed to free one arm and push him back.

"Just stop it!" Levi exclaimed. "Let me explain."

Deb thought about kneeing him in the testicles, but was scared of angering him.

Instead, she stomped down on his foot.

His other hand released her, and she rushed past him.

She couldn't go out the front door, but maybe she could grab her phone and lock herself in a bathroom and call for help.

His arm reached around her waist, pulled her into his body, and something terrifying occurred to her. She realized what Levi might do to her; surprisingly, it hadn't occurred to her before. Her guard had dropped too far.

She'd trusted authority.

Deb went wild with fear, kicking back and pushing at his arm until she heard Levi grunt and curse. He pushed her forward, hard, into the wall. She crashed into it and stumbled back and fell, holding her nose. She looked down at her hand. Saw blood.

Levi was standing over her, a gun in his hand.

"Calm down," he said. "I'm not going to hurt you."

Deb looked back down at the blood.

"Okay, that was an accident. Will you just listen to me?"

She pointed. "Your gun."

"Yeah, I just need you to stop fighting . . . I don't know what else to do. Okay?" He slid the gun into his holster, lifted his hands. "I'm not going to hurt you. I just want to talk, okay?"

"Okay."

"I'm sorry about this," Levi said quietly. "It's not how I wanted things to go down."

"Okay."

"I really am sorry."

Despite her fear, Deb was reminded of Grant, his habit of apologizing over and over again after an argument. Days would pass, and he'd send her flowers, jewelry, mention the fight before they fell asleep at night. It had been both annoying and endearing.

Lately she'd wondered if his contrition had been in service to some greater guilt. As if he'd felt the need to always beg forgiveness from her.

"Why am I here?" she asked.

"Because I wanted to tell you all that. And I want to show you something, and I couldn't do it anywhere else."

Just stay alive, Deb told herself, doing her best to keep her face calm. *Do what he says and stay alive.*

She nodded, playing along.

Relief started to break through his pained expression.

He loves me.

He didn't bring me here to hurt me.

Deb took a breath, tried to keep things light, normal.

"So, I'm pretty complex," Levi told her seriously.

Deb had no idea where he was going with this. But she kept quiet.

That pained expression returned. Levi walked over to the couch, slumped down on it. "This is all so messed up."

Deb glanced at the front door. It would take her four steps, she calculated, to reach it. Four steps.

"Why?" she asked.

"I never should have fallen in love with you. And I knew it was happening. Temple told me to watch you, keep an eye on you after Grant died. And I felt it happening."

"Temple? What temple? Are they the ones who killed Grant?"

Levi ignored her. "I'd see you at the store or sitting in your backyard, or sometimes through the window while you were eating or getting ready for bed, and I could feel it."

"You watched me that much?"

Levi misinterpreted her statement, took it as a compliment. He looked up at her with a slight smile. "Once I saw you, I did a lot more than he asked me to."

"Who asked you?"

Confusion replaced the smile. "Temple."

"What Temple?"

"Scott Temple."

The name meant nothing to her. She tried another approach. "So you watched me?" Deb crossed her arms over her chest, casually took a small step back.

Three steps to the door.

Levi nodded.

"Why?"

Two steps.

"It's what we do. Scope out someone once they sleep with one of our prostitutes. See if they're worth anything. I watched Grant for a few weeks after he was with Maria, looked into him, found out he had money . . . especially after he helped out Maria. We started blackmailing him, and everything was going the way it always does until he snapped. Threatened to go to the cops."

"So the people you work with killed him?"

Levi nodded. "But the thing was, I wasn't just watching Grant. Not after I saw you. Once that happened, I . . ." Levi's sentence trailed away.

One step.

"And then Temple told me to keep an eye on you, see if Grant had told you anything." Pain on Levi's face. "Look, I never wanted to hurt you. You know that, right? I could have caught you and tortured you for the information. I could have hurt Kim. I could have done anything else, if I wanted to."

Deb leaned toward the door, hoping it wasn't enough for Levi to notice.

"Temple made up the story about some insane hooker. It wasn't some woman killing those men, those men we weren't sure about, those men who knew too much. It was us."

"Us?"

Deb was so close she could reach out and touch the handle.

Levi jumped up from the couch, walked over to Deb, took her wrists in his hands.

"Can I show you something?"

He led her away from the door, down the hallway. She saw a fish tank in a small alcove, small brightly colored fish darting around. They walked into a small bedroom, and he turned on the light.

"You see?" Levi asked, as if in awe of his own work.

"What . . . what is this?"

The room only had a television in the corner of the room, a metal folding chair in front of it. Compared to the rest of the house, it was empty. No personality, no design. No emotion.

And something about that terrified her.

Deb stared at the television. It was sitting on a television stand, showing black and white footage. She couldn't tell what it was showing, a room on some sort of security feed. She looked closer.

A bedroom, shown from a camera high in the corner.

"What is this?" she asked again.

On the screen, a woman walked into the room. She opened a drawer in a dresser, pulled something out and headed to the bathroom.

Something occurred to Deb, a notion reluctantly tugging at her.

How did I know it was the bathroom?

"That's you," Levi said.

"What?"

"That's your bedroom last night," Levi said at the same moment she realized it. Deb should have known it before, but the angle of the camera confused her.

"How did you get this?"

"When you were out one day. I came in and set up the cameras."

"Cameras?" she heard herself ask.

"I wanted to watch you. I wanted to see what you did when I wasn't there. You're so beautiful. I could watch you all day. Some days I did. I'd even talk to you when you were cooking or changing or crying."

"Where . . . where did you put the cameras?"

"Everywhere."

And Deb realized how trapped she really was.

31

"LEVI PRICE IS the guy we report to," Smith told Cessy and Chris. "Lives in Virginia, in Arlington. Used to be FBI or something. We go to him when we can't get to Temple."

"You're Jewish?" Chris asked.

"What?" Smith asked back.

Cessy sensed the conversation veering. "You holding out on anything else?"

Smith looked down miserably at the ropes binding him to the chair. "That's everything."

"Why don't I believe you?" Chris asked. He tipped the chair back again, peered down into Smith's face, now so far back his head was parallel to the ground.

Smith's arms and legs were flailing, and he was trying to push his body forward, trying to right himself.

"Be careful, Chris," Cessy warned.

"Cessy, I got this."

"But he's really far back."

Chris turned toward his sister. "I know what I'm doing."

One of Smith's legs kicked too high. And kicked Chris's arm off the chair.

His fall was a short scream, not more than seconds.

The landing was a mix of shattering sounds, chair and bones breaking all at once.

"Fuck!" Cessy exclaimed.

Chris was staring down to the alley, twelve stories below. "Oh, shit."

"Is he dead?" Cessy didn't want to look over the edge. Her body felt cold, like a sheet of ice was being pulled over her.

Chris nodded, still staring down. "He kicked my arm. It's not my fault."

"What?"

"I'm innocent."

Cessy squatted down, covered her face.

Tried to calm herself, tried to corral her rushing thoughts.

"We need to go," she said. "We need to go right now."

"Where?"

"I don't know where."

They hurried into Chris's car. Cessy listened for police sirens, looked for the flash of lights. Nothing. She knew they were lucky. Rockville was a ghost town at night.

They drove down the parking garage's ramps, looking for cameras. Didn't see any.

"We need to find that guy," Chris said decisively. "The one he told us about. Levi Price. And we need to find him now. Find him before they realize what happened, before they find us."

"Why?" Cessy's stomach was churning, fear and nausea rolling over each other.

"Because we need to get to them before they get to us." He paused as they pulled into the street, then drove away from the garage and the crumpled body in the alley.

It was hard for Cessy to concentrate. Hard for her to focus on one thing. She wasn't even sure what had happened.

Had Chris let him go on purpose?

And did she care? Was she truly upset that a man had died . . . or did she think she needed to be upset?

After all, Chris was right. They needed to control the situation.

She pulled out her phone, punched in the name *Levi Price* and *Arlington*.

An address appeared, less than an hour away.

Cessy looked out the window as they drove, at the trees and yellow headlights racing past on the other side of the highway. Everything felt like a blur and had since Hector died. No, before that. Ever since Hector first hit her. That was when her life changed again.

Moving to Baltimore gave her the chance to start over, and Cessy had, and she'd been happy. And then Hector had hit her, started hitting her, and she was lost. Thinking about running, about fighting. No matter what happened, about changing.

Just like now.

They were crossing Roosevelt Bridge from Maryland to Virginia when Chris broke the silence. DC's lights glowed to their right, the dark Potomac River gleamed to their left. According to Cessy's phone, they were about ten minutes from Levi Price's house.

"It really wasn't my fault," Chris said, his words echoing what she'd been privately telling herself:

I didn't do anything wrong.

"No?" she asked.

"He kicked my hand," Chris said stubbornly. "I wasn't going to let him go. I had more I wanted to ask."

"Yeah? Then what were you going to do with him? Call him an Uber?"

Silence again as they entered Virginia. Cessy had only been to Virginia once since moving to Baltimore. A date with Hector, in the early stages of their relationship, to Old Town Alexandria, a cobblestoned area filled with shops and restaurants and crowds that reminded her of Fells Point. Hector had taken her to eat at a seafood restaurant, which was so good that it was almost worth the ridiculous cost of the dinner. Afterward, they walked along a trail next to the water, held hands, ate ice cream cones.

That was the first time they had ever held hands.

"You act like you're blaming me," Chris said suddenly. "What was I supposed to do after I was done talking to him?"

"Call the cops?"

"The last thing I need is the cops looking into me."

"You didn't have to be there. We had him tied up. I could have waited with him."

"Yeah, okay, you say that *now*. We didn't exactly have a plan *then*."

Cessy understood what her brother was saying; more than that, she agreed with him. But she didn't let herself get deterred. "You wanted to kill him," she insisted stubbornly.

She wondered if she was just speaking to Chris.

"And you didn't? After he tried to kill you?"

"It's too easy for you," she argued. "You like it."

"I don't like it. I do it because it has to be done. Like that fucker who hurt Mom. Remember him? Remember helping me bury him?"

"It's why I left Arizona." The sentence was short and honest. And incomplete.

"That's the thing. You always run, Cessy. But like you were saying, it's not who you are."

"What are you talking about?"

Cessy felt like Chris was digging a deep hole in the dirt, and the shovel was about to strike a hidden box.

"It's that thing, that thing we learned in school. You know, when you run or hide or something?"

"Fight or flight?"

Chris pointed triumphantly at Cessy. "That's it! You act like your instinct is to run, to flight. But it's not. You want to fight. That's what you always do first. Then you think about it, and you think about me, and you don't want that to be you. So you run off."

This wasn't a conversation she could have now.

She wanted to pour dirt back into that hole.

"Bullshit. Turn here."

They took an exit off the beltway, headed into Arlington. The businesses thinned out as they drove into residential neighborhoods.

"You know I'm right," Chris said, a tone in his voice that Cessy had found annoying ever since childhood. His "I told you so" attitude.

"Look, Chris, it doesn't matter what I *want* to do; it matters what I actually do. You get that? Yeah, I want to kill the people who burned down Rose's house. Of course I do." Her voice thickened. "But that's not what I'm going to do. You understand that? I'm going to find those people and . . . do something. And then I'm going to go in a different direction. Maybe I'll move. Maybe I'll stay. I don't know, and right now I don't care. All I care about is ending this."

"Eh." Chris's only comment.

But this was better. Cessy felt like she was on even ground. Her breathing slowed. The flush in her cheeks receded.

"And I care about you, *pendejo*. I need you to be safe and not, like, a little sadistic serial killer."

"I'm not little."

"Of everything in that sentence, I wished you'd picked another word to disagree with. Turn here. It's at the end of the next street."

Chris turned a corner, slowed to a stop at the curb.

"So what do we do here?" he asked. "With Levi Price? Knock on his door and ask if he can chat?"

"No," she said. "We do what we did with Smith. Except for the last part where you dropped him off the roof."

Chris leaned forward, peered through the window. "It's only one story. So it wouldn't really bother him that much. And I really don't think your "Kumbaya" approach is going to work."

"That's not my approach, and I know these guys don't operate that way. We need to get the jump on him, force him to do what we want. And we can do that without killing anyone."

Chris looked doubtful. And disappointed. "I guess."

32

The killer stands blocking the door to the hall, watching panic overcome Deb. That same panic the killer saw in Maria's face, right before he struck her with those brass knuckles, turned her face into a cave. But this is different, something about this is worlds away.

The killer wants to step forward, peer deep into Deb's face. Bite her lips. The killer can see all that emotion swirling inside her, and he wants more, wants to experience it, taste it, let it wash over. Like sex, the way you can see a woman's emotions and feel them tightening over you.

And like sex, his cock is so hard its straining, pulling him like those children's games with magnets and metal, his skin and soul dissolving as he follows it.

Deb wants to run past them. He can see her weighing the option, her legs tightening. He'll catch her and maybe hurt her if she tries, and he knows Price doesn't want that. Price will turn to him and fight, and they could get so distracted she ends up escaping. That's happened before. Happened with Becky Morales when she ran out of her apartment and he told Price he needed to take over, and caught her by the dumpster, smashed her head into it until her hair came loose in his hand, until her arms stopped pushing him, until he came so hard he fell to his knees.

He didn't care, but Price had been upset.

So upset that the killer vanished for a year or two, only reemerged when Price first saw Deb. Started thinking about her too much. And realized he might be needed.

This was it; tonight was it. No point in hiding anymore. No reason to wait for Price to call him.

It felt good for Deb to see him, to realize what he was. Like when those married men, near broke from blackmail, told their wives what had happened, what they had done. That sense of relief washing over guilt, regardless of consequence.

Of course, if they'd felt that emotion earlier, they'd never be in this situation. Men never understand emotion in the moment; it's always after, upon reflection or forced realization. The killer didn't care for women, but they seemed to understand things as they happened. They needed to. Men didn't. Prey need to be conscious of everything. A predator only focuses on the hunt, on himself.

It wasn't that the killer hated women, although he did hate a number of things about them and—actually, yeah, he hated women. Hated how they drew Price in, how everything was a reaction, waiting for him to do something. Always watching. Or if they weren't reactionary, then they took charge, threw off his expectations. Acted like men.

But there was a point with most women, when they were struggling and knew they were losing the struggle . . . *that* was the point. That's when they were perfect. That's when they would do anything, be anyone he wanted, offering spread legs or love or money or isolation.

If he could just keep them at that state.

The television snapped off and the lights went out.

Deb was invisible in front of him, lost in the dark.

"What happened?" he and Price asked.

33

"WHAT HAPPENED?" LEVI asked.

Deb heard a rustling sound from him and then a small snap. He'd taken out his gun.

"Stay here," Levi said softly. "Something's not right."

It was so dark Deb didn't see him leave, only heard the floor creaking underneath his feet as he walked away from the room.

Deb waited a few moments, then stepped into the hallway.

A faint light from the bay windows; Deb cautiously walked toward it. She was scared and confused, but realized that this was her best and maybe only chance to escape. She peered down the dark hall to the living room, willing her eyes to adjust to the lack of light, to pull shapes.

The floor creaked far in front of her, near the direction of the front door. She turned and went the opposite way, deeper into the house.

Searching for a window to crawl out of.

Deb kept an arm ahead of her and barely lifted her feet, slowly shuffling forward. She finally touched something, a wall, and realized she was at the end of the hall. Reached sideways and touched another doorway. Grasped the knob, turned it, pushed open the door soundlessly, tried to keep her breathing quiet.

She knew Levi could restore the power any moment now, and she'd be discovered.

The room was dark, pitch-black, but she stepped in anyway. Bumped something with her shin. Reached down, felt wrinkled sheets and a mattress.

A bedroom.

Which meant there might be a window.

Deb reached down, felt the edge of the bed, made her way around the room.

A hand grabbed her wrist.

Another hand clamped over her mouth, just before she could scream.

She felt a body press behind her.

"Don't make a sound," a woman's voice whispered into her ear.

Deb stood still, frozen.

The hand lifted.

"Who are you?"

Deb didn't say anything.

"Oh, you can answer that."

"Deb," she said, and panicked that she couldn't remember her last name.

"How do you know Levi Price?"

"Not well."

"Huh?"

"He lied to me."

"Yeah, okay. We'll see. You're coming with us for now."

"Us?"

"Me and my brother." The hand released her wrist, and Deb felt the woman quickly, efficiently pat down her body.

"Are you a cop?" Deb asked.

"No. Not even sure I did that right. Shut up and come on."

The woman took Deb's hand, led her out of the bedroom.

Deb followed her, too scared to be anything but blindly obedient. This woman didn't seem like she would let Deb refuse her, and Deb didn't even know if refusing made sense. It was all so confusing. And dark.

And impossible not to think about the video Levi had shown her. The earnestness in his voice when he'd claimed to do it out of love. Something in his voice had a sickness to it, addiction and helplessness.

It wasn't a voice she'd be able to forget.

The woman led Deb down the hall, abruptly stopped.

"What?" Deb asked.

"Deb?" Levi said.

The woman grabbed Deb's shoulders and yanked them, and Deb fell face-first into the carpet.

Moments later, a gun fired, a terribly loud explosion that left Deb's ears ringing.

Another gun. The wall next to them exploded.

Levi was shouting, she was shouting, her ears ached. The other woman's body was covering her, shielding her. The woman's hand covered her mouth and Deb tried to lie as close to the carpet as possible, panic engulfing her.

Finally, a series of repeated words from the other woman broke through:

"He's gone, he's gone, he's gone, he's gone."

She removed her hand from over Deb's mouth.

"Who's gone?"

"Levi Price. He ran out the front door."

"He did?"

A rough, coarse hand reached down, felt Deb's wrist, found her hand.

"Who's this?"

"I found her in his bedroom."

"Huh. Let's go."

They pulled Deb to her feet. Her legs were shaky, but she followed them, walking clumsily, down the hall and outside.

The door was open and, finally, there was light. Faint, but enough to break the dark.

The man darted forward, looked outside, waved for them to follow him. The woman did, stopped on the porch with Deb and looked around. Then she waved to the man, and he ran to the next spot, stopped, and waved at them to follow him.

It seemed unnecessary to Deb, given that Levi's car was gone, but she was so scared that she wanted to be as safe as possible. She ran with the woman, so tense that breathing was a struggle. She gasped for air whenever they stopped.

They kept going until they reached a car parked down the street. The woman opened a door. Deb climbed inside the back seat.

The woman slid into the driver's seat. The man took the passenger side.

He turned as the car pulled away from the curb.

"My name's Chris, and this is my sister Cessy." His smile looked like a shark swimming toward her. "How do you know Levi Price?"

PART FOUR

THE HUNT AND THE KILL

34

"WHO HELPED HER?" Scott Temple asked.

Freddie Harris listened to the phone conversation and rubbed his sweaty palms over his thighs, but subtly. He tried not to fidget as he sat in the wooden chair facing Temple's desk.

"What do you mean, you don't know?" Temple asked. "That's not particularly self-aware."

Harris watched Temple's free hand tighten into a fist, then slowly relax.

"Well, yes, Levi, I do think you should find her. That would be an excellent idea. Remember, some people make things happen, some watch what happened, others wonder what happened. Which of those are you?"

Temple paused, listened to the phone.

"Yes," he said after a moment, "you probably have heard that before, but the point stands. Find Deb Thomas."

Temple hung up the phone, examined the fingernails on his right hand.

"What happened?" Harris asked.

"Oh, nothing. Just Levi fell in love with the Thomas widow and thought it'd be a good idea to tell her who he really is."

"He *did*?"

"Promptly and predictably, she ended up running away from him. With help. Shots were fired. Of course, he has no idea who was helping her or where she went."

"Levi told her? And there were gun shots? Someone helped her?"

Temple nodded, pulled open a drawer, took out a metal nail file. Rubbed the file slowly, methodically over his ring finger.

"And he used his real name," Temple said as he inspected his nails. "Actually used his real name. Because—and this is a quote—he wanted to be honest with her."

Harris eyed the long file. It had been created to resemble a dagger, complete with a sharp pointed end.

"Any word from Smith?" Temple asked, his voice still calm.

"Not yet." Harris paused. "Are you going to have Levi killed?"

Temple slammed the file into the wooden desk. The blade sunk deep, stood like an exclamation mark.

Harris had jumped out of his chair. He cautiously sat back down.

"I should, right?" Temple said, his voice unchanged, still casual. "But not right now. We need more information from Levi first. He's on his way here."

"You're bringing him *here*? After he was involved in a shooting?"

Temple waved a dismissive hand. "This is a satellite office."

Harris glanced around the office. A couple of shelves with law books and Orioles memorabilia. Framed certificates congratulating Temple for finishing various legal programs. Posters of nature scenes with inspirational sayings underneath them: "The highest peak is inside yourself." "When there's no trail, make one." "You're already starting at the top— climb higher." "Plunge depths to reach heights." The desk was mainly clear except for a computer, a green-shaded desk lamp, and a stack of manila folders with white and pink paper. Harris had never been to Temple's other office, but he imagined it was nicer, more expansive, better suited to the needs of Baltimore County's District Attorney.

"Did you try Smith again?" Temple asked.

Harris pulled his phone out of his pocket, texted his partner a second time. Set the phone on his knee to wait for a response. "He's probably asleep. He was looking beat earlier tonight."

"You two never should have let Cessy Castillo leave the hospital," Temple said mildly.

"It was crowded in there. Couldn't finish her off." Harris kept his tone calm. He'd seen firsthand how ruthless Temple was. Surprising for a man who looked like he'd be happiest mowing his lawn. Temple had mild features: brown parted hair, neatly combed; always wearing a bland navy-blue business suit; clean-shaven; kind, watery eyes.

But Harris knew this wholesome appearance was a façade.

He'd seen Temple put a comforting hand on a man's shoulder, smile, and then slide his hand over and choke that man's life away.

Once he'd watched Temple swing a hacksaw into a pimp's limbs, eventually cutting off both arms as the man screamed for his life and his god and then his death. Smith had been holding the man's wife; Harris had been holding his ten-year-old son. He remembered how resolved James had been, his grip firm on the wife's arms as her eyes squeezed closed and her knees buckled. And he remembered the boy's thin shoulders in his hands, how violently they'd trembled.

And his own trembling hands.

Temple's smile had never left.

Harris hated being alone with Temple; really, hated doing anything without his partner. James Smith was the leader of their duo, a man who never seemed afraid or unsure of himself. Harris took strength from James the way plants absorbed sunlight.

Without James, Harris felt like he was withering.

It had always been this way with Harris; he was always subservient and secondary to other men. He could do anything or be anybody provided he could mimic someone else. He'd followed his two brothers into crime and, when his older brother was killed, followed the younger one into prison after a home invasion turned into a homicide. His brother convinced the judge that Harris was nothing more than an unwitting accomplice, so he was spared a life sentence. Harris left after four years of prison, without any idea of what to do, and realized that, aside from the beatings, he missed prison's structure. And he missed his brother.

Knowing what he needed, his brother hooked him up with a friend outside, someone who owed him a favor, a man named James Smith.

And Harris had dutifully followed James ever since.

"You know," Temple said slowly, "a crowded hospital didn't keep Barry alive."

Harris blinked. "You had Barry killed?"

"A crowded safe house didn't stop it from being burnt to the ground." Temple pointed to one of the inspirational posters behind him. "If you believe in yourself, Freddie, then anything is possible. But you have to *believe*."

"I understand."

"No, you don't. Right now you don't believe in yourself, so I don't believe in you. You don't think you can ascend that peak. Become the you that you need to become to become a better you."

"What?"

"That's why I've reached out to someone else."

"What?"

A knock on the door.

"Look at that timing!" Temple exclaimed. "Holy cow! Nothing that cool will ever happen to either of us again! Come on in."

The door opened and a man walked into the room. He wore a long brown coat and a black baseball cap pulled low. He walked past Freddie without a glance, stood before Temple's desk.

Harris shivered, as if cold was trailing the new arrival.

The new arrival took off his cap and gave it to Harris. Freddie took it, looked up at the man, reared back into his chair.

"Got to tell you," Temple said, "for a bounty hunter, you're not exactly inconspicuous." He squinted. "Did you get burned?"

The man nodded.

Harris stared at the back of the man's bald head, the yellow and red rough skin, seemingly clumped together in places.

"Ouch," Temple remarked. "How'd it happen? Car accident? Grilling?"

When the man spoke, his voice was scraped and rough. "Someone set me on fire."

"Yikes," Temple replied. "On purpose?"

The man nodded.

"Was that before or after you became a bounty hunter?"

"Before."

Temple beamed. "Destiny reflects where you're going, but strength is how you get there."

"Okay," the burned man said.

Temple wagged his finger. "You've caught every person you've ever hunted down. Is that true? One hundred percent?"

"Yeah."

Temple beamed. "See, Freddie? Those are the kind of numbers I like. Your name's Seth, right?"

"Yeah."

"Seth, I bet you're self-actualized as all get out. Do you have a last name?"

"Just Seth."

"I can work with that. Can you work with that, Freddie?"

Harris was still staring at the back of Seth's scarred head. "Sure."

"The terms are ten thousand for Cessy Castillo, five for anyone helping her. She may have a couple of people working for her. We're not sure."

"Doesn't matter."

"Didn't think it did! When you're at the top of your personal pyramid, you realize that all obstacles are already beneath you."

Freddie blinked.

Seth didn't say anything.

"I don't need to see the bodies in person or anything," Temple continued, "just some photos. No one left breathing." He considered something, his head bobbing a little as he thought. "And I want you to work with a man named Levi Price on it. Bit of an idiot, but he's my cousin. You can't choose your family, only your path. Anyway, Freddie here will put you in touch. Do we have a deal?"

35

KIM WAS A little scared, a lot confused, and had no idea why she was sitting next to her mom on the edge of a bed in room 16 of the Paradise Motor Lodge in Manassas, Virginia.

"Who are these people?" Kim asked, quietly.

"I'm not sure," her mother replied.

A woman, probably a few years older than Kim, sat on a chair by the window and stared outside. She'd been sitting there since Kim had knocked on the door and her mother pulled her in with a quick, fierce embrace. The curtains were drawn, but the woman stared out through a narrow slit between the shades and the wall, relentlessly, as if it was inevitable that someone else was coming.

A man was in the bathroom. He hadn't introduced himself, just exclaimed, "Nature's calling!" when the motel room door closed behind Kim, and then he'd hurried into the bathroom. Kim couldn't tell if he and the woman were siblings or married—they looked alike, but there was distance between them in the way they regarded each other. A distance Kim associated with marriage.

Kim thought about that, made a note to think more later about why she did.

For now, she just wanted to figure out why she'd been urgently called to meet her mom in a motel in Manassas. She'd been watching a movie with Rebecca, Rebecca's parents out of town, drowsily lying against her girlfriend, enjoying the warmth of Rebecca's arms over her shirt and the warmth of the blanket spread over them both. And then her phone had buzzed.

She'd risen from the couch, the message *URGENT CALL MOM NOW URGENT* jarring her awake. She called her, and the worry in her mom's tone compelled Kim to dismiss the excuses she'd already been planning. She told Rebecca she had to go.

Rebecca followed her into the hall, the blanket wrapped around her like a cocoon. "Is your mom okay?"

Kim slipped on her shoes, felt the stress in her face. Her mom had sounded near hysterical, close to crying.

All this was so new. Kim was used to her mom being in control, confident, easily self-assured. She'd never seen her mom so reactionary, such a victim of circumstance, since Dad died.

"She doesn't sound okay," Kim said.

"You want me to come with you?"

"No, I'll be okay. I'll call you, though."

Kim put on her jacket, fished her car keys out of the pocket, walked to the basement back door. Rebecca followed her, still wrapped in the blanket.

"I'm sorry," Kim said. "Sorry to cut another night short."

"It's okay. You don't have to apologize." She paused. "I understand."

There was something in her tone Kim wanted to stop and discuss, something belying the words *I understand*, but Kim didn't have time to talk.

She hugged Rebecca and left.

* * *

The toilet flushed, the sink ran. Chris stepped out of the bathroom.

"All right, let's start with the intros," he said. "We'll introduce ourselves and say why we're all here. And maybe share something with each other no one else knows."

The two women sitting on the bed were looking at him strangely. No one said anything.

"Good," Chris said. "My name's Chris Castillo. That's my sister, Cessy, by the window. She lives in Baltimore. I'm here from Phoenix. Nice town you have here! Now, how do we all know each other?"

It took a moment, and then Cessy spoke. "Those men killed my husband."

"What?" the younger woman asked. "What men?"

"Mine too," the older woman said, and she caught herself. "Sorry, my name is Deb Thomas. This is my daughter, Kim." She turned toward Cessy. "When did your husband die?"

"About a month ago."

"That's about the same time my husband died. His name was Grant."

Chris wondered if he'd left his gun in the car or the bathroom.

"Friday night, November eighth," Cessy said.

"That's the same night for Dad," Kim said, and the hurt way she said *Dad* hung in the room. Softened it. Chris wanted to say something, but the tension in the women's faces kept his mouth closed.

He was just so damn happy, and that made it tough. Happy to be back with Cessy, especially now that she seemed to have stopped coughing. Happy to have made it out of that dark house alive. And really happy that his blind gunshot hadn't accidentally struck his sister.

But no one seemed as happy as he was—no one else was smiling, that was for damn sure—so Chris kept quiet and worked on relaxing his smile.

He wondered if the motel had a vending machine and if Cessy would be mad if he went looking for one.

Probably. She got mad at him a lot.

"Mom," the girl continued, "what's going on?"

"The men who killed your father . . . they threatened me tonight. These two saved me."

"What?" the girl asked, her voice faint. "I don't understand. What men?"

Now Chris felt like he could talk. "Our investigation has revealed them to be a group of assholes," he said.

"Pimps and crooks," Cessy elaborated. "They blackmail men."

"But how was Dad involved?" Kim asked.

"So they used prostitutes," Deb said slowly, "to extort men."

"Yeah?" Kim asked. "And?"

Silence.

"Well," Chris said brightly, "this is awkward."

*   *   *

Deb watched comprehension fill her daughter's face.

"He did?" Kim said softly.

Deb nodded.

Kim stood, walked away from her mom toward the opposite wall. Deb wanted to do more, reach out to Kim and comfort her, but so much was happening. Her mind felt like a pile of papers tossed in the air, and she wanted to catch each one as it fell. But there were too many—she couldn't. Deb couldn't understand everything that was happening.

Levi Price had lied to her about everything.

Followed her.

Watched her.

She'd barely escaped his house. Not only that, but she'd *had* to escape his house.

She'd been in gunfire.

She and Kim were with two strangers in a motel room.

It was too much, and Deb wanted to tell Kim everything was going to be okay. But that was a lie, one Kim would see through. One Kim would feel in Deb's arms, hear in her words.

"How'd you end up with Levi Price?" Cessy asked.

"He introduced himself to me," Deb said. "He told me he was investigating Grant's death with the FBI."

"Levi, the man who was at our house?" Kim asked. "Why?"

"Because he was stalking me," Deb replied, her voice quieting as the sentence ended.

She looked down, felt guilt. As if she had somehow led Levi to do the terrible things he'd done.

And wondered why she felt it.

Why she was compelled to take blame for his actions.

"He told me a lot of stuff," she went on. "Told me he was working for someone named Scott Temple."

"Scott Temple?" Cessy asked.

Deb nodded.

Cessy and Chris glanced at each other.

"The Jews," Chris said solemnly.

"That's not what this is, dummy," Cessy told him.

Deb ignored them. "He even took me to the prostitute Grant was with."

"He did?" Kim asked.

"Where is she now?" Cessy asked.

"She's dead. I think he killed her."

"Oh no," Kim said softly, and the soft words broke something inside of Deb. She wanted to comfort Kim, wanted to say the right thing, wanted to keep her safe.

And didn't know how to do any of those things.

* * *

"Plenty of people associated with those men have that in common," Cessy said. "Being dead, I mean. Probably us soon, too."

"Do you mind?" Deb asked, and gestured at her daughter.

Cessy took her response as a challenge. "Not at all. They burned down a group home I was in, just to get at me. Killed four people, including my friend Rose. They killed my husband, your husband, and they almost killed you. I have nowhere to run, no place to hide, and no way to defend myself. But, hey, sorry for being negative."

"What about the cops?" Kim put in.

"No cops," Chris said.

"Why not?"

Now it was Cessy's turn to feel uncomfortable.

"Probably for the best that the cops don't look into me," Chris offered.

"Jesus," Deb said. Cessy watched her rub her eyes, stare down into her hands.

"So what do we do?" Deb asked. "Stay here, wait for those men to find us?"

"I mean," Cessy said defensively, "we just saved your ass. I haven't really had time to think of something since then."

"Also I'm hungry," Chris put in. At another time, Cessy would have probably felt the urge to snap at Chris, tell him to calm down with the non sequiturs, but she was too stressed to care.

Fortunately, both Deb and her daughter seemed content to ignore him.

"Okay," Deb said, and stood. "We don't know the two of you or anything about you. I appreciate you getting me out of Levi's house and bringing us here, but my daughter and I are going to the police. I won't tell them about you, won't say a word, but someone needs to tell the cops."

Cessy considered that.

"If you want to leave," she said, "you can leave. We won't stop you."

"And we can go to the police?" Deb asked.

"I don't care where you go," Cessy said. "Just don't tell anyone about us."

"Really? I take off and go to the cops, and you'll just let me walk out that door?"

"Yeah, but I'm going to the cops with you. I want to make sure you keep my brother's name out of it. He's done some shady shit in his past and doesn't need the police looking into him. Or knowing where he is."

Cessy and Deb locked eyes, neither women backing down.

"Okay," Deb said, and she stood.

Cessy followed suit, put on her jacket. Looked at Chris standing against the wall.

"I'll bring you something to eat," she said.

He nodded, smiled.

Chris's smile . . . he was enjoying this. And, for some reason, given everything that had happened, his smile worried Cessy.

She wondered if she should tell the cops everything.

Everything, including how she put Barry in the hospital. The body she helped bury in Arizona. The bodies Chris had buried.

Tie all the violence together, like loose threads, and then snip that complicated knot away.

"Let's go," she said.

CHAPTER

36

DETECTIVE STEVE ROBECK was exhausted. He was pulling a double, covering the midnight Manassas shift for a buddy on vacation, and the slot was brutal. Most of his nights dealt with drunks—drunks driving, drunks pissing in public, drunks fighting outside bars. He could deal with that, but what got to him were the most serious cases, the shootings, the robberies; the mothers and children occasionally showing up, running in the night from some abusive asshole, scared and quiet. During the day he was called out to investigate the aftermath of a crime; during night, there was more immediacy, an urgency to his work, the disruption of sleep leaving people even more unsettled. Crime was never predictable to the victims, and the more their natural order was disturbed, the more unraveled their lives became.

And then there were the crazies, people following crime like it was a wave sweeping them along, making up stories, putting their lives in newspaper narratives. Stories that fell apart the moment they were touched, like a house made of dust.

Like the three women sitting in front of him at one in the morning.

"That sounds insane," he told them after they'd finished their story. Not the kind of thing Robeck would usually say, but again, this wasn't his usual shift.

"What sounds insane?" one of them asked, an older Asian. "Which part?"

"All of it."

The Asian looked at the two women sitting next to her, her daughter and a Hispanic friend.

"But it's the truth!"

"So a group of pimps killed your husbands," Robeck said dubiously, "and now they're trying to kill you too?"

"We don't know if they're all pimps," the Hispanic said. "Just some of them."

"Sorry," Robeck said, and he did regret getting that piece of information wrong. Hard to be dismissive when you're inaccurate. "It's been a long day."

"You saw that they were both killed on the same night," the older Asian said. "Our husbands. Both shot."

"I did," Robeck acknowledged, but he didn't say more. He didn't tell them that it wasn't unusual for people dealing with grief to clutch at strands, to find answers wherever they could. No matter how crazy.

Particularly women.

But he couldn't say that.

Just think it.

Robeck stifled a yawn. "Do you have the name of the man that's been threatening you?"

"Levi Price," Asian mom said. "He told me he was an FBI agent, but he was lying."

Robeck rubbed his elbow. False identity usually meant some sort of financial scam. Someone targeting vulnerable widows. Not a surprise.

And this late at night, given how tired Robeck was, not much of a concern.

"Are you sure Levi Price is his real name?"

"Oh. No, I guess not."

"I can make some calls," he offered. "Check to see if anyone's come across this man. Do you have anything else you can give me?"

"I don't think so," Asian mom said, and she glanced over at her daughter and the Hispanic. Daughter didn't move; Hispanic shook her head again.

"Let me have your number," Robeck told her. "I'll look into this and—"

"What?" Mom Asian said. "No, we need protection. We need help right now!"

"Sorry?"

"Those men are after us."

"I don't have evidence of a crime, just your word."

"But we're telling you the truth!" Asian mom leaned forward, hands on the table, a cresting wave of worry poised to crash.

"I told you," he said, his voice level and patient, "the most I can do right now is look into this. If you feel you're in immediate danger, call me. I'll give you my cell number. But we need time to investigate. Does that make sense?"

"Not really."

"There was a shooting in Virginia," the Hispanic said.

"When?"

"Earlier tonight. We were there. He shot at us."

Again, not uncommon for people to find a crime and link themselves to it. Especially if they were working some angle. Robeck thought again about his scam theory and wondered if these three were in on it. Maybe setting up some long con.

Going to the cops now to make their story plausible later.

Robeck pressed a button on his receiver. "Ericson, any word on a shooting in Northern Virginia earlier tonight?"

A few moments passed. "None reported."

"Maybe it hasn't been reported yet," Asian mom said.

Robeck wouldn't have believed they were involved even if it had. At this point, he was sure this was a scam. Or some weird manifestation of grief. Or both.

Hard to imagine the best when people constantly showed you their worst.

"I promise I'll look into it," Robeck said. "But for now, that's all I can do. And if you have any problems, call me directly."

The women glanced at each other, and the fear in their expressions almost broke his resolve. Nearly made him doubt himself.

Something occurred to him.

"We actually have a human trafficking task force set up," Robeck said. "It's a new thing, interstate, working with Virginia, DC, and Maryland. Specifically relates to prostitution."

"Okay," the Hispanic said.

"If there's something to this, then we'll find out. I'll report what happened, see if the name Levi Price rings any bells, see if his name or this network of pimps shows up." Robeck noticed the lack of hope in their faces. "I know it doesn't seem like much," he pressed, "but they're taking this seriously. It's being spearheaded by the DA up in Baltimore County. Temple."

Now there was a change in their expressions, but it wasn't what he expected. Fear, different shades of it across all three women.

"Temple?" the Hispanic asked. "Scott Temple?"

Robeck nodded, now convinced this was a con. He'd seen this before, the fear in amateur scammers the moment their story was going to be vetted.

"Temple wants all incidents of human trafficking, especially prostitution, brought directly to his desk. And I can give him your names and numbers. How's that sound?"

As he suspected, they didn't want to pursue the matter.

But he'd still report it to Temple's task force first thing in the morning.

Just in case.

37

"WHAT HAPPENED TO you, anyway?" Levi Price asked the burned man.

Seth didn't respond, didn't even look up from the map he was staring into.

Price sighed. Temple had called Price on his way to Temple's office, told him to head to some apartment instead. Work with a man named Seth. But he didn't tell him Seth was a walking scab.

Seth had opened the door after Price knocked, glanced at him, walked back over to his small dining room table, and stared down into a map. Price didn't see much else in the apartment—a recliner in front of a television set, a couple of closed doors that presumably led to a bedroom and bathroom, a small outdated kitchen. An out-of-place movie poster showing two people sitting on a bench, staring at a bridge.

"I'm guessing you live alone?" Price asked.

No response.

Price squinted down at the map, saw that it detailed Maryland, DC, and Northern Virginia. A couple of spots had been circled in red.

Price pointed at one of the circles.

"What's that for?"

"Smith was found here."

"Smith's dead?"

Seth grunted.

"You think it was the same people who came to my place in Virginia?"

Seth grunted assent, placed a discolored finger on the map. "Cessy Castillo was in the hospital here. She lives here. Over in Baltimore. You see a Panamanian woman at your place earlier tonight?"

"No."

Seth stared at him, his blue eyes peering out from a pale, typographical map of flesh.

Price stared back coolly. Felt that killer rustling inside him. That other person he could just give way to, like a costume slipped on and off.

"You said the people who came to your place were professionals."

Price wasn't sure if it was a question. "Yeah."

"Smith was taken out cleanly. Caught and dropped off a high floor. Whoever got him questioned him, found out about the next person to attack, then went there. It's the same people. Now they have Deb Thomas. What does she know?"

"What does she know?" Price repeated.

Seth's voice lowered, turned menacing. "What did you tell her?"

Price was very conscious of the gun on his hip, the weight of it against his side.

"Look," he said, "Deb doesn't know anything she didn't know before. Like I told you, she started asking questions. I did what I could to close her off."

"She knows you. Knows your real name. Temple may decide to kill you for the lines you've crossed."

Price rested his hand on the table, just inches from his hip. He tried to make the move look natural.

"But I think we need you alive," Seth added. "They may try to find you."

"So I'm bait?"

Seth didn't respond, just kept staring at him.

"Wait," Price said, an idea forming. "Her daughter, Kim. She has a friend, a girlfriend, in college. Name starts with an "R." Rachel, maybe? If Kim and her mom are hiding somewhere, this girl might be able to found out where."

"Where is she?"

"I'm not sure, but I can find her."

"Do it."

Price nodded.

He'd checked out Seth when he came in, didn't see any sign of a weapon on him. Even so, he had a feeling Seth could kill him.

That other person inside Price, the bloodthirsty one, the one who occasionally emerged with a howl, the killer who had gleefully caved in Maria's skull . . . that man was just a part of Price.

But he could tell it was all of Seth.

Temple had told him that Seth never failed. Even fire hadn't stopped him, a fire that must have ravaged him, a fire like his body had been thrown into hell's flames.

Price recognized something in Seth, the kind of recognition animals in the wild experience, not kinship, not hate. Wolves watching each other across a field, before turning and disappearing back into the wild.

Death didn't come for Seth.

He brought it to others.

Price knew he'd bring it to Deb Thomas.

"Be back," Price said, and went to the bathroom.

He locked the door behind him, gripped the sink with both hands, stared hard into the mirror.

He'd fallen in love.

He'd fucked up.

All he was supposed to do was look into Grant Thomas's financials. Make sure the money Grant had given them—and the money he'd given Maria, which she'd dutifully given them—couldn't be traced. Break into his house, run through statements, search for desperate letters Grant may have left his family, explaining everything he'd done. But Grant had left his family lost. Price hadn't found anything.

That is, anything other than love when he first saw Deb Thomas. Something about her, the way she had a foot in two worlds. Grieving, but comforting her daughter. Devastated by her husband's death, but determined to press on. Overwhelmed by concerns about money, but desperate to find a way to stay in her home and keep Kim in college. That duality; Price loved her struggle so much his eyes stung.

It helped, of course, that she was beautiful. Through cameras, he'd watched Deb after a shower, a towel flashing between her legs as she bent to dry herself. Watched her run a tired hand through her thick hair, imagined that same hair through his fingers. And then, when the distance from a camera was too much, he'd sneak into her house and watch her sleep at night, his face inches from her own. Her lips so close to his.

Price looked at the mirror, realized he was smiling.

He'd watched the way Deb walked into the building where Maria lived, clearly lacking confidence but pressing on. Watched Deb cry on the ride back home from that apartment, turned away from him, her body a ball, staring at the half-hearted rain as it splashed the window. Watched the way Deb answered the door, a questioning expression on her face, and then that mix of relief and worry when she recognized him. Laughing at dinner with her daughter and her daughter's girl-friend (Roxanne, Renae?) after that bitch had finished grilling him, when the evening had relaxed. When Deb had briefly looked at him and must have momentarily forgotten everything that happened at Maria's and smiled, and her smile swung his heart like a hammock in summer sun. The way her fingers reached between his at Ruth's Chris (was the girl's name Ruth?).

Price knew where love's path ended, where it always ended with him, because the killer inside could never allow him to be with anyone. But Price wanted to have the chance to walk that path with her. After the last bullet was fired, after the blood was wiped away like it had never existed, after the bodies were buried and forgotten, he wanted to hold Deb. Kiss her tears, her lips.

Press his head to her chest and listen to her heartbeat slow.

38

CESSY, DEB, AND Kim filed back into the motel room.

"That was quick," Chris said.

"Cop didn't believe us." Cessy collapsed on one of the beds like she'd been thrown on it. "Pretty much thought we were crazy."

"So now what?" Chris asked.

"Now we go the hell to sleep," Cessy said, and yawned. "This night has lasted way too long. What is it, three in the morning?"

"I don't know what to do," Deb said. She stood against the wall, nervously rubbed her hands. It had been a quiet drive back to the motel, the three women each deep in her own thoughts. "Kim and I will be okay if we just don't say anything, right?"

Cessy could hear the panic beating under Deb's words, the desperation and exhaustion and fear that led victims to break and beg for help from their captors.

"I mean, I'll tell them myself we don't want anything to do with them," Deb went on. "I'll tell them we just want to be left alone."

"Doesn't matter," Cessy said. "Not if they're not comfortable with you knowing what you know."

"Spoiler alert!" Chris exclaimed. "They're not comfortable."

"Then what do we do? Try different cops? The FBI?"

"You could," Cessy replied, "but you'll catch Temple's attention. And Baltimore doesn't exactly have the best rep for witness protection."

"So what do we do?" Deb asked again, that panic coming forth like shark fins breaking through the surface of the water.

"We sleep," Cessy said, and stretched. She saw that Deb was close to breaking, could see her composure unraveling, but didn't offer consolation. She was thinking about her own options.

There weren't many.

These men were tied to the police. Chris had already killed one of them (and Cessy fervently hoped Smith hadn't been a cop), and they'd probably left fingerprints and DNA all over Price's house. She and Chris would eventually be caught if they ran, caught if they didn't.

The only thing they could do was go deeper into the web, try to find the spider. Catch and expose him before he caught them.

Scott Temple.

*   *   *

The sound of the bathroom door closing woke Deb.

She couldn't believe she'd actually fallen asleep.

She lay in bed, confused, wondering how much time had passed. The heavy curtains did an effective job of keeping sunlight out, so much so that Deb was surprised when she looked at the alarm clock and saw it was one in the afternoon. Chris and Cessy were snoring in the room's other bed, alternating like jazz horns trading fours. Kim had been lying next to her, but now Deb was alone in bed.

Deb walked over to the bathroom, knocked quietly on the door.

"Yeah." Kim's soft voice.

Deb walked in, closed the door behind her. Her daughter was sitting on the toilet's closed seat, hands clasped between her eyes, looking down. She glanced up at Deb, and her eyes were scared and wet.

Her face looked so young and so helpless that Deb felt a rush of pity. And strength. She knelt before Kim, placed her daughter's forehead on her shoulder, held her.

"Are you worried?"

Kim nodded stiffly.

"We'll be okay. I promise you. We'll be okay. I'll find a way to . . ."

Kim pulled away from her mother.

"Why'd you lie to me?"

"What?"

"Why didn't you tell me the truth about Dad?"

Deb sat back on the cold floor. "What do you mean?"

"Why didn't you tell me about the prostitute?"

The prostitute.

The word seemed so serious, so mature, coming from her daughter.

The pain from what Grant had done returned, the rawness, like a red canyon tearing open inside of her.

"I didn't know if I should tell you," Deb said. "And I just found out. I didn't know anything about this until after he'd died."

"Really?"

"Honestly. And I didn't want to change anything in your feelings about your father. Some things need to stay inside a marriage. I thought this was one of them."

"Yeah, but not anymore."

"Not anymore," Deb agreed sadly. She looked down at the blue and white tiles. "I'm sorry. I'm sorry that we're in this mess. If I hadn't asked any questions, we wouldn't be in a gross motel room bathroom with two complete psychos outside."

Kim smiled through the tears on her face. "It's kind of funny when you put it like that."

Deb allowed herself a small smile. "I promise you, honey, we're going to find a way through this. We'll keep our heads down until we get somewhere safe. I won't let anything happen to you."

"We need to tell Rebecca, Mom," Kim said, urgency returning to her voice. "That Levi Price guy met her. He knows what she looks like, knows where she goes to school. He might go after her to find us. He might hurt her."

Deb pursed her lips.

Kim was right.

Rebecca was in danger.

And so was Nicole.

So was anyone Price had met.

It was hard for Deb to think with any sort of precision in this panic. Any time she tried to focus on a thought, it squirmed away.

The only thing that seemed like it would immediately make her feel better would be to leave this motel room, get as far away from these people as possible.

"Let's go find Rebecca and Nicole," she decided. "We'll tell them, and then I'll deal with everything else."

Kim looked relieved, but the shadow hadn't entirely left her face.

"What?" Deb asked.

"Mom, do you think those two out there will just let us leave?"

Deb thought about it.

"Stay here," she said. "And lock the door. Do you have your phone?"

Kim nodded, eyes wide.

"I'm going to talk to Chris and Cessy. If you hear something happen to me, call nine-one-one. But don't do it until then. Just be ready."

"I'll go with you."

"I don't want to put you in any more danger than I already have. If we're safe, I'll knock."

Deb hugged her daughter, felt Kim's head press against her shoulder. Then she rose and stepped outside.

Chris and Cessy were still snoring.

Deb waited for Kim to close and lock the bathroom door. Once she heard the lock click, she said:

"Hey guys."

Louder.

"Excuse me."

A moment passed.

"Hey!"

The siblings started, woke simultaneously, sitting up and blinking in confusion.

"My daughter and I are leaving," Deb said. "Her girlfriend isn't safe. Levi knows about her, so we need to get to her before he does. We're going to get her and then figure out our next move. But I can promise you we won't say anything about you. I promise you."

"Okay." Cessy stretched. "Bye."

Chris waved.

"You're not going to try and stop us?" Deb asked, incredulous.

"Does that hurt your feelings?" Cessy asked.

"No, it's not that. I just, I just thought . . ."

"You're not our prisoner," Cessy said, "and you don't know a thing about us. And we won't be in this motel for that long."

That sounded vaguely ominous, but Deb decided to let it go.

"So then, goodbye?"

"We'll miss you," Chris said. Cessy was already lying back down.

Deb knocked on the bathroom door.

*　*　*

"Should we have just let them go?" Chris asked sleepily once Deb and Kim had left.

"I was serious," Cessy replied nonchalantly. "They're not our prisoners. They're free to go. Besides, we could use their help."

He yawned. "What do you mean?"

"I mean they're going to end up drawing those men back out in the open." Cessy sat up, reached for her jeans on the floor. "Let's follow them."

39

"Yeah, I know," Price said into the phone. "Yeah, I *know*." He sighed and glanced over at Seth in the driver's seat. Seth stared through the windshield, his damaged skin hidden behind sunglasses, a baseball cap, a black hoodie.

Price turned his attention back to the phone call from Harris.

"This entire mess needs to be cleaned up," Harris was saying. "You understand that, right? How far did this spill reach?"

"I told you. Everyone. Her, her daughter, her daughter's friend. Some other woman I can't remember, I think her name was Natalie or something . . ."

"No names. Just contain the spill."

Price smirked. Harris was so scared of saying anything incriminating that he always talked in some pseudo-coded language. This despite the fact that no one was investigating them for anything, and they—unofficially—worked for the DA.

Then again, maybe his family relation to the DA had relaxed Price too much. He and his cousin, Scott Temple, had grown up with each other, played together like siblings because they were both only children, never more than a town or two apart. They'd gone to the University of Maryland's University College together, studied criminal justice, both with the hopes of following in the footsteps of Temple's father, a career cop who was a father to them both (Price's father had disappeared right after his birth). Those goals changed after four long years.

Temple studied law, and Price went to work for Homeland Security, dealing with immigration and customs.

Price lost touch with his cousin when he went to work in DC, spent a few years mired in paperwork and boredom, and then a few years in raids. That's when he found an attitude developing inside him, an "us versus them" mentality. A superiority complex when he'd bust through doors and see people living like savages. Treating each other like garbage. Children, naked and shivering, standing near open ovens just to stay warm, looking quiet and scared. He imagined they were grateful to be led away from their ill-equipped, terrified, gibberish-speaking parents.

And that's when the killer first emerged, the whispering presence that had been inside him all his life, the side he'd never showed anyone, the part of him that always wanted to push boundaries further. Happened after some foreign father threatened them with a knife, his wife and children wailing behind him. Cut Price's arm, not bad, but enough for a few stitches. They arrested the father, took the children.

A day later—still angry, seething at what these "savages" had done to him—the killer returned for the wife.

A couple of guys in Security told him about places they went to relieve stress, to do things their wives and girlfriends wouldn't. Massage parlors. Apartments. The back of an Asian market. Price went to those places pent up, left relieved. Price didn't think much about the whores he was with, just knew it was a way to keep the killer calm, a way to dissipate that red rage.

Then the sweep happened. He and about a dozen of his fellow agents, arrested for soliciting prostitutes, unceremoniously kicked out of Homeland. It was in all the papers, although, because of their jobs, no names were mentioned.

And it was about a week later when his cousin reached out to him, a year into his term as the district attorney of Baltimore County, and swore him to confidence. Told him about a side scheme, using prostitutes as a form of blackmail.

Price signed up immediately.

"Do you have any sense of the direction the spill is headed in?" Harris asked now.

This stupid code. "We have a couple of ideas."

"And you can stop it before it spreads? Or do you need help?"

"We'll stop it," Price said.

"Well, it reached Manassas," Harris said tersely. "Like I told you, one of our offices there."

"And like I told you, Manassas is a big town. That doesn't help much. Keep looking, but Seth and I are trying a better angle."

"No names!" Harris exclaimed, and hung up the phone.

Price did the same. "That guy. He make you talk in a code too?"

"I don't talk to him." Seth drank from his coffee.

"Who do you talk to?" Seth didn't answer, and Price didn't expect him to. They'd been together a day, and Seth barely spoke, which in turn made Price speak more. Just to fill the silence. It made him feel foolish.

"I wanted to help Deb," he said, "but I don't see what I can do now. She probably thinks I killed her husband, and I guess I can't blame her. No reason for her to trust anything I tell her."

Seth stared forward.

"It was a mistake on my part," Price went on. "I don't know what I was thinking."

But he thought about Deb and still felt that sorrow of unrequited love. The love that confused him, overwhelmed him. The unceasing thoughts, the way her face burned into his mind, a powerful iron cattle brand pressed and seared into his brain. Price hoped it was different this time, but his love only ever ended in one place, in one way.

All the women he'd loved were dead.

Seth scratched the side of his scarred neck. Stayed silent.

"I'd like another chance to talk with her, another chance to clear things up, but I know I won't get that. The only thing I ask is that you end it quick for her if you're the one to do it."

Price watched Seth and thought he saw Seth nod. It was almost imperceptible, but Price figured that was the best he was going to get from the burned man. He settled back in his seat, picked up his coffee, let the hot, dark liquid warm his tongue and throat.

And he stared at the entrance of the dorm building on the other side of the parking lot and waited for Kim Thomas's girlfriend, Rebecca Blake, to emerge.

CHAPTER

40

K IM WATCHED HER girlfriend walk through the doors of the Silver Diner, look around, spot her and her mother in a back booth.

Rebecca waved, sauntered over in that casual unhurried way she walked, like she was determined to experience the world on her terms. When she reached the table, Kim abruptly stood and buried herself in Rebecca's arms. Kim wanted to kiss her, wanted to cry. But she felt the stares of the customers around them. She returned to the seat next to her mother.

"Wow," Rebecca said as she sat across from them. "Are you two okay?"

It took Kim a moment to realize what exactly Rebecca was referring to, the contrast between them. Rebecca was wearing a white sweater and jeans with calf-high suede boots, looked perfectly put together. Kim and Deb were disheveled, hair messed, wearing day-old clothes. Faces tightened by tension.

"It's been bad," Deb said, staring at two men eating by themselves.

"Why? What's up?"

"So," Kim started, "we found out that that guy named—"

"Here's the thing," Deb interrupted. "We can't tell you much. Okay? It's not safe for you."

"Um, okay."

Deb's voice lowered. "You know that Kim's father died. We found out it wasn't random, like we thought." She cleared her throat. "And the men who did it may be after us."

"*What?*"

Kim watched Rebecca's face change, eyes widen, mouth open. She looked at Kim for confirmation.

Kim nodded.

"Are you two serious right now?"

"It's not safe," Deb said, "and there's a chance they may come after you."

An emotion Kim had never seen filled her girlfriend's face. Something raw. Terror.

"Do you remember that man named Levi?" Deb went on, as if she hadn't noticed the panic overtaking Rebecca. "The one who had dinner with us? He works with them."

"It's blackmail," Kim said. "They—"

Deb interrupted her daughter. "The less you know, the better. Don't say anything until this is all straightened out. Can you do that?"

Rebecca's voice was so quiet Kim had to strain to hear her. "I'm home for finals. My family—"

"The less you know," Deb repeated herself firmly, "the better. They won't hurt you if you don't know anything."

Two tears streamed down Rebecca's face. "Are you sure?"

Deb nodded. "It's us they're after."

Kim wondered if her mother really was this certain or if she was simply trying to calm Rebecca down. She reached across the table and held Rebecca's hand.

Rebecca took her hand away, held it in her lap and rubbed her hands together, the way she always did when she was nervous. Kim remembered when she had first noticed that habit, the night she told Rebecca that she loved her, the two of them sitting in her dorm room on her bed, having just kissed after hanging out together for weeks. Rebecca had smiled that lovely, shy smile and asked, "Really?" in such an unconfident, uncertain, heartbreaking tone.

And now Rebecca wouldn't look at her.

"Are you all right?" Kim asked.

Rebecca met her eyes but quickly glanced away.

Kim hated this. She desperately wanted Rebecca to look her in the eyes, wanted to let Rebecca know she wasn't in danger. Kim wanted to lie to her, to tell her that everything her mother was saying was made up, this was all a fevered hallucination brought on by grief. Assure Rebecca that nothing had changed, she was fine.

They would be okay.

"Keep a low profile," her mother was saying, that urgency still in her voice. "And if you see Levi, tell him you haven't seen us. Tell him you and Kim broke up. This will all be over soon, I promise."

"Okay."

Everything is fine, Kim didn't say.

She wanted to, but the truth of the situation held her back. Her mother, the Castillos. All that had happened over the past few weeks.

Kim wanted to comfort Rebecca, but she didn't want to lie. And couldn't give her false assurances.

"You and Kim can't talk for a few days," her mother was saying. "Not until this is over."

"All right."

Rebecca accepted the idea of distance more easily than Kim would have preferred, but Kim didn't have a right to call her out on it. And she had no anger toward her girlfriend.

Rather, it was directed at her mother for taking over this conversation, taking over her relationship, ruining her life with the mess her father had left them.

Kim searched Rebecca's downcast face, still trying to find a way to look her in the eye, to shake her of the notion that their relationship was a tree her parents had poisoned, infection spreading through the branches and trunk and down into the roots, sickening everything it touched.

But she didn't say anything.

And she and Rebecca didn't say goodbye when Rebecca left.

41

"So basically," Temple asked, "you have no leads, no clues, and no idea where anyone is. Is that a good summation?"

Price stood in front of Temple's desk, shifted weight uncomfortably. "That sounds like we haven't made any progress."

"Oh!" Temple's voice took on a mock excited tone. "You've made progress? Do share!"

Price glanced behind himself. Seth was standing at the door, hoodie and hat and sunglasses still obscuring his face, seemingly indifferent to what was being said.

Harris stood behind Temple, looking worried but clearly trying to hide his concern.

"We went to the daughter's college to find her friend. Rebecca Blake."

"And what did Rebecca Blake tell you?"

"She wasn't there. I asked around and found out she's at home. Comes from money. One of her parents is a big-time lawyer."

Temple sighed. "Okay, so you won't bark up that tree too loudly, right? Stay away from people who can draw attention to us. What other leads do you have?"

"That's it," Price said. He glanced back at Seth again, who still seemed impassive to everything being said. "But we're looking."

"You hung out with Deb Thomas for weeks. And she just disappeared on you?"

Price felt a mix of anger and concern rising inside him, and he wasn't sure which was going to win out. He trusted Scott but hated having his back to Seth. His spine was tense, as if a bullet might end up in it at any moment.

"For now," he admitted, "but we just started searching."

"What if she goes back to the cops?" Temple asked.

"You are the cops."

"Not all the cops. Her story's crazy, but not if someone believes it and starts digging. She needs to disappear before that happens. And you need to find out who shot up your house."

"They didn't really shoot up my house . . ."

Temple looked past Price, to Seth. "Is he slowing you down? Would it help if he was out of the picture? Is he pushing the goalpost further away?"

"Out of the picture?" Price asked. He thought he saw sympathy in Harris's eyes.

Seth barely shrugged. "He's all right. For now."

"What did you mean, 'out of the picture'?"

"Because if he is," Temple went on, "then just let me know. He's always been one to look around instead of forward." He stared at Price. "And you never know what you're walking into when you're looking back."

"You'd kill me?" Price asked.

"Everything is murder and death with you." Temple frowned. "But yes."

Price felt his stomach tighten, throat thicken. "We're family."

Definitely sympathy in Harris's eyes.

"My God, Levi," Temple said, "what do you think kept you alive this far? Anyone else would have had you shot in the back of the head and thrown you into a ditch. Do you know how much danger we're in, all because you thought you fell in love?"

"To be fair, I didn't *think* I was in love . . ."

Temple let his exasperation get the best of him. "Seth, remember how I said you had to check in with me before you killed Levi?"

The burned man nodded.

"No need to check in anymore. If he's being unhelpful or even if he just annoys you, go ahead and put a bullet in him."

"We're family!" Price exclaimed.

"Cousins. Not like we're brothers, for goodness sake."

"Look, give me a few days. I can find her."

"Oh, I don't have a problem giving you a few days. Seth might, but I'm okay with it."

Price looked at Seth again, saw himself reflected in the burned man's sunglasses.

"I'll find them," Price said.

"Or die!" Temple agreed cheerfully. "See how important it is to set realistic goals?"

*　　*　　*

"You're really going to kill him?" Harris asked Temple after Seth and Price left.

"Of course not," Temple replied. "Seth will."

Temple's mood had lightened since they left, which relaxed Harris. Not completely, but a little.

"You're not going to stop him?"

"I don't think I could. Seth is a very determined young man." Temple frowned, indicated the chair in front of his desk. "Have a seat."

Harris had been standing close to the door, hoping to leave soon. But he sat in the hard wooden chair, nervously crossed his legs.

Temple walked around his desk, sat on the edge. "Freddie, do you know Herman Cortes?"

"Is he from around here?"

"Not quite. Herman Cortes was a Spanish conquistador who helped lead Spain's conquest of Mexico in the 1500s."

"So, not from around here?"

Temple smiled widely. "Exactly. He landed in Mexico at a time when the Aztecs were thriving. Cortes's men were exhausted from their sea voyage, and arrived tired and disillusioned. Certainly not ready to fight. Cortes saw the exhaustion in his men's faces as they docked on the beach and, despite his own weariness, knew they had to press on. After all, the Spanish hadn't arrived at Mexico simply to frolic at the beach. They'd come to conquer the country for their king."

Harris nodded.

"Cortes, realizing that the men needed to be inspired, put forth one of the great motivational lessons in history. One morning he stood in front of his sullen soldiers and exhorted them to fight. He told them that this expedition was their God-given purpose. He told them that they needed to press on, that their journey and glory had yet to be realized. He told them that their kingdom was as far as they dared let themselves see."

Harris shifted in his chair.

"It was an outstanding speech. Many of the men were inspired, and they raised their swords and shields to the sun, the dull metal glinting in the morning light. They cried Cortes's name, and the name of their King, King Charles. But not all of the men were motivated."

Temple's voice lowered, grew more intense.

"Cortes knew he needed complete, unwavering support. And so he burned the boats."

"What?"

"He burned his own boats. Set them on fire. The men watched them burn, these magnificent vessels that had taken them across the sea. Taken them from their families and friends. The ships burned in the water, and the soldiers realized they would never have the opportunity to return home. They would stay here, and they would fight. Their only option was to fight. What a feeling that must have been! To watch the boats engulfed by flames. To feel the sword in your hand and realize, now, this was your only passage."

Harris listened, spellbound.

"You haven't seemed comfortable making that kind of sacrifice. You and James, rest his soul, haven't been motivated to stop Cessy Castillo."

Harris blinked. It took a moment for him to slip out of the story, return to the present.

"Wait—what? I'm motivated! I am!"

"I just don't know," Temple said. "Sometimes I get the sense that, among those burning boats, you would have tried to swim back to Spain. After all, you let Cessy leave the hospital."

"No way. No way."

Temple leaned back on the edge of his desk, smiled.

His foot smashed Harris's throat.

Harris was off his chair and on the ground, choking. Breath came to him through a maze, a maze taking too long to solve. He felt his hands on his throat, trying to squeeze air in. His mind was a dark spreading cloud.

Something heavy on him.

Temple.

"You just don't have the vision I need," Temple said calmly.

Only one thing was clear to Harris, one thing breaking through the terror and the pain. Temple was holding a sharpened pencil he'd taken from his desk, and pressing the point into Harris's right eye.

Temple's knees had pinned down Harris's shoulders, and the man's thrashing didn't dislodge him as the pencil sank deeper. Temple pulled out his phone with the other hand, flipped it on.

"Siri, show me a diagram of the human eye."

As the pencil pushed further, Harris's struggles weakened. But his screams increased.

"How interesting," Temple told him, talking loudly. "We've extended past the pupil and into the vitreous cavity. Which is what is producing this fluid. And that," and he wiggled the pencil, "is the orbital bone, but we don't want to stop there. We need to go through the optic nerve, but it doesn't seem like the pencil will fit."

Temple wiggled the pencil some more. Frowned.

"Surprisingly fragile orbital bones in the human eye. Apparently with enough force . . ."

Temple leaned forward, over the pencil and over Harris's head. Pushed down with all his might.

The pencil sank in to the eraser.

Harris's arms and legs kicked wildly. Then his movements and screams abruptly ceased.

"Apparently with enough force," Temple went on. "You can break through those bones and penetrate the brain. So I learned something! And a day where someone gains painful knowledge measures a year of happiness for someone else."

Temple stood, wiped his hands.

Picked up his phone from the floor.

"Siri, take a note. Poster idea. Man standing at the edge of the ocean, looking out. Photo is black and white. Underneath is text saying, "A day where someone gains painful knowledge measures a year of happiness for someone else. Call it 'Vision.'"

42

"THAT LYING MOTHERFUCKER!" Nicole exclaimed. "I'm going to kill him."

"No, you're not," Deb said into the phone. "You're going to lay low and keep an eye out for him. Or anyone suspicious."

"Let them come!" Nicole declared. "You know I have a gun."

"You do?"

"This is *Vir-gi-ni-a*," Nicole said, saying the state name slowly. "Of course I have a gun."

"Northern Virginia. And how come you never told me about this?"

"Well, whatever. But good thing I have one, right?"

"I don't want you to have to use it. So lay low and don't do anything."

"Come stay with me. You and Kim. I'll keep you safe."

"I knew you'd say that," Deb said. "And I love you for it. But I'm not going to put you in any more danger."

"So you're just going to stay in hiding forever?"

"I'm thinking of a plan," Deb said. "It's just taking a while."

"Will you let me know what it is when you know what it is?"

"I will. Hey, you know, I think Levi was trying to convince me that you were involved in this somehow."

"What?"

"He kept dropping hints that I couldn't trust you."

"Please tell me you didn't believe him. Even for a second."

"Not even for a second."

"What an asshole." Nicole was quiet for a moment. "Hey, I have a place you can use." My folks bought land in Chincoteague before they died. It's in my name, and I never go there."

"Chincoteague? That little sailing place in Maryland?"

"Yeah, the little town where they have the ponies? Out there."

"You never mentioned you had another house."

"Well, it's not really a house so much."

"So much?"

"So much as it's a plot that's never been developed."

"You're saying we can go stay on your pile of grass?"

"It's more marsh than grass. But it is next to a creek. So, pretty?"

"Well, thank you for that. I'll keep it in mind."

"Hey, sweetie?"

"Yeah?"

"I love you. Can I give you my gun?"

"I love you too. And no."

* * *

It took two days for Deb to finally sleep.

After meeting with Rebecca, she and Kim had driven Kim's Jetta until they found a small, nondescript motel in Alexandria. She thought about going farther out for safety, but the towns outside of the area were too small. Strangers made an impression. Here, it was easy to get lost in the crowds, to be forgotten. The motel she picked was the kind in need of paint, with a billboard missing letters, not visited by anyone in serious search of rest. They parked in back and rented a room for fifty dollars a night. Deb paid in cash, checked her balance at a nearby ATM.

Her account was low. Deb wondered, of all of Grant's cruelties, if leaving his family without resources was the worst.

"What are we going to do?" Kim asked when they checked in. Deb didn't have an answer.

Kim slept that first night in the new motel while Deb sat up in the room's other bed and wondered about Levi. Wondered how she could have been so mistaken, never seen him for what he was. He'd seemed so confident and believable when she thought he was working for the FBI, and all that confidence had vanished when he'd told her the truth. As sudden as the removal of a mask.

It made her feel stupid.

Like she had with Grant.

That was the worst feeling. Stupidity. Having to admit she'd been so easily fooled to Kim, to those siblings, to herself. She saw herself through everyone else's eyes, saw herself as helpless.

As sunlight crept around the motel's windows and the night turned to morning, Deb touched a tissue to her eyes—by now, the bed was covered in crumpled tissues. She'd felt helpless ever since Grant died. Ever since she'd realized that her freelance income would need to be full-time, but hadn't been able to find work. Ever since she'd desperately wanted to talk to Grant about the changes Kim was going through, and remembered over and over that she was alone. Ever since bullets had flown in that dark house.

Ever since her fear had grown stronger than she was.

Kim woke up about an hour after dawn. Stretched, looked around the motel room as if remembering where she was.

"What's the plan for today?"

The plan was to watch TV, which they did after Deb walked over to a nearby convenience store and bought water, cereal, bananas, and an assortment of junk food. They ate Pop-Tarts and watched game shows and soap operas.

"Got any idea what we're going to do?" Kim asked around noon.

Deb shook her head.

They watched TV until evening, Kim sleeping intermittently through the afternoon. Sometimes Kim talked about Rebecca, and once or twice she cried about Rebecca, but she seemed to be handling everything fairly well. And for that, Deb was grateful.

By the second evening, Deb's own fear started to recede. Television introduced a sense of removal from their own lives, and both women were appreciative of it. It was nice to be reminded that they were part of a larger world.

"What are we going to do?" Kim asked again.

Deb still didn't know, but she was relieved that a sense of calmness was starting to grow.

Kim slept soundly that night, and for the first time in two days, Deb did as well.

"We need to figure this out," she told Kim the next morning.

"We really do," her daughter replied. "I can't wear these same clothes one more day."

"There's that," Deb acknowledged. "And we also can't live in this motel room for the rest of our lives."

"Should we try the cops again?"

"I don't think so. I thought about it, and there's nothing we can tell them that will help us. We don't have any proof of anything. I think we should go back home."

"You do?"

Deb weighed her plan as she spoke.

"The only help we're going to find is if we get it from the source itself. And the only person who can tell us we're safe is Levi, and I know he doesn't want to hurt me. He thinks he loves me, so let's use that. He'll come back once we go home, and he'll find me, and I can tell him that we're not going to tell anyone about him or whoever he's involved with. I'll tell him that we're going to forget any of this ever happened."

"You really think that'll work?"

"It's the only option we have. I can't think of anything else that truly guarantees our safety."

"Can I talk to Rebecca? Can I visit her?"

"After I talk to Levi. I want to make sure we're safe before we step too far out into the world. Does that make sense?"

Kim looked down at her hands, her empty palms, as if she was wishing something could fill them. "Yeah, I just miss her, is all."

Deb felt a stab of empathy at that, a reminder of what it was like to be desperately in love. "I promise you'll be able to talk to her soon."

"She probably thinks I'm crazy."

"Just tell her *I'm* crazy. Blame it on me."

"Good idea."

Kim smiled. Deb smiled back. The sensation felt foreign to her, but nice.

"We're going to be okay," she said.

CHAPTER

43

W*HAT I SHOULD do,* Price thought, as he paid for a 7-11 hot dog
wrapped in tin foil, *is keep driving. Just head west until they can't
find me anymore. Or north or south or east.*

Anywhere but here.

But he walked back to his car, sat inside, opened his hot dog. And
knew he wasn't going to drive away.

For one thing, and Price knew how stupid this was, how irrespon-
sibly, hopelessly dumb . . . he didn't want to leave Deb.

There was no chance she'd ever trust him again, and he understood
that. But what he couldn't believe, as he bit into his hot dog and tasted
the swirl of packed meat and coarse bread and ketchup and mustard,
was that her feelings for him were gone.

It didn't seem possible, given how deeply he'd cared about Deb,
how much of a figure she'd been in his mind. He thought about her so
often that he imagined she could actually feel his thoughts, his feelings
like echoes pushing toward her.

He remembered their hands touching.

He should have wrapped his fingers around hers, leaned over and
held her, told her how deeply his feelings really ran. A kiss would have
explained everything, shown his intensity. Deb likely wouldn't have
pulled away, not until a few moments had passed. And that was all he
needed. Just a few moments.

He wanted to talk to Deb again; he needed to. Before the burned
man and Temple got their hands on her. He needed to tell her to run,

and to run with him. He could keep her safe, but she'd have to trust him. Price imagined the scene in his head, him pacing in front of Deb as she looked up at him. Taking out his gun and saying something like, "If anyone comes after you, they have to get through me." He liked that image, kept it in his mind until he realized he was smiling blankly out the windshield and people were watching.

He took another bite out of the hot dog.

Would Deb trust him again? Probably not. Especially if he had Seth with him, all quiet and disfigured and murderous. The burned man wasn't exactly the type to put someone at ease. Levi certainly didn't feel relaxed when he was with Seth, especially now that Seth had the green light to kill him whenever he wanted.

That definitely didn't put him at ease.

He was just happy that the burned man wasn't with him now, that Seth had agreed to let him hunt on his own. That surprised Price, given the potential that he'd run. But he also realized the reasoning behind Seth's decision. Seth figured he could track him down easily enough.

Price finished off the rest of the hot dog and threw the wrapper onto the passenger seat.

Started the car, pulled out of the parking lot, headed down the dark highway.

He was going to have to kill Deb.

In some ways, this was better. Better that he do it than Seth, that Deb's last look be at him rather than into Seth's cold eyes and scarred face. If Price was the one to kill her, at least he could explain to her again how he felt before she died, tell her how much she meant to him, how he'd broken into her house and watched her while she slept. How he'd never taken advantage of her. How he'd risked his life just to tell her the truth about himself.

And she'd tell him she'd loved him too. Just to get him to stop.

It might not be the truth, but it'd be enough.

Price was so lost in his thoughts that he barely realized he was driving. Driving was secondary to him, something his subconscious mind handled while he thought about Deb. Ever since he'd first spoken to her, his mind had functioned this way. As if the real world was shadowed, and the truth was in his thoughts.

Two hours later Price parked in front of a large house just outside of Annapolis. The house was in a quiet neighborhood, spaced far from its neighbor. That was one way you could tell this was an expensive area. Seemed like the trend in the DC/MD/VA triangle was to jam houses and condos together as close as possible. Wealth was measured in distance.

The only thing that would save him now would be to do what Temple wanted. It was inevitable, to be honest. Eventually Deb would have to die, and so would Kim. He'd known it the moment he'd shown Deb the videos of her house. Her reactions had never been close to his—Deb had been surprised, dismayed, even disappointed. Never felt what he'd felt.

Price slid into the seat, glanced around the dark, quiet neighborhood, thought about Deb some more. Unzipped his pants.

When he was done, he cleaned himself up with the hot dog wrapper and threw it out the window. And kept watching Rebecca Blake's house.

It was hard not to doze off for a few minutes, especially after he'd finished masturbating, so he opened the glove compartment and pulled out a warm energy drink. Opened it and drank deeply.

And turned his attention back to Rebecca's house.

She was his only lead. Price had nowhere else to turn, no other ideas on who to follow. After she hadn't shown up at the dorm, Seth had assumed following her was a waste of time, but Price thought she had potential.

He'd have to kidnap her, force her to tell him what she knew, and kill her. Or have Seth kill her. Probably better to take her to Seth and Temple to prove to them that he was serious.

And then Price saw her.

Rebecca was walking out of her house. She closed and locked the front door behind her.

She climbed into her car, a black BMW. The taillights reddened.

She drove right by him.

Fortunately, his seat was still down, and it was the middle of the night, so Rebecca didn't see him. Price's head felt like it was on fire. He had no idea where Rebecca was going, but she was making this easy for him. No matter where she went, chances were there wouldn't be very many people around at this time of night.

He followed her.

CHAPTER

44

"HONESTLY," CESSY ASKED Chris, "how long are they going to stay in that motel room?"

Chris shrugged.

She and Chris had been watching the motel for the past three days, waiting to see if Deb and Kim emerged, if someone suspicious came by. Quite a few suspicious people had shown up at the motel, but no one stopped by their room, aside from occasional deliveries of pizzas or sandwiches. Most of the rooms around them were occupied by men, checking in alone, and then a woman coming by and leaving within an hour.

"I had no idea there was this many prostitutes in Northern Virginia," Cessy observed.

"Anywhere there's men," Chris replied, "there's prostitutes."

Cessy considered that.

"That's pretty astute," she told her brother.

"I don't even know what that means," he replied cheerfully. "Astute?"

"No clue!" Chris happily stared out the windshield.

Cessy regarded him, realized she was smiling. Yes, Chris had his issues—which, Cessy knew, was the nicest possible way to term a psychopath—but there was something in him that she deeply, desperately loved. Something innocent to him, bright-eyed, wide-eyed.

Something that could be saved.

Cessy wondered if that was how their mother had felt toward him, if that was why she'd always favored him. If their mother had seen that vulnerability in him, despite everything.

Cessy had yet to want a child during her twenty-three years, but she'd always imagined herself a mother someday. She often remembered the way their own mother used to come home before prostitution drained her, her face softening as she walked inside, turning cute with her and Chris, cooking, flirtatiously talking on the phone, gossiping with girlfriends in an excited mix of Spanish and English. Cessy had loved that about her, loved how she was able to be two different people so easily: simultaneously young and old; mature, but only reluctantly. Cessy and Chris had been bodies she breathed life into.

"You think mom favored you?" she asked Chris.

"I always thought she favored *you*."

"You did?"

"She let you do whatever you wanted. Treated you like a friend. She babied me. Made me feel like I had two moms, you and her."

"I never thought of it that way."

Chris shrugged.

"You really felt like that?"

"Yeah."

"That's so weird to me."

"We all see things differently. Even the same things."

Cessy stared at her brother.

"I really need you to learn what *astute* means."

The door to Deb's motel room swung open.

Kim emerged.

"Check that out." Chris pointed at Deb's daughter as she nervously glanced around, hurried away from the motel room.

"I see her."

Kim walked down the street, turned at the corner.

"Maybe she's going to get something to eat?" Chris guessed.

"At one in the morning?"

"I mean, I'm hungry. I could eat. Do you want to eat?"

"No."

"Do you want to follow her?" Chris asked.

"I don't think so," Cessy said. "Her mom's who they want. We stay with her. Wait to see if she leaves, or if they show up."

They watched Kim walk away.

45

KIM OPENED THE motel door slowly, careful not to wake her mom. She stepped outside and closed the door behind her.

It had taken three days for Rebecca to finally answer one of her texts, for the two of them to have anything close to a conversation. Three days where Kim's heart felt like a thin branch on the verge of snapping. She walked through the night, arms crossed over herself in both cold and worry, and headed to the gas station down the street. Slipped in her earbuds and played music from her phone.

One of her favorites, a song Rebecca had introduced her to, "Shoulda Known" by the rap group Atmosphere. A song about the dangerous drug-like intoxication of love, the senseless slip into someone else. Heavy, dangerous bass—a plea to action from the damned lost in the dark.

"Lost in the rush don't know what to do . . ."

Even at one in the morning, cars sped down Route 1. The sides of the street were broken-down strip malls, old restaurants, and stores no one would ever enter—random electronics, mattresses, carpets. Kim headed down the road, ignored the beeps of a couple of cars as they passed, driven by men who slowed to gawk at her.

She stepped into a gas station's convenience mart.

Her mom would kill her if she woke and found the note Kim had left, a note explaining that she'd gone to meet Rebecca somewhere nearby and would be right back. She'd never seen her mom like this, so broken and terrified, not even right after her dad died. There had been a sadness in her mom then, a sadness deep and life-changing, but not accompanied by fear.

Now fear consumed her mom, so much so that Kim felt her own foundations were shaking.

She really needed Rebecca.

Kim turned off the music, pulled the earbuds out.

She didn't see anyone in the convenience mart except for the cashier, a tall, thin, dark-skinned man who looked up at her and smiled. She smiled back briefly, hopefully enough to be friendly, but not enough to encourage conversation.

"Hello," the man said in a thick accent Kim couldn't place. "You good?"

"I'm good."

The man didn't reply, just smiled again and looked down at a magazine spread open over the counter. She heard another man talking to someone in a back storeroom. Tried not to let herself get distracted, and examined a spinning rack of sunglasses.

She wasn't sure what she'd say when Rebecca showed up. Their talk at the Silver Diner had been a disaster, mainly because her mom had been such a freak show.

She'd texted Rebecca afterward, received no reply. Sent texts intermittently over a couple of days, staring at her phone for minutes afterward, waiting. Finally received a *Hey.*

Things aren't as bad as they sounded, Kim had texted, deciding to downplay the threat. *My mom's having a bad time.*

Rebecca's reply:

Ok

Can I see you? Kim asked.

Minutes passed.

The wait was interminable to Kim.

Yes

Kim walked away from the sunglasses and headed to the back of the store, near the frozen food. Pulled out her phone and glanced at it, read through Rebecca's texts again. It surprised Kim to see that she was the pursuer, and Rebecca, often reluctant. Kim had never been the aggressive one in a relationship. But Rebecca, despite her intelligence and confidence, had a shyness to her, a shyness Kim found alternately lovely and tiring.

"Hey."

Rebecca's voice came from behind her.

Kim turned and saw her.

Her heart turned to water.

Rebecca wore jeans and a gray hoodie, and her hands were shoved in the hoodie's front pocket. Her face bore a worried, hopeful expression. Kim knew her expression was the same.

"Hey, you," Kim said, and she embraced her girlfriend. There was a moment when the hug lasted, tightened in intimacy, and then Rebecca pulled back.

They stood apart.

Kim glanced to the front of the store. The cashier was still staring down at some magazine.

"How's your mom?" Rebecca asked.

"She's definitely doing better. It took a couple of days, but she's calmed down."

"Are you guys safe?"

Kim nodded. "I think so. My mom's . . . like I said, she's having a bad time."

"So what are you going to do now? Are you going back home?"

Rebecca's voice was tense, her questions rapid. Her cool confidence gone.

"I'm not sure. My mom thinks she can figure stuff out. So we'll probably go back home. I just don't know when. We've spent the past couple of days holed up in a motel, watching TV."

"Mother–daughter bonding time?"

"Right."

The two women were quiet again.

Kim glanced back toward the front of the store. The clerk was typing something onto his phone, squinting down at the screen.

"Why do you keep looking over there?" Rebecca asked.

"I do?"

"Yes."

Kim thought it best not to admit to her worry about someone coming in. "I'm just nervous seeing you, I guess."

"Why?"

Kim felt weight in her shoulders when she shrugged. "Something doesn't feel right between us. Something's changed."

Rebecca took a moment. "I know."

Kim was surprised at how small her voice sounded when she spoke. "Did you . . . did you meet someone else?"

"No."

Relief rushed through her. Kim felt like she could deal with anything but that. "Then what is it?"

"It's the way you keep looking around."

"Why?"

"I can tell you're scared."

"That's not true." Kim caught herself. "Well, okay, a little. I mean,
mainly because my mom was so worried."

"She's not the only one."

Rebecca refused to meet her eyes, but Kim could see the sadness in
her face.

"You're scared."

"Terrified."

"Why?"

"I don't want to be involved in this," Rebecca said, her voice small.
"I don't want anyone after me."

"No one's going to come after you. Look, some guys were blackmailing my dad, and then they . . ." Kim paused. "Once they find out
my mom and I aren't a problem, they'll let us go."

Kim's words, even as she said them, sounded fake to her ears. Naïve.
Something she wanted to believe more than she actually did.

But she didn't take the words back despite how they sounded.

She needed Rebecca to believe her.

"You're not taking this the way your mom did," Rebecca said.

"Like a freak show?"

"Like it's real."

An edginess had pushed through both their voices.

"I am."

"Your mom was so scared the other day at that restaurant. Like she
could die. I don't want to be part of that."

"So you're too afraid to stay with me?"

Kim knew how her words sounded, like a taunt, a childish dare for
Rebecca to ignore her concerns and stay with her out of pressure, but
she didn't care.

She hadn't thought, until now, that she could lose her over this.

"You don't need to leave me," Kim urged her. "Things are going to
be fine, and then you and I can go back to what we had. Please. I lost
my dad, my mom's going insane—I don't want to lose you too."

Kim knew that she was using her dad's death and her mother's fear
as a cheap ploy to get Rebecca to stay with her.

She didn't care.

At that moment, she'd use anything she could.

"It's just, I just have so much going on right now," Rebecca said quietly. "I'm doing really good in school, and I'm thinking about going to law school."

"You are?"

Rebecca nodded, and now she met Kim's eyes.

"I want to be that person," Rebecca said. "The person studying for law school and not worried about anything else. Definitely not in this situation. I know that might be selfish, and I'm sorry. I am."

There was something Kim wanted to say. There were a thousand things she wanted to say.

"But I love you," Kim said.

"I love you too," Rebecca told her. "But not enough."

CHAPTER

46

P RICE SAT UP straight in his seat as Kim pushed through the doors of the convenience mart.

Kim.

He hadn't been able to see inside the store after Rebecca had gone inside, had no idea she'd even been meeting someone. Price had assumed she was making a stop on her trip somewhere else.

But she'd gone to meet Kim.

His hunch had paid off.

Price started his car and followed Kim as she walked down Route 1. She was walking fast, distracted. He probably could have driven right beside her without her noticing.

He felt the killer waking up. Whispering how easy it would be to pull her into his car. So dark, and traffic was sparse. He could pull over, hop out, grab Kim from behind, and throw her into the backseat like a bag of garbage. Punch her in the face until she was unconscious. Tie her wrists and ankles and gag her mouth. Take her wherever he wanted for whatever he needed. He'd done it before.

He slowed, veered toward the curb.

But this wasn't the time.

Price picked up his phone from the passenger seat, thought about calling Seth. Decided to wait until he had more information.

Kim turned the corner and headed through a nearly empty parking lot to a dingy motel. She looked around again, walked to one of the doors, pulled out her key, and pushed it into the lock.

The light inside the room flooded on, and the door swung open.
He saw Deb.

It was only for a moment. Deb's hair was wild and her expression distraught. She grabbed her daughter by the arm, yanked her inside, slammed the door shut.

Price felt like his guts were being tied into a knot.

He realized his hands were gripping the wheel, and did his best to relax them.

He had to run to the motel room, grab Deb, run off with her.

Price was standing outside the car when he came to his senses.

He thought about Temple.

And he thought about Seth.

Price reluctantly climbed back inside, pulled out his phone.

*   *   *

Across the street, sitting in Chris's Civic, Cessy and Chris watched Kim walk back to her motel room. Saw Deb angrily usher her inside.

And, to their surprise, saw a man step out of a sedan and stare at the motel room.

"Well," Cessy said. "Shit."

"I could go for a burger," Chris put in.

Cessy ignored him.

Levi Price.

Price chewed a knuckle and got back into his car. Cessy stared at the car intently, waiting to see if he got back out.

But Price stayed in his car. After about ten minutes, the taillights glowed, and he drove off.

Cessy and Chris followed him.

47

KIM HAD NEVER seen her mom so angry.

"Of all the dumb things you could have done, you snuck out to see your girlfriend?"

"No one saw us. No one even knows we're here."

"You don't know that!" Deb walked over to the curtains, peered outside through the slit between the curtain and the wall. "How'd you even get in touch with her?"

"I texted her."

"You've been texting her? They can track your texts!"

"Christ, Mom, this isn't the movies. No one's tracking my texts. They'd need . . . a warrant or something."

"Did you give Rebecca the motel name and room number? Does she know where you're staying?"

"I just told her to meet me at the little convenience store down the street."

Deb sat on the edge of the bed, rubbed her eyes. "Jesus."

"Mom, it was fine."

"It's not *fine*, Kim. You need to be more careful than this."

"Well, I don't think I'm going to see Rebecca again, so you don't have to worry about it."

Deb caught the pain in her daughter's voice, the tears behind her words. Despite her fear, empathy rustled inside her.

Her daughter wouldn't even be in this situation if it wasn't for her.

"We need to leave," Deb said, her voice slow as she tried to steady it. "We need to leave, and then we can figure out everything else. We need to find somewhere else to stay."

"Back home?"

"Another motel."

"I thought you said we could go back home."

"I know I did. I know." Deb tightly held her hands together. "I just need to think. I'm not sure what to do right now." She stood and paced back and forth, talking largely to herself. "I know that Levi is going to be looking for us. I know he's going to have questions about who shot at him the other night. He needs to know he can trust me. They have to be looking for us everywhere, don't they? If we go home right now, then they'll find us, but maybe we can end this, maybe we can let them know that they can trust us, promise them whatever they want if they just let us be free . . ."

"Mom?"

Deb stopped and looked at her daughter.

"I'm sorry," Kim said brokenly. "I just really wanted to see her."

Part of Deb still wanted to yell at Kim, wanted to shake her, even strike her. But there was that other part, the complex parenting mired in love and anxiety, that led her to sit next to Kim, open her arms, and draw her daughter toward her.

"It's okay," she said. "We'll be okay."

Kim was crying.

"Everything's so fucked," Kim said. "I know I shouldn't have gone out, I know how scared you were, but I had to see her. And she told me she doesn't want to be with me anymore. She's too scared. She doesn't care enough. She's too scared."

Deb held her.

Watched the door and let her daughter grieve.

48

Deb stared out the window while Kim finished drying her hair in the bathroom. Near noon, the parking lot was half full. She recognized some of the cars, old paint-worn sedans and a dented tan pickup truck that hadn't left its spot since they'd checked in three days ago. Deb didn't see anything unusual. No one milling around. The lot, empty of people.

"Got everything?" she called out to Kim.

"I didn't bring anything."

Deb checked under the bed to make sure they weren't leaving something behind. Kim was right; they hadn't brought much, aside from what they'd been carrying. And her clothes felt stale and gross. No matter how thoroughly she showered, Deb's body still didn't feel clean after three days of being cooped up in this room.

And she wasn't looking forward to moving to another motel. She'd hoped they could return home, return to their house and their lives and normalcy. Explain to Levi that there was no point in him pursuing her; no romance, no threat of exposure. Promise him that the reason for Grant's death would never leave her lips.

But Kim's meeting with Rebecca had scared her, brought back that sense of panic. Deb wanted to hide for a few more days. Wanted to let her breathing slow.

Deb had thought nothing could be worse than the grief she'd felt after Grant's murder. And yet, now she wanted to return to that state, to the time when her life had been nothing but loss. Because at least there had been a path to recovery, something to follow, even if she couldn't see it.

But ever since Levi Price and the Castillos and the gun shots in that dark house, the path had been lost.

Deb opened the motel room door, expecting bright winter sunlight.

Shadows covered her.

A hand clamped over Deb's mouth, pushed her back into the room. Two men stepped inside, left the door open behind them. A gun was pointed in her direction. Deb heard loud breathing from someone.

Levi Price and another man.

Levi looked different. Tired, even a bit sad.

The other man's face was hidden behind sunglasses and a baseball cap.

"Levi?" Deb asked.

She bumped into Kim's body behind her.

Deb hadn't realized she was backing up.

Something strange with Levi's face. His mouth was tight, but his eyes were soft.

"Deb, you're going to need to come with us. You and your daughter."

"Why?" Her throat was so dry that the word came out rough.

"We need to talk to you."

"No."

Levi's voice, lower. Insistent. "Come on, Deb."

The man with Levi walked past Deb. Grabbed Kim by her hair. She cried out. Deb reached to him and Levi pulled her away.

Kim struggled, hands flailing. She knocked the baseball cap off the other man's head, knocked his sunglasses off. Looked at him and screamed, and his hand pressed down over her mouth, silenced her. The man turned and glared at Deb.

Deb's knees weakened as she looked at his burnt face, the discolored layers of skin.

Fear inside her, churning like an engine on the verge of overheating. Worse than fear—panic. She hadn't been able to protect Kim. Deb had failed despite everything she'd done, despite trying to go to the police and leaving the Castillos and hiding in this motel room.

Nothing had worked.

And all the hope that had built inside her, the whispers of safety that came from the peace of the motel room, from seclusion, were overwhelmed.

"This is Seth," Levi said, indicating the burned man.

"Please don't take us," Deb said. "We don't have anything for you."

"Not my choice," Levi told her.

"You have a choice." Deb heard the fear in her voice, the wobbling lack of control. Fear devouring her, her hands and legs shaking.

"You have a choice," Deb said again, not sure what she was saying, only knowing that everyone in the room had stopped and seemed to be listening to her, and she needed that. To have everyone, everything stop. To wait, *just wait*, before life irrevocably changed again, and she and Kim were helplessly dragged along. To stop violence from engulfing them the same way it had ripped Grant away.

To find a direction to go in because now her path had vanished, and the light was gone, and Deb couldn't see in the dark.

49

Kɪᴍ's ʜᴇᴀᴅ ʜᴜʀᴛ from where that man named Seth had pulled her hair, but the pain was secondary, distant in her mind.

None of this seemed real.

Kim watched her mom struggle with Levi, his arms wrapped around her waist, his strangely content expression in sharp contrast to the fear consuming her mother. Kim watched Seth turn away from her and toward the door in one smooth motion, the gun back in his hand.

She wanted to scream for help, but Kim worried anything she did would make these men angrier, worried about forcing them to do something they weren't yet planning. After all, there was still a chance for safety, still hope that the worst wouldn't happen. Maybe Levi just wanted to talk with her mother, make sure one last time that she didn't love him. Maybe Levi and Seth just needed a guarantee that whatever they were involved with would stay secret.

Maybe it was one of hundreds of things that wouldn't hurt them.

"What's wrong with your face?"

At first, Kim thought the question came from her mother, but it didn't sound like her mother's voice.

The question came from the doorway.

The man from the other night, Chris Castillo, was standing in the entrance to the room. Holding a gun pointed at the floor.

A shout, or something like a shout.

Kim jumped. Her mother screamed.

Kim had never heard her mother scream. She'd heard her cry, shout, laugh, shriek in surprise, but never the type of lost scream that sounded like it had been torn out of her.

Chris stepped back, looked down at his shoulder, at the suddenly ripped cloth. Another shout, and Chris took a second step. His face changed expression, turned pained. He tried to lift the gun, but it fell from his fingers.

Chris stumbled into the room, roughly pushed past Kim, sat on one of the twin beds. He lay down, breathing hard.

The white bedspread beneath him turned red.

Kim wanted to scream, wanted to make some sound, but it was as if the air had been knocked out of her.

She turned toward her mother helplessly. Saw Levi pulling her mother, the two of them tripping, Levi falling into Seth, and the three of them sprawling onto the concrete outside.

Her mother rose and stumbled back into the room, slammed the front door, locked it.

"What's happening?" Kim asked. Her voice was strangled and small, still scared to speak. As if saying something would make all of this real.

As if this was a nightmare and there was a chance that if Kim stayed quiet, she'd wake.

Otherwise, the nightmare would be real. Her life replaced by dreams, a change she hadn't asked for.

Like her father's death.

"Go into the bathroom," her mother was telling her. "Lock the door."

Chris Castillo gasped on the bed behind her.

This was her fault.

That thought was a whisper in Kim's ear, but it had been there ever since she saw Seth and Levi at the door. This was her fault for texting Rebecca and meeting her at the store and somehow revealing where she and her mother were hidden. Her fault for falling in love and believing that anything done out of love couldn't have these consequences. Her fault for loving someone who didn't love her back.

The doorknob rattled, the door shook as someone slammed against it.

Her mother grabbed her shoulders and shook her.

"Kim, now!"

Kim hurried to the bathroom, not looking, not thinking. She closed the door behind her and locked it, and sank to her knees, forehead against the metal door handle, the handle cold against her skin. The chill rushed over her body.

CHAPTER

50

WELL, CHRIS THOUGHT. *Shit. This isn't good.*

He could feel the bullet wounds torn into his stomach and shoulder, the bed beneath him; could vaguely feel wetness under him, but he didn't seem able to move his arms or legs. It was hard; one of those things where, if he really wanted to, really wanted to give the effort, he could lift his arms and shake his feet. He just didn't want to. Kind of like eating a bucket of fried chicken to the point where you were full, and then realizing there was one piece left. You could eat it, sure, but did you want to?

A crashing sound from somewhere in front of him.

"Get to the back!" a man shouted.

If he really wanted to, Chris could raise his head and see the door. But he didn't. He just wanted to lie in bed.

He heard Deb screaming, and there was another smashing sound and the door must have flown open, because sunlight bathed the room. A shadow rushed past him, and Chris tried to reach out to grab it, but missed.

And then he wasn't sure if his hand had really reached out.

Deb screamed, somewhere, and glass shattered. Strange that there were no sirens yet, but this probably wasn't the kind of motel where people helped each other out.

And this wasn't the kind of thing people got involved in.

"Can someone get me a doctor?" Chris asked, but no one seemed to hear him.

He coughed, sat up, one hand over the wound in his stomach, the other on his shoulder. Deb and the burned man were gone. The room was empty. He stood, shakily walked to the front door, stared out into blinding sunlight.

No, that wasn't right.

Chris hadn't moved. He was still lying on his back, and Deb and that burned man were screaming and shouting. He wondered why the burned man didn't just shoot Deb.

Didn't seem fair that he'd been shot and Deb hadn't.

Chris wondered if he'd really asked for a doctor. Wondered if he actually could stand if he wanted.

And he wondered where Cessy was.

Chris thought maybe he was dying, and the idea of dying alone, while Cessy was somewhere out there, made him sad. Not scared, just sad. He'd really liked spending time with Cessy.

It had been so nice to love.

He had to keep breathing. He knew that. Just keep taking slow, deep breaths.

He missed Cessy more than his stomach and shoulder hurt, missed her so much that tears burned his eyes—at least, he thought they did.

Missed her in a way that would never end.

CHAPTER

51

CESSY HEARD THE gunshots from the other side of the motel. She slid off the hood of Chris's car and hurried across the parking lot, toward the sounds.

Chris had told her he'd wanted to take a walk, stretch his legs. Told her he was tired of watching the street that led to the motel parking lot, waiting to see if anyone showed up.

Gun shots hadn't been a planned part of his stroll.

Anxiety thrummed through Cessy as she ran, concern about Chris, about her plan, her assuredness suddenly in doubt. She knew Chris could take care of himself, but it was others she worried about. Fear that she should have restrained him, stopped him, that the murderous side of her brother—and maybe it was more than just a side—would be exposed and unleashed. That he'd bring hell to people, and Cessy had done nothing to prevent it. Nothing to spare the lives of the innocent people Chris would kill, if he hadn't already. Their deaths would be her responsibility, and that responsibility tightened Cessy's stomach like the ends of a hard knot pulled in opposite directions.

The parking lot was on higher ground, and Cessy had to make her way down a small hill to reach the motel. She slipped, gathered herself before she fell, looked up, and saw Levi Price race around the side of the building and stop at a back window.

He broke the window with two hits from the handle of his gun, hastily pushed loose glass off the sill, pulled himself up and dropped inside.

Cessy felt detached, almost like she was watching a television show.

Hours of tailing Levi since last night had led to this. Hours of tension, her muscles like a cat's haunches poised to jump, and now it was time and the attack was happening in front of her, and she didn't know what to do.

And then Cessy remembered the shots and her brother. Reality rushed back.

She hurried down the rest of the hill and ran to that smashed back window. Heard a woman crying inside the room and Levi shouting.

"Do what I tell you!" he was ordering someone. "Out the window!"

Hands appeared on the windowsill, a woman's thin fingers. A head next. Kim's crying face, looking down in surprise at Cessy.

Cessy lifted a finger to her lips, then reached up and helped Kim down.

"About time," Levi said, and his head loomed over the window sill.

Cessy grabbed the top of his head. Drove his forehead down into the wooden window pane.

His head popped up and she did it again. And maybe it was part of her that she shared with Chris, some biological communal violence, but Cessy found the feeling and sound of Levi's head smashing down deeply satisfying.

He slumped out of sight.

"My mom," Kim said. "My mom's inside."

"I'll get her," Cessy told her. "Our car is on top of that hill. Get inside it and wait for us. It'll be me, your mom, and my brother."

"What kind of car?"

"A blue Civic. It's old and ugly. I'll bring your mom back to you, I promise."

For a moment, it seemed like fear had rooted Kim to the ground. Something she wanted to say. But she turned and hurried up the hill.

Cessy watched her, waiting to make sure Kim followed her instructions, and then she ran around the motel, heading to the front and her brother.

Neither Cessy nor Kim looked back as they raced away.

If they had, they might have seen Levi Price, his face bloodied and angry, pulling himself out of the bathroom window.

And following Kim.

CHAPTER

52

S ETH BACKHANDED DEB into a wall. She collapsed, unconscious. He
regarded her for a moment. Then he lifted his foot, kicked through
the bathroom door. Seth walked in, took in the scene—the broken window, the glass on the floor, the blood on the sill. He guessed what had
happened.

Seth left the bathroom, stepped back into the bedroom. Examined
the bloody man on the bed, held his index finger under the man's nose.
Didn't feel air. He glanced down at Deb, her body crumpled in a corner
of the room. Thought about tying her up, carrying her outside, tossing
her into his trunk. He had zip ties in his pocket, but the ball gag and
blindfold were in the car. Seth knew from experience that people didn't
stay unconscious for long; at most, minutes. And fastening her wrists
and ankles, then lifting her, all carried the risk of waking Deb. If she
woke when he was carrying her, Seth could simply hit her again, or
choke her until she faded. But another hit might break her neck, send
her into shock. Inadvertently kill her. Temple wanted her alive.

Seth's car was parked outside, the trunk facing the room door. He
could go to his car, grab the blindfold and ball gag out of the glove
compartment, come back to the room, secure Deb. By that time Price
should have found Kim, although it was more likely, given the mess in
the bathroom and Price's general incompetence, that he'd lost her. Kim
was probably consumed by panic after seeing that man shot to death,
after hearing her mother beaten. Probably racing up Route 1, screaming
the entire way. Seth had seen scared parents offer up their children in

exchange for their own lives, spouses viciously turn on each other, long-time partners sell each other out. Very few people, when violence erupted, held their beliefs. Panic overtook them, the desperate need for control, for normalcy.

Seth touched the scarred skin on the back of his neck.

Ninety-nine percent of the time, this was true.

He'd been surprised once, surprised at someone who fought back—a woman, no less. He hadn't expected to have trouble with her. Hadn't expected her ferocity. Seth had been winning the struggle, overwhelming her, and suddenly a lighter was in her hand and she was smiling and his body was aflame. She'd pushed him away, and his clothes had melted into his skin, and his skin melted into his bones, and nothing could stop the fire. Not rolling on the ground, not stumbling away for help, not screaming. Seth had woken in a hospital, tubes everywhere, one eye refusing to open, his body in a stunned, exhausted state. And then, moments later, the pain had returned and he'd screamed again, pulling the tubes, until nurses and doctors held him down, and his good eye closed. This had happened for days, although Seth had assumed it was months, even years, in his hazy mix of anguish and unconsciousness.

"He should be dead," he'd heard one of the doctors say.

Seth regarded Deb again, strode past the bodies in the bedroom, stepped into the sunlight outside of the motel room.

A foot landed in his gut.

Seth was more surprised than hurt.

"Where's my brother?"

A young woman stood in front of him. Cessy Castillo, by what he'd been told. She didn't seem surprised by his scarred face, didn't have the repulsed reaction or fear everyone else did. She punched his chin and Seth smiled, the same smile that woman had given him, the one woman who had escaped, the woman he'd someday find and question and kill. Question her about their fight, about how she'd managed to fend him off despite his ambush. About the fire. About her smile.

Something smashed into the back of Seth's head.

He turned, saw Deb Thomas holding a small metal garbage can with a dent the size of his head.

Heard a siren in the distance, and Seth realized he didn't have any more time to waste.

He pulled his gun back out.

Both women stepped back and Seth came up with a plan to take them. Force them at gunpoint into the car, drive him somewhere quiet, have them tie each other up. But Seth discarded the plan in seconds. Too much potential for things to go wrong, for Deb or Cessy to panic and run off. His only hope was that Price had kidnapped Kim. That Price had managed to do one thing right in his life, and they could use Kim as leverage to find out where Cessy had hidden those photographs, find out everything Deb had learned about Temple's operation.

"Either of you talks to the cops before you hear from me again," Seth gestured at Deb, "and her daughter dies."

He turned away, kept the gun out.

Pulled the hoodie over his burned head and walked off into the cold sunlight.

53

Deb and Cessy watched Seth walk away.

"What's he talking about?" Cessy asked. "Kim's in Chris's car. Up the hill, behind the motel. Edge of the parking lot."

"Your brother . . ." Deb started to say, and stopped.

"What?"

"He's inside."

Cessy looked at Deb, wondering what she couldn't say, then stepped into the room as Deb hurried off to find her daughter.

Chris was still. A stillness she immediately recognized.

Cessy knelt by him.

She pulled Chris's face to her, pressed it into her neck.

Cessy felt like she could somehow rewind time, return back to when he was living, before the bullets. She'd found him seconds too late. Mere seconds. Seconds were nothing. It didn't seem possible that they could be so catastrophic. So callous.

Hands on her, urgent hands.

"Kim's not there. Your car's not there."

Cessy heard Deb's voice, but it was coming from another world.

Cessy didn't move, didn't respond.

"Please," Deb said. "Please! Cessy! They're gone."

PART FIVE

THEY'RE GONE

CHAPTER

54

THE ROPES BIT into Kim's wrists. Her arms were bound behind her. Shoulders ached from being stretched.

But all that pain was secondary to fear. Fear coursed through her body like electricity; fear made the world seem like it was happening in flashes; fear forced her to shake; fear wouldn't let her stop crying. Kim was almost grateful for the hood over her head. She didn't know what was going to happen, and was scared to find out.

She wanted to be home with her mom and dad, well before she'd gone to college, back when they would light a fire against those freezing Virginia winters and celebrate their Christmas tradition of drinking eggnog, which none of them liked, but Mom insisted it was tradition, so they had to. And watching *A Christmas Story*, which Kim always griped about but secretly enjoyed. She wanted to be back in the warmth of that house and those memories, when her dad would laugh his great booming laugh that always held surprise.

Her mom.

Kim couldn't think about her mom without despair, without the floor disappearing underneath her. Couldn't bear to think of what could have happened to her.

It was all too much. If these men were going to kill her, then Kim wanted it to happen soon. She almost wanted to ask for it, to tell them that dread and worry were eating her and she couldn't bear to wait anymore. That any sound near her face made her body spasm, that her heart was beating so fast her chest ached.

She wanted to live and she wanted to die.

The two men who had driven her here were arguing.

"So we take her to my cousin, and then what happens? Come on, Seth. Let me call her mom. Then we'll take both of them to Scott, maybe all three."

"We take her now," Seth said. The certainty in his voice, the rough assurance, struck terror in her.

Kim had to force herself not to whimper.

"I'm just saying we can find all three," Levi argued, "and get everyone together. End this at one time."

A pause in the conversation.

"You want to see Deb now," Seth said slowly. "You'll see her soon enough."

"That's not . . . entirely it," Levi argued, and his voice was muffled as a door slammed.

It took a few seconds, but Kim realized the men had left whatever room she was in. She was alone.

Instinctively, her arms pulled against the ropes as she tried to rise. But there was no escaping her bonds. And even if she did, she had no idea where she was or where she could run.

Kim sat back in the chair, tried not to let fear devour her as she heard the two men walk back into the room.

She sensed them standing in front of her.

55

CESSY AND DEB waited in Chris's car behind a McDonald's, about a mile from the motel, out of the range of the sirens.

Cessy sat in the driver seat, arms loosely folded over her stomach, staring forward, staring at nothing, her brother's blood on her.

It didn't seem real that Chris was gone.

She kept expecting him to appear. She had an urge to call him, to tell him what had happened. She wanted to talk to Chris about his own death, about how she'd felt when she learned he was gone.

And there was another part in her, another part that had always expected to receive word that Chris had been killed in Arizona, the same sudden way their mother had been killed. As if Cessy had always been steeling herself for the only way his bloody path could end.

She wiped her hands on her jeans, rubbed them back and forth. Blinked back tears.

It wasn't the murder that surprised her. Cessy would have been more surprised if he had died naturally of old age in a rocking chair or from the horrors of cancer. But that would have never happened. She imagined Chris smiling, taking his gun and leaving the doctor's office after some awful diagnosis, finding a way to go out in a blaze of gun smoke.

Chris was always meant to be killed.

"I don't know what to wait for," Deb said suddenly. "Are they going to call me?"

It took Cessy a moment to come back. "Who?"

"The men. The ones who took Kim."

Cessy thought the other woman sounded strangely calm. She'd assumed Deb would be overcome by panic. This was a surprise.

She wondered if Deb was in shock.

"I need to call Levi," Deb said. "Tell him that he can have me for my daughter." She looked at Cessy, and Cessy saw the helpless expression on the other woman's face. "Right?"

"I don't know."

"Dammit!" Deb exclaimed. "Maybe we should just go to the cops. They can't all be crooked, right?"

"It's not that they're crooked. It's that their boss is."

"So what do we do?"

Cessy wiped her face, smeared tears. "We go at Temple."

"What?"

"We put a gun to Temple's head," Cessy spoke, and listened to herself speak. It was almost as if she had no control of what she was saying, Chris's spirit guiding this ruthlessness and daring. "We tell him that we want your daughter for his life. Get him to confess to everything, put it on tape. We get your daughter back, get Temple in jail. Or I kill him."

"Can't we just go to the FBI or something?"

"He's the district attorney. He is the law. The minute we poke our heads up, he'll see. And he's not going to keep us alive. We know that now after everything that just happened." Cessy blinked, paused. "The only thing keeping your daughter alive is that they don't know where to find us. The minute they do, they kill her."

Deb was silent for a moment.

"I know," she said heavily. "I'm trying to keep my head straight because I know Kim needs that now. But it's hard. I'm so scared. I don't know where to turn or what to do. I know you're right. I know we can't go to the cops or anyone else."

Cessy watched her.

"I'm sorry for what happened to your brother," Deb said, her voice small. "But I'm just so scared for Kim. I'm scared for her, and I feel like panic is about to rush over me, and I can't let it. Right now those men have my daughter and she has to be scared, and I don't know what they're doing to her. And I can't even let myself wonder what they're doing to her. I can't let myself think too much about her right now because if I do, I feel like I might die."

"I know."

Cessy felt the other woman's panic.

And she felt Deb's need to trust in her, her desperate hope that Cessy would be able to help.

She wanted to say something to give the other woman courage, something that would dispel darkness. But she couldn't think of anything, no phrase or promise that would put Deb at ease.

She fought a sudden urge to drive back to the motel, throw herself on Chris, will his body back to life. Give it her spirit and her blood. Give him anything, just so he would rise and walk and laugh.

"Let's find your daughter," she said instead. "Let's go find your daughter."

Temple gunned his Prius down the road, driving way too fast, something left over from his days of riding around with cops. Cops always sped when they were off-duty, like they refused to settle into being typical citizens. You put someone in a job like that, Temple thought, and they'll never understand complacency afterward. Kind of like Seth. No way that guy would ever be anything other than a killer.

Temple had time to reflect as he drove down the dark, starless highway, and he thought about Kim. Tried to imagine the girl's terror as she was kept, blind and bound, in a house with two dangerous men. The panic whenever the floor creaked above her. Her sleepless, painful night.

Nope. Nothing.

Temple took the exit to Columbia. It had always been this way, like emotions were some sort of bewildering foreign language. It confused him as a child until the teasing of other children, and the rigidity of his father, taught him the importance of mimicry. And that mimicry had taken root, become as imperative to his life as breathing. It wasn't until college, when self-examination was expected, that he realized what he was.

But he still kept it a secret.

Temple was good at secrets.

Pimps had the tendency to leave trails, and Temple had to make sure those trails came to abrupt ends. Nothing he did himself, of course. He had men throughout the DC/MD/VA triangle, small men who imagined themselves as giant businessmen, hopeful entrepreneurs who saw dollar signs where other men saw tits and ass. Men who understood the necessity of a stranglehold.

His men cracked down on corners, caught the new pimps as they slunk forward, let them know the old way of doing things had changed. Let them know that if they wanted to run girls on these streets or clubs or cities, someone was overseeing them. And that someone was building an army.

The pimps caved or died. Two bullets. A trademark.

The money came in cash. They gave him part of their take, and in return Temple sent the cops and detectives in different directions. Protected the pimps who swore to him, arrested those who didn't.

Cops, judges, attorneys, journalists, and politicians—they'd all been his customers. They didn't know who was blackmailing them, but he knew everything about them, the growing number of powerful men who had discovered they were only a photo or confession away from ruin.

Temple was one of the world's greatest pimps and ruled his empire with whispers and bullets.

He pulled into his townhouse community, parked in the driveway, stepped out of the car. He could afford more than this slender home—much more—but he knew the importance of a modest appearance. His home in Aruba was far more extravagant.

His father's career as a police officer had placed his family on the poorer side of town, and Temple would never return there. He'd hated that life, the distinct economic separation at law school, the mocking tone friends and colleagues assumed when they learned he'd grown up in blue-collar Dundalk, the constant jokes about Baltimore's crime and poverty. Temple would smile and laugh and play along. Inside him, a match flared. Burned.

And so Temple's idea had developed. A plan to expose the nature of men in the highest reaches of society, or hold them hostage. And to do it by taking advantage of the poorest, the most wretched, the people he'd grown up with and reviled.

And like any scheme built on greed and lust, it had worked perfectly. Until recently.

Carelessness and killing was running through his men like an infection. It hadn't mattered before. Nobody—police, media, family—worried about a pimp losing his life. Those murders were counted as casualties of the country's never-ending drug war, shrugged away. As long as it didn't explode like crack had in the eighties, or stretch into the suburbs, Temple could use violence like a surgeon used a scalpel.

Unfortunately, his business had exploded. And was reaching into the suburbs.

Maybe the price of his blackmail had gone too high, and bankruptcy was harder for men to admit to than adultery. Maybe he'd ordered more kills than necessary, not bothering to spread them out, even occasionally two in one night. Maybe he needed to scrutinize the men he worked with more thoroughly (*Dammit, Levi,* he thought). But whatever the reason, the past months had turned into a bloodbath. A necessary one, but a bloodbath.

Because of men like Grant Thomas threatening to inform the authorities, all in a misguided effort to help a whore.

Because of men like Hector Ramirez, splashed in so much blood that he'd grown repulsed. And wanted to flee.

Because of men like Freddie Harris, a pointless coward, useless after the loss of his partner.

Scott Temple had built a business based on the unreliability of men, and now that same unreliability was undoing his work.

But Temple had done enough. He had the home in Aruba, fake passports, and a second life waiting in case this life was revealed. All he needed to do was snip the last few threads, find and burn those photographs Hector had taken, and he could take the money and disappear. Become a new person. Someone completely different from that poor Dundalk kid who'd pathetically stayed to work in Maryland.

He'd finally leave that person behind, discard his skin like a snake.

Become someone new.

Reach his highest potential.

Temple breathed in the cold night air, locked his Prius.

Glanced around, saw two people hiding in a car and definitely watching him.

He headed into his townhouse.

The alarm system beeped as Temple walked in. He shut it off. Normally, the first thing Temple did was change out of his business suit into something more comfortable, like jeans or sweats, but he could tell that this wasn't going to be a normal night.

On the other hand, he was really hungry, so he tossed a frozen burrito into the microwave and slapped the door shut.

Temple glanced out the window, saw the two people still sitting in their car. He couldn't see anything other than their silhouettes, but could tell they were definitely watching him. He wondered if he'd have time to change.

But then two women stepped out of the car, took pains to softly close the doors.

Temple realized who the women were and was momentarily impressed.

He went upstairs, got his .22, and slipped it into an ankle holster. Let his pants leg drop over it.

Then he went to the kitchen to eat his burrito and wait for them.

Waited to snip these threads.

57

CESSY RANG THE doorbell.

Deb looked at her. "You're ringing the doorbell?"

"Yeah, why not?"

"I thought we'd sneak around or something. Try and take him by surprise."

"We're not exactly a pair of Navy SEALs."

"Right, but I just thought—"

The door swung open. Cessy and Deb looked at Temple.

He was taller than Deb expected. And a lot more plain-looking than she'd imagined. Parted brown hair, mild eyes, looked like he'd be happiest talking about how well his rose bushes were doing.

Definitely didn't look like the mastermind behind a murderous crime wave and extortion ring.

And he was holding a burrito.

"Why, hello there," Temple said cheerfully. "How can I help you two ladies?"

"Where's my daughter?" Deb asked.

"I'm sorry?"

"My daughter, Kim. Where is she?"

Temple looked confused. "Ma'am?"

"Stop fucking around," Cessy said, "and answer her."

"But I don't know what you're talking about." Temple frowned. "Why don't you two come inside? I have burritos."

"Or," Cessy said, "you could come with us."

"Well," Temple said, "no."

Deb felt like she was losing control. "Where's Kim?"

Her voice was higher and harsher than she expected.

"I really don't know who you're talking about," Temple said, "but maybe we should talk about this inside?"

"Fine," Deb said, and she stepped through the doorway.

"But we—" Cessy started, then she sighed and followed her.

And noticed the bulge near Temple's ankle.

"Come to the kitchen," Temple was saying as he passed through the small foyer. "Like I said, I'm *starving*."

"The idea was to get him to come with us," Cessy whispered to Deb harshly. "Not to step inside his house."

"My daughter might be in here," Deb replied.

Cessy gritted her teeth, followed them.

Like everything else Cessy had seen of the house, the kitchen was sparsely decorated. No pictures on the wall, clean countertops, smudge-less stainless steel appliances. Temple stood near the sink.

He took a small bite out of the burrito. "So who's this Kim?"

"You know who she is."

"Do I?"

He sounded so confident that Deb second-guessed herself before she pressed on.

"Where do you have her? Is she okay? Just tell me if she's okay."

"I don't know who this Kim is."

"Tell me the truth!"

"I am telling you the truth."

"Hey," Cessy said, her voice louder than either Deb's or Temple's, "we're not going to come to an agreement here, and Deb and I don't have all night."

Deb and Temple looked at her.

"So I have something else to suggest. Another approach."

"What's that?" Temple asked suspiciously.

Cessy lunged at Temple, ducked down, and grabbed his leg.

"What are you doing?" Deb asked, surprised at both Cessy's action and how quick she was.

Temple lost his balance and fell face-first into his plate. He swore, the mild-mannered demeanor gone, and violently kicked Cessy away. Temple reached down and lifted his pants leg over his ankle.

Deb saw his holster.

She pointed. "He—he has a gun."

"Why do you think I went for his leg?" Cessy asked, and she scrambled to her feet and launched herself again.

Temple took out the gun and Cessy grabbed it, wrenched it away.

It clattered on the floor. Deb picked the gun up, held it loosely.

It was the first time she'd ever held a gun. It was lighter than she'd expected, smaller. Almost like a toy version of the real thing.

Cessy lifted Temple's head up, grabbed a knife from the counter and pressed it into his neck.

"Let's try this again," she said. "Where's Kim?"

"I don't—"

That was all Temple managed to say before the edge of the knife dug into his neck.

Temple went rigid. He looked forward, hands flat on the table, burrito stuck to his cheek.

"Where's her daughter?" Cessy asked again.

Temple looked directly at Deb. It was as if his dark eyes were burning through her.

"If I knew where your daughter was," Temple said, speaking slowly, "do you really think this is the best way to find out? Do you think I'll help you now?"

"Bitch," Cessy said. "I have a knife pressed against your neck."

"We know about you," Deb said, and she hated the unintentional quaver in her voice. "People told us what you do."

"Did they?"

Those unblinking eyes stared hate into Deb.

"They said you run an extortion ring of prostitutes. That you're at the center of it. That my husband was being blackmailed, and then they killed him. That Cessy's husband was part of it, and they killed him too. Killed plenty of people."

"Ex-husband," Cessy added.

"Ladies, let's assume that's true," Temple said. "Let's assume I have two identities. One as the district attorney of Baltimore County, and one as the head of this . . . gang. Do you think either of those jobs makes me the type of person to give in to a pair of inexperienced women coming in here and threatening my life?"

The gun was starting to feel heavy in Deb's hand. She didn't know how to hold it, didn't want to aim it at anyone in case it accidentally went off. She shifted hands and held it loosely, pointing at the floor.

"All we want is her daughter," Cessy said. "Then we'll go, and you never have to hear from us again."

"Because regardless of either of those jobs," Temple went on, ignoring Cessy, "you can be sure I'm protected, correct? And if I do both those things, then I have both the good guys and the bad guys watching my back."

That uneasy feeling started to spin in Deb's stomach.

"Stop delaying," Cessy said, and she wormed the tip of the knife in a small circle. "Where's her kid?"

A thin line of blood raced down Temple's neck.

He closed his eyes, squeezed them in pain, lips nothing more than thin lines.

When his eyes opened, he looked straight at Deb again.

Deb's chest tightened.

"You don't have to worry about the good guys too much," Temple said. "You'll spend four to five years in jail. I'm assuming neither of you have anything on your records yet, so this is breaking and entering and assault, and that's just to start, although a judge might have leniency, depending on why you're here. If, like you said, your daughter's really missing, rather than just down in Ocean City for a few days with some guy she didn't tell you about. My guess is the judge will ask me if I think you should face the full extent of your charges."

He lifted his left hand, touched the blood on his neck.

"I do."

Neither Deb or Cessy said anything.

"That's the good outcome," Temple said. "Here's the bad one."

He looked at the blood on his fingers, picked up a paper napkin and wiped his fingers with it.

Cessy kept the knife firm.

"Let's say I am mobbed up," Temple went on, crumpling the napkin. "Let's say I do have a gang of pimps and killers. That means there are a lot of dangerous men out there who need to make sure no one finds out the truth about me. Because if I go down, then they go down. So they need to make sure I stay safe."

Cessy glanced around the room.

Deb realized she was sweating underneath her shirt.

"Now, you'll need to listen closely to this part," Temple said, and he gestured at Deb. "Especially you.

"If I really do have your daughter tied up in, oh, some basement somewhere, with, say, two killers watching her, and all of these people are watching my back to make sure I'm okay, then obviously your daughter . . . Kim, right? You said her name was Kim?"

Deb's mouth was dry, barren. She nodded.

"Then Kim is my big chip right now. And the only reason I'd keep her alive is for information. But if I'm not alive, or if those two killers don't hear from me at regular times, then it stands to reason that we'd cut off any expendable threats."

"What are you saying?" Deb asked.

"I'm saying there's no way out of this for you two," Temple replied. "You're going to end up in jail, or you and your daughter are going to end up dead. But there's a third option."

Cessy wormed the knife point again.

This time Temple's eyes stayed open, although they narrowed.

He and Deb stared at each other. Until she understood what he was suggesting.

Deb pointed the gun at Cessy.

"My daughter for her," Deb said.

58

K IM COULD BARELY walk when they untied her.
Her left leg was so cramped that it was difficult to stand. Her spine felt swollen.

She cried out when someone grabbed her wrist, grabbed her where the ropes had bitten into her. They bound her wrists with some sort of zip tie, but not in the same place the ropes had burnt her.

They held her elbows, led her forward. She shuffled between them, the hood still over her head.

"Where are we going?" Kim asked.

"Stairs."

The first steps sent electricity through her sore thighs. She climbed carefully, slowly, until they reached the top of the staircase. They didn't rush her.

She was guided through quiet rooms until a doorway led to a temperature change, a fifteen- to twenty-degree drop. She heard a car door hollowly open, and Kim realized she was in a garage. She was pushed into a seat. A door shut behind her.

Other doors opened and shut. The car shifted as people sat inside. She heard and felt the engine rumble to life.

"Where are you taking me?" she asked again.

"You'll see."

"Are you going to kill me?"

"No."

Kim wondered if they'd lie about that.

She was still afraid, but her emotions felt like they'd hit a wall; as if, at this point, she couldn't be more scared. She remembered stories of people who had lost their entire families in horrific tragedies, and how hearing of each death eventually numbed them; the sadness still there, but pushed too far.

Her fear was there, and it was everything, but it didn't seem like it could get deeper.

Kim kept quiet as they drove, her head down.

She wanted to ask more questions, ask where they were taking her, but she didn't want to draw attention to herself.

She heard cars speed past on the dark highway.

"Where are we going?" she asked again.

Neither of the men acted like they heard her.

Kim stayed quiet until the car pulled to a stop and the engine died. Someone pulled off her hood.

She looked up and blinked. Recognized Levi Price in the passenger seat, the burned man in the driver's. He wore a hooded sweatshirt, but she could see the charred skin on his hands as they rested on the wheel.

The burned man turned in his seat, faced her.

"We're going to walk with you from the car to a townhouse. You're going to hold a jacket over your wrists. You're not going to stop on the way. You're not going to run for help. You're not going to say a word. You're not even going to breathe too loud."

"Okay."

"What?"

"Okay."

"Your mom's inside," Levi Price said.

She looked at him, surprised. He was fixing his hair in the visor mirror.

"She is?"

The burned man nodded.

"She's okay?"

Levi flipped the visor up. "She came to save you. Seems like it worked. Let's go."

They led her from the car to the townhouse, and with each step, fear left a little. Some of it was the relief of seeing her mom. And maybe it was being outside, in a community of houses presumably filled with people. So many opportunities for someone to save her.

It only occurred to Kim when they opened the door and pushed her inside that these men could have been lying.

She tried to take stock of where she was. The warm house, the bright lights.

"Kim?"

Her mother's voice. Kim turned, saw her mom and ran toward her, clumsily, hands still bound.

59

"Isn't anyone going to hug me?" Cessy asked.

Temple grinned as Price and the burned man filed into the room. "I'm afraid not."

Cessy watched the burned man as he looked around, sizing everything up, taking in every detail, giving Temple a handgun with just a touch of judgment. Then she turned her attention to Price, who was clearly waiting for Deb to stop hugging her daughter and pay attention to him.

Cessy shifted her weight uncomfortably, and the burned man and Temple immediately turned their attention toward her. Price was still watching Deb.

"Relax," Cessy said. "Just a cramp." She straightened out her leg and rubbed her thigh.

"You asked what happens next," Temple said. "I'll tell you."

"Awesome."

Temple smiled again. "We're going to question you about everything that's happened, and then figure out what to do with you."

"You mean you're putting a bullet in my head."

"It's a small bullet."

Kim and Deb stopped hugging.

"What'd he say, Mom?"

Cessy looked over at Kim and Deb, saw the concern on Kim's face, the guilt on Deb's. Deb's hand holding Temple's .22 was pointed down, but Cessy noted the tension in her arm. She didn't trust Deb's experience but, with Kim here, Cessy trusted her willingness to shoot.

Well, she thought, *that's interesting.*

And then Price stepped in her line of sight and faced Deb.

"Are you doing okay?" he asked, his voice earnest.

"For Christ's sake, Levi," Temple said, "she's not interested. She'll never be interested." He sighed and sat in a chair facing Cessy, chin resting on the back, arms wrapped around it. The burned man walked over and stood next to him.

"Mom, what are they going to do to her?" Kim asked, peering around Price.

"I'm curious about that too," Cessy said.

"We're not taking you that far away," Temple replied. "Not far at all."

Cessy knew it was destined to fail, but she didn't see what she could do other than scramble to her feet and try to get the gun out of Temple's hand. The burned man probably had one too, but it wasn't out yet. Of course, Price had his gun out, and there was a chance he could accidentally fire and kill Deb or Kim.

She was absolutely fine imagining Deb with a bullet in her chest, but she couldn't do that to Kim.

Even if, as irritated as she was, Cessy understood why Deb had done what she did. If she'd had a daughter, or anyone she cared about, she'd probably have double-crossed Deb to save them.

Anyone she cared about.

Chris's memory slammed into her.

"Get her up, Seth," Temple instructed the burned man. "Let's get her out of here."

Seth pushed away from the table and walked toward Cessy.

Walked between Cessy and Temple.

The best chance I'll have, Cessy thought, *is now.*

Her legs tensed to rise.

"Wait a minute," Price said. His voice brought the room to a halt. "Wait."

"Levi?" Temple asked.

Price pushed himself to his feet and slowly backed away from Deb and Kim.

Cessy craned her neck to look at Deb.

Deb was pointing the .22 at Price.

Deb gestured toward Cessy with her other hand. "I'm taking her and my daughter, and we're leaving."

"Dammit, Levi!" Temple exclaimed. "How are you so useless?"

"I'm sorry," Price told him helplessly.

"Deb, right? Your name's Deb?" Temple asked, and waved dismissively at Price. "Just shoot him."

"The gun's not aimed at him," Deb said. Cessy watched her shift her aim to Temple.

"Of course," Temple sighed. "Of course."

But he didn't lower the gun aimed at Cessy.

"You do realize," Temple said, "that we're about to have a complete and total massacre."

"If we do," Deb replied, "you'll be the first one shot."

"Maybe," Temple acknowledged. "Or maybe you'll miss me. Have you ever fired a gun before?"

Deb didn't reply.

"You're not going to kill all three of us," Temple said, "but you and Cessy will die. And so will Kim."

"But you'll die first," Deb said resolutely.

"Maybe."

"You'll die first," Deb repeated, and she walked over to Temple. Stood next to him, the gun inches from his head.

Every other gun was pointed at Cessy. It was not reassuring.

"Let's look at this another way," Temple said. "Right now you and your daughter can leave. You can leave, and as long as you stay silent about all this, no one will come after you. But if the three of you leave this house, you're going to be hunted. And I have more capabilities to find you then you can imagine."

"I know all that," Deb said.

"What you don't know is what we'll do when we catch you. We won't use a bullet. And you won't die before Kim does."

Cessy watched Deb carefully.

"Then come after us," Deb said, "because the three of us are leaving together."

CHAPTER

60

Deb and Cessy stared at Kim through the windshield of Chris's car, watched as she slept in the passenger seat.

"She's tired," Cessy said.

"She should be."

They'd driven all night and much of the following day after leaving Temple's house, without any idea of where to go. They thought about fleeing back to Virginia or somewhere deep in DC, but finally decided on Nicole's suggestion of Chincoteague, Maryland. In the summer, Chincoteague crawled with tourists, and the harbor was filled with boats. But now, in winter, the town was desolate.

Even so, Cessy and Deb stayed outside of the small town and any outlying residential areas. They'd driven into the woods, taken a small road off the highway, and found a quiet camping area hidden by enough trees to effectively block the car from the road. A low stream was nearby, and dead leaves crackled underfoot. Circles of blackened stones, the remains of abandoned campfires, dotted the clearing.

"We can't stay here forever," Cessy said, still staring at Kim.

"I know."

"And I have no idea where we can go next." Cessy thought about Anthony Jenkins, the brief phone call she'd made to him earlier that day. He'd sounded so worried, so different in the way he spoke to her after helping her dump Barry's body at the hospital. Distant.

Cessy could tell, without asking, that she couldn't turn to him. Ever again.

"I guess maybe we could stay here," Cessy went on. "Tell your daughter we're forest people now."

Deb smiled a little.

"Do you know how to catch fish or cook squirrels or really anything outside of a house?" Cessy asked.

"No."

"Damn. Me neither."

The women were quiet.

"Thanks for saving me," Cessy said. "I mean, you also double-crossed me, but I'm glad you came through in the end."

"I couldn't leave you there," Deb replied. "Couldn't have lived with myself." She ran her hands through her hair. The single-minded determination Cessy had noticed ever since Deb had aimed that gun remained. Something had changed inside her.

"But what are we going to do?" Deb asked.

Cessy didn't have a good answer to that question.

* * *

Later that day, close to evening, Deb and Kim walked down to the stream. Winters had been warm in recent years, and they were comfortable in the light jackets they'd bought at a store on the drive down.

"I can't believe I slept for that long," Kim said. "And I still feel tired."

"I'm so tired that I feel like I'll always feel tired," Deb said. "Like right after your father passed. Like nothing will ever be the same, including completely relaxing. Like there's a tension that will never leave."

Kim sat on the ground.

Deb sat next to her.

"But it will go away," Deb went on. She could hear that parental, advice-giving tone in her voice, and it bothered her. But she felt like this was important. "It'll go away just like that other pain did. Once we get out of this and time has passed, we'll recover. I promise you."

Kim rested her head against her mother's shoulder.

A gray shape stepped through the shadows on the other side of the stream.

Kim and Deb froze.

The shadow walked out, detached from the darkness. A pony. It lowered its head to drink from the still stream.

"It must not see us," Deb said.

"Or it's just so used to people," Kim replied.

"It's cute."

The pony kept drinking. Deb and Kim looked to see if there were any others. But this one was on its own.

"Remember when we went horseback riding at the Grand Canyon?" Deb asked. "That whole white water rafting trip that started at the dude ranch?"

"Oh yeah, that was fun! I mean, it was a rough ride, and I'm pretty sure that horse took my virginity, but it was fun."

Deb laughed.

"It's weird when they gallop," Kim said.

"What do you mean? Scary?"

"It's just . . . you have control when the horses are trotting along, you know? Seems like you can make it do anything you want. Like it's some sort of cool bike or car. And then a horse gallops, and all that control is gone. You're not in charge anymore."

Deb watched the pony drink. It lifted its front right hoof, tapped the ground twice before setting it back down.

"A horse could do anything it wanted and you'd be completely powerless," Kim went on. "It's scary."

The pony finishing drinking, wandered back into shadows, disappeared.

"I'm sorry that I got you into this," Deb said. "I didn't know it would go this far. When I found out about your father, I wanted to find out everything I could. And there was a point where I thought maybe what I was doing was dangerous, but I kept going forward. I didn't think anything bad would happen to you and me."

"Mom, you don't have to keep saying you're sorry. I get it."

Deb looked at her daughter. Kim was staring at the water, her face untroubled.

She's not worried, Deb thought. *She's too young to understand how bad this is.*

"So that guy's in love with you or something?"

"Looks like it," Deb said.

"Gross. I mean, not gross because of you."

"I get it."

A car engine cut through the silence. They turned and saw Cessy driving back to the campsite.

"Wonder what snacks she got?" Kim asked. "I'm not sure 7-11 carried everything on our shopping list."

"It was pretty extensive," Deb agreed. She and Kim headed up to the car to see what Cessy bought. Ideally, Deb thought, she'd been able to find water, bread, and some types of meat and fruit.

And also a temporary cell phone.

61

Levi didn't like how closely Seth was standing behind him. And he wasn't thrilled with how Temple was berating him.

"Tell me again," Temple said, sitting behind the desk in his satellite office, "how that housewife got the jump on you?"

"She leaned over to whisper something," Levi said, nerves hollowing his voice, "and I saw it pointed at me."

"What'd you think she was going to whisper? *I love you, Levi?*"

It took Levi a moment. "Maybe?"

Temple closed his eyes, rubbed his forehead. Levi turned and looked at Seth. Seth looked back at him and shrugged.

The gesture made Levi feel a bit better. There was still a good chance Seth was going to kill him, but it seemed less likely given the shrug. It was a shared moment.

Had to count for something.

Levi smiled at Seth. Seth ignored him.

Oh well.

Temple lifted his head, gazed at his cousin. Picked up a pencil.

"Aren't you going to put out an APB?" Levi asked.

"They can't be caught and taken in anymore. They're three witnesses who can describe all of us *and* have seen the inside of my house. And Seth's house, if the daughter somehow remembers where she was. Any lawyer would sense something's not right. So would any cop."

"Are you going to try to kill me?"

Temple looked longingly at the pencil. "Oh goodness, Levi, I really want to. You have no idea. You're like an itch that would go away if I just let myself scratch it. Mediocrity is your height."

That rustling inside him. The killer stirring, jostling, like a wild animal having nightmares.

Levi didn't think he could kill both Seth and Temple, but he was ready to try.

His phone buzzed.

He pulled it out of his pocket, looked at the number.

"Oh, sorry, excuse me," Temple said. "Do you need to take that?"

Levi shook his head, slid the phone back into his pocket.

"Get out of here," Temple told him. "Let me think about what to do next."

Levi did as his cousin wanted. Left Temple and Seth in the office, stepped into the hall, immediately checked his phone. Saw the number, dialed it back.

"Hello?"

Levi knew the voice.

"Deb?" he asked.

"Hey, Levi," she said, sounding small, uncertain. "Can you meet with me?"

62

"THIS IDEA," CESSY told Deb again, "is terrible."

"I don't have anything else," Deb said resolutely. "Do you?"

Kim and Cessy glanced at each other.

"I thought you said something about us becoming forest people?" Kim asked.

"Right?" Cessy asked drily.

Deb smiled, but it was a small smile. "Temple will find us. And when he does, we won't have anything to offer him. But if I can get Levi on my side, then maybe that will help."

"He's sick, mom," Kim told her. "Sick and obsessed. You're not going to be safe with him."

Deb knew her daughter was right.

And part of her was happy with her daughter's insight. It made Deb feel that, no matter what happened to her, Kim would be okay.

"What are you going to offer him?" Cessy asked. "You going to marry him or something?"

"I hope it doesn't come to that."

"You're not going to double-cross me again, right?" Cessy asked.

Deb shrugged. "I don't see how I could make that promise."

"Shit." Cessy crossed her arms over her chest, stared moodily into the dark. It was near nighttime, and without the lights of a prominent city nearby, the forest quickly turned pitch black. "When's he going to be here?"

"He said tomorrow morning."

"So why do you want us to leave now?" Kim asked.

Deb didn't respond.

"Because she doesn't trust him," Cessy answered for her. "And she wants to make sure you're far away from here."

Kim turned toward Deb.

Deb looked away. "I don't know what else to do. I don't. We can't go to the cops and we can't run. The only hope we have is that someone from their side might help us out. If that's the only chance we have, then it's a chance we have to take."

"You really need to come up with a better plan," Cessy said.

"Do you have one?" Deb asked.

"Is time travel a thing? Because . . ."

"I'm not leaving you," Kim said, her voice thick. "And I can't believe you'd ask me to. After we lost Dad, you think I'd risk losing you too?"

"Levi won't hurt me," Deb said, more decisively than she felt. "He won't. But I don't know what he'd do to you two."

Kim kept her arms crossed tightly over her chest, turned, and walked away.

"Keep an eye on her," Deb told Cessy.

"Yeah, I will. But stay safe because I'm not going to raise her or anything." Cessy paused. "I can't afford the two-bedroom apartments in my building."

"If something happens to me," Deb said, "then help Kim find my friend Nicole Boxer. Nicole can take care of her."

The thought seemed right to Deb. Nicole had been alone for so long, and she knew Kim so well . . . Nicole becoming Kim's new mother seemed natural.

"Nicole Boxer," Cessy repeated.

"She's my best friend. She can help Kim out."

"Okay."

"Really?"

"Sure. After all, I owe you. You saved my life." Cessy thought about it. "Well, you put my life in jeopardy and *then* saved it. But still."

"Thank you."

The two women stared into the darkness.

"How are you doing?" Deb asked. "About Chris?"

Deb wasn't sure how to broach the subject. Cessy hadn't said anything about her brother.

But she didn't want to let the other woman suffer without offering to listen. And Deb knew Cessy was suffering. The moments of taut silence, the distraction, the long rubbing of her eyes that came from more than stress and exhaustion.

"I don't know how I'm doing," Cessy said.

Again, silence.

"When Hector died," she went on, "I really didn't care. Not that much."

"Why not?"

"Hector wasn't a good man."

Deb listened, grateful that the dark hid her surprised reaction. She felt that it was always right to grieve when someone dies, regardless of the kind of person that man or woman had been.

"But it's different with Chris?" she asked, tentatively.

"Chris was just as bad," Cessy said moodily. "I was just on the right side of his bad side. He hurt a lot of people. That's why I left home. Why I moved here from Arizona."

Deb wasn't sure of what to say. Fortunately, Cessy kept talking.

"I knew he was going to die. Not just die. Get killed. Get killed or taken to prison. No other choice."

A sound. They turned and watched Kim head into the car, where the three of them had slept last night. The car's interior light flicked on, suddenly illuminating the car and the forest around it, and then snapped off as she closed the door.

"She's mad at me," Deb remarked.

"She should be. You're going to get yourself killed."

Deb didn't want to think about that. "Do you feel like you could have helped Chris?"

"No," Cessy said flatly. And then, "Maybe. I don't know. It was how he saw the world. He was a killer."

"Still, though . . ."

Cessy didn't let Deb finish her thought. "These men are all murderers," she said. "They're all evil. You understand that, right? You *believe* that, right?"

"They killed my husband. Of course I do."

"And they'll do the same to you and your daughter. You want to give this Levi guy a choice. I'm telling you, I'm warning you . . ." Cessy turned toward her, and Deb felt like she could feel the other woman's eyes in the dark. "I know how he's going to choose."

Deb's courage flagged immediately after Kim and Cessy drove off.

She felt Levi coming. Could sense his car speeding to the woods like there was some sort of connection between the two of them, a connection Levi had made that she had no choice but to follow. He wanted her too much for her to escape.

The night was warm, but Deb still rubbed her arms and paced. Sometimes she used the flashlight to peer into the woods, but generally kept it off. She worried about draining the batteries, being trapped in darkness.

So she waited. And listened.

And thought about Kim. Where she'd gone. If Cessy had managed to guide her somewhere safe. If she'd see her again.

And that thought, that last thought, made her question her plan.

What was the plan exactly? To try to convince Levi to let her and Kim and Cessy go free? To give herself over to him and hope he could convince Temple to let them escape? What was she going to offer? Her love? Her body? Her life?

A twig snapped.

Deb whirled around, stared into the darkness. Kept her flashlight off, not sure she wanted to reveal exactly where she was to someone waiting in the woods.

And wasn't sure she wanted to see whoever was out there.

She stayed still for several minutes. Didn't hear any other sounds save for a soft warm wind rustling the leaves.

Maybe it had been a deer or a pony.

Another snap.

Deb stood statue-still, held her breath.

No one came into the clearing.

That pattern continued for much of the night, until the random sounds in darkness stopped scaring her. Deb sat on the ground, her back against a tree, but sleep never came.

She thought about Grant, thought about him in a way she hadn't since his death, even before his death. She remembered him simply, as the boy she'd known in college, the times he was nervous or unsure, those sweet moments when he was puzzled or lost and she wanted to touch his face, to absorb that cute, helpless expression.

She had loved him, and right now, despite the past hellish few weeks, that love felt like an important thing to remember. A comforting thing.

Like the night she'd spent with her mother in the hospital, after the doctors had confided to Deb that her mother would likely die the next day. And her mother seemed to know, but never addressed it. Instead, for one lucid hour, she and Deb talked about her childhood, marveled over memories, chatted at times like excited girlfriends. Held hands. Lay next to each other. Looked up and laughed.

In the end, Deb didn't want to reflect on pain.

The morning sun began to lighten the world. Deb heard a distant car slow down and stop.

A door closed. Footsteps approached.

She stood warily.

Levi Price stepped into the clearing. He looked as tired as she felt. He wore jeans and a jacket, unzipped over a green T-shirt.

"Hi, Levi." Deb tried to keep her tone light.

"Why'd you do that the other night?"

"What?" Deb was taken aback.

She hadn't expected him to be confrontational.

"The gun. Why'd you do that? I could have kept the three of you safe. Or at least you and Kim. But you pulled out that gun and messed everything up. What were you thinking?"

"It couldn't be just me and Kim," Deb said.

"I wanted to save you," Levi said plaintively.

"I know you did, Levi. I know it."

She said it softly, trying to keep her appeal to him. Trying to make sure she could use him for whatever she needed.

"I showed you all that stuff, and I thought you'd understand." Levi grimaced. "Took you back to my house and showed you everything." He bit his lip. "I thought you'd understand, and then I saw your face and it was like I saw everything from another angle. You know? I didn't like it."

Deb spoke cautiously, not wanting to say the wrong thing. "I didn't really have time to process everything."

Levi turned toward her, a pained expression in his eyes. "I don't think you would have loved me the way I loved you."

"Grant just died."

"Yeah," Levi said plaintively. "He did."

"Did you kill him?"

"No."

"I didn't have much time to think about it," Deb said, still trying to make sure she didn't lose Levi. "But what you were doing for me . . . that meant a lot. You helped me. I did start to care for you."

"Really?" She watched Levi's face, watched hope replace pain.

"Christ, Levi," a voice said. "I should have known you'd maximized your potential years ago."

Deb and Levi both turned as Temple stepped into the clearing. Like Levi, he held a gun.

Unlike Levi's, it was pointed at Deb.

And now she desperately wished she hadn't given the .22 to Cessy.

"You told him where I was?" Deb asked Levi.

"No!"

"I followed him," Temple said. "And I'm irritated and tired, so you don't have a whole lot of time. Where are the photos?"

Deb didn't reply.

"Okay," Temple said, and he aimed his gun at Deb.

Deb's stomach dropped, and she took a step back.

"Wait, wait!" Levi shouted.

"The pictures are with a reporter at the *Post*," Deb said. "That's where they are now."

Temple looked at her carefully.

"You're bluffing," he announced. "What's your plan? Try and blackmail me? Tell me you won't say a word if I let the three of you go?"

That was exactly the plan.

Deb didn't know what to say.

"Hey," Levi said, his voice soft. "Did you really send them to someone at the *Post*?"

Deb nodded and her head felt loose.

"Here's the thing," Temple said. "I could shoot you right here, leave your body in the woods. But maybe the photos *are* with some reporter. And maybe Kim and Cessy come back here looking for you. And then there's an investigation. There's no way we can possibly clean up the scene and remove all of our evidence. Too many loose threads."

Something in Temple's face softened. He smiled, and the smile seemed genuine.

"That was smart. I have to admit, that's smart.

"But here's the thing you don't know," he went on. "I am one careful man. I've had this side gig for a few years now, and there's nothing that can link it back to me. I know how to follow a paper trail. I know how to tie together disparate leads. I know how to catch the bad guys. So there's no way I came here without an alibi. And unlike you, I'm not bluffing."

Deb realized her hands were balled. It was hard to swallow, hard to breathe, hard to get words out. She tried to fight off the panic, tried to remember that if she was killed, Kim would be next.

She tried to speak. No words would come.

"All right," Temple said. "Bye."

"Wait!" Levi cried, and stepped in between Temple's gun and Deb. "You don't have to do this!"

"Levi. Not this again."

"She won't say a word about this, right? None of this." Levi looked at Deb. "You and Kim and Cessy will just go your own way, right? You promise?"

Deb nodded.

"Oh, well," Temple said, "if she said she promises, then I have to believe her."

"But she does," Levi said helplessly. "She does."

"Levi, the best thing about Deb being dead is that maybe you'll come back to being a little normal. Because this teenage lovesick is just about reaching the end for me."

Levi whirled around, faced Temple, his gun suddenly out.

Deb saw Temple's face over Levi's shoulder, saw the surprise and then, anger. Anger until she heard the gun shot, and then his face crumpled, turned pained. Temple disappeared from her view, fell to the ground.

Levi turned toward her, and then Deb heard another gunshot. Levi winced, his knees buckling. He grimaced, sat down roughly.

Deb wanted to run, but she was rooted. The gun shots echoed in her ears like they'd never stop ringing.

Temple held the gun up, but it was pointed away from her, into the trees. His arm dropped, and he lay back. Took a deep breath. Didn't take another.

Levi lay at his feet, looking up at Deb. Blood was spreading on the bottom corner of his shirt. His face was white, scared.

"Help me," he said.

CHAPTER

64

"I DON'T WANT ANYTHING," Kim told her.

"You need to eat," Cessy replied. The words came naturally, made her feel very much like a mother, even though she was only a few years older than Kim.

"I can't right now," Kim insisted. She put the International House of Pancakes menu back on the table, slid it to Cessy, past her untouched cup of coffee. "I keep thinking about Mom."

"She'll be okay," Cessy said with a confidence she didn't feel. "They need her help."

"Yeah," Kim said gloomily.

Cessy watched her, wondered if she should say more, decided against it. They'd driven for a couple of hours in silence, Kim occasionally crying quietly in the passenger seat. Cessy had stopped at an IHOP somewhere in Maryland, more for rest than food. Sleep had pulled her powerfully, particularly as her adrenaline passed.

She took another sip of coffee.

The restaurant, now around five AM, wasn't crowded. Mostly empty tables and dark sections. A young couple, Cessy guessed close to Kim's age, sat side by side in a booth. A middle-aged man in a pink polo and tan slacks sat by himself, staring into his phone.

"Can I get y'all anything?" a waitress asked. "Besides coffee?"

"Steak and eggs for me," Cessy said. "Medium and over easy. Strawberry pancakes for her."

"I'm not hungry," Kim said.

The waitress looked at Cessy.

"Steak and eggs for me, pancakes for her," Cessy repeated.

The waitress left silverware on the table and walked off. Kim didn't say anything. Cessy glanced at the entrance. It was hard for her not to check the door, even if they were in the middle of nowhere with no chance Temple or his men could find them. But Cessy couldn't help it, couldn't fight the fear inside her.

"How's she going to contact us?" Kim asked. "How's she even going to get out of there? How will we know this worked? Or didn't work? Or if she's okay?"

"These are all good questions."

Kim looked at her expectantly.

"And I don't have any answers. But those were good questions. Your mom seemed like she had a plan. I just don't know what it was."

The burned man walked into the restaurant.

Toward their table.

Cessy's blood felt like it had frozen in place. And she remembered the .22 Deb had given her, sitting in the glove compartment.

"I just—" Kim started to say, and stopped when she saw Cessy's expression. "What?"

The burned man seemed like he was walking in slow motion, like time itself was subject to his control. He wore jeans and an unzipped black sweatshirt. Cessy could see a gun in his side holster.

"You're here?" she heard Kim ask, faint and frightened.

The voice stirred something in Cessy, helped her emerge.

The steak knife on the table.

She imagined grabbing it and pushing it deep into the burned man's stomach and pulling it sideways, imagined the pain in his scarred face.

He sat across from her.

"You're the one who killed my brother," Cessy said, her voice low. Shaking.

"Where's my mom?" Kim asked.

"You'll be with her soon," the burned man said.

The connotation of death. Cessy wondered if Kim noticed.

Cessy glanced around the restaurant again. The young couple and middle-aged man were in the same places they had been. A waitress poured coffee from a pot with an orange lid. Another woman, the hostess maybe, listlessly waited at the cash register up front.

"How'd you find us?" Cessy asked.

He paused, as if considering whether or not to answer.

"Price's phone. Passed you as you were leaving Chincoteague. Decided to turn around, see where you went."

"Yeah, I'm new to all this murder stuff," Cessy said. "But I'm getting used to it."

The burned man took Kim's coffee cup, glanced inside, drank. Set the cup down.

Stared at Cessy.

She stared back.

"What are you guys doing?" Kim asked, her voice still small.

"He's thinking about killing me," Cessy said.

The burned man didn't say anything. Just watched her.

"What?" Kim's voice, somewhere distant from Cessy.

"And I'm thinking about killing him."

He nodded. "I feel it."

"Me too," Cessy said. The feeling was like embers inside her, glowing red embers pricking up under a gasoline wind. She looked at him and all she remembered was Chris. Chris lying down on that motel bed, face frozen in a contorted mix of fear and pain.

"Where are we going to do it?" the burned man asked. "Drive off and find a place? Somewhere out in a field? Out back behind the restaurant?"

"I don't care where," Cessy said, her words hot.

He slid his chair closer to Cessy. She did the same, so close their legs almost touched. She knew it was her imagination, but she thought she could smell traces of burnt flesh. Burnt hair and flesh.

"She did a number on you," Cessy said.

"What?"

She noticed how Seth's expression tightened.

"It was a woman, right? A woman did this to you? Set you on fire? Someone you were hurting?"

Cessy didn't know how she knew, but she did. A woman had done this to him. Some woman had fought him and won.

"I'm going to kill you," the burned man said, and now his voice was lower, menacing. "I know what Hector did to you. How he hit you. Kicked you. How you took it like a dog."

"I want to take that knife," Cessy said, "and I want to push it inside you."

"Please . . ." Kim was saying. "Please no."

"Then do it," he said. "Kill me."

"Don't," Kim said.

Cessy reached for the steak knife but her hand slapped down empty on the table. She looked down. The knife was gone.

The burned man was reaching toward her, and then leaned back in his chair, as if he wanted to regard her. Cessy stood, chair pushed back, touched her side. Felt her shirt and something else, something hard, the knife's wooden handle, like it was stuck to her shirt. Looked down, saw the blade buried inside her.

Pain knocked Cessy to her knees.

Someone screaming. A lot of people screaming. Cessy looked down at the floor, the drops of her blood. Thought about Chris lying on the bed, like he was on the floor beneath her, serenely smiling up.

Felt her elbows give.

Saw Kim backing up, the burned man walking toward her. Kim screaming, other people screaming, shouting.

Chris whispering in her ear.

Cessy pushed herself back to her knees. Everything around her growing faint. Climbed to her feet. Dragged herself to the burned man, leaning against the table for help. Kim against a wall, hands up. The burned man pulling the gun out.

Cessy's knees shook. Her hand on the table slipped. She grabbed the steak knife, pulled it out with a cry. Stumbled toward the burned man, felt herself fall. Fell and pushed the knife into the burned man's back.

Bodies everywhere. People running like moths to a light, ants toward a corpse. Chris's voice again. The burned man on the floor, shouting, bodies under him. The bodies on Cessy too, pushing the knife deeper, as if Chris's hands were over hers.

CHAPTER

65

"HELP ME," LEVI Price asked Deb.
 She'd never seen someone shot before, someone killed, the
moments someone had been alive, and then gone. How sudden it was.
The abruptness.

Levi was trying to push himself to his car, his back on the ground,
feet kicking the dirt.

"I can't sit up," he said, frightened. "I can't sit up."

Deb walked over to him, cautiously, avoiding Temple. She knew
Temple was dead; he hadn't taken a breath or moved a muscle in minutes, and his eyes were open and still. But she kept her distance from his
corpse, as if he might lunge at her.

"Deb," Levi said. "Please."

Something heartbreakingly young in his voice, the fear. Young in
the way that scared children beg for their parents.

"I don't know what to do," Deb said.

"Can you get me . . ." Levi paused, hands lifted over his stomach, as
if the wound had grown too painful to touch. "Can you get me to a
doctor?"

Deb reached down, grabbed Levi's hands, pulled. He tried to use
his legs to help, but they barely got any traction. Pulling him was like
pulling dead weight.

"I can't," she said.

"Can you call someone?"

Deb searched for her phone, saw it on the ground.

"I'm sorry," Levi was saying. "I'm so sorry about taking Kim and lying to you. I just fell in love with you."

Deb listened to him, listened to Levi as his words slurred, like someone speaking just before they're overcome by sleep.

"I'm sorry about what I did. Maria told him about us, told Grant. He wanted to help her. Scott made me do it."

His words growing faint.

"He did?"

Levi nodded. "He made me do it. Grant was going to talk. He made me do it."

Levi stopped speaking, licked his lips. Looked up, his eyes peering out of his stark white face.

"Is that your phone?"

"No," Deb said.

A moment of comprehension crossed Levi's expression, and then that expression changed, contorted into rage and hate.

Levi's gun was warm in Deb's hand.

The Baltimore Sun
District Attorney's Death Remains a Mystery

Baltimore, MD

*A*UTHORITIES ARE STILL *trying to unravel the circumstances that led to the death of District Attorney Scott Temple.*

Temple's body was found in a forested area of the quiet vacation town of Chincoteague, Maryland. He had been shot in the chest at close range, suggesting an assassination.

The body of a second man, identified as Levi Price, was also found at the scene, shot in the back and the forehead.

In a curious twist, a suspect has been apprehended in connection with the shootings. That suspect, a man named Seth Yates, was arrested in a nearby International House of Pancakes after attacking another customer. According to witnesses, Yates used a table knife to stab a female customer, a twenty-three year old Baltimore bartender named Cessy Castillo. Castillo stabbed him back, and other customers in the restaurant quickly overpowered Yates and held him down until authorities arrived.

Yates and Castillo are both expected to recover from their injuries.

A gun was found on Yates, and his car was spotted leaving the site where the bodies of District Attorney Temple and Price were found. Although experts have concluded that the gun was not used in the execution-style deaths of Temple and Price, Yates has since been linked to both men. And his checkered past with law enforcement and agitated state that morning raises substantial concerns, an investigator associated with the case said.

Both local and state officials were stunned by the news.

"Scott Temple was a champion of the rule of law," the governor's office said in a statement. "His initiatives, such as increased patrolmen in neighborhoods and his human trafficking task force, are representative of his passion and determination. He will be missed, and not easily replaced."

KIM BLINKED WHEN she saw Cessy at the door.

"Oh shit," she said. "How are you?"

"I'm okay. How are you? How's your mom?"

Kim gazed at Cessy for a long moment. Cessy couldn't read anything in her expression.

"You'll have to see," she said. "Come on in."

Kim led Cessy to the kitchen. Cessy walked slowly. The wound in her side throbbed, although the pain was only an echo of what it had been days earlier.

Deb's house was almost exactly what Cessy had imagined. Suburban classy, which meant the latest trends—hardwood floors covered with expensive rugs, walls removed for an open floor plan, rooms filled with light. The kitchen was all stainless steel appliances and led directly to a family room.

Kim pulled out a chair at a table next to the bay window, overlooking the garden.

"She's outside," Kim said. Cessy stood rather than trying to sit in the chair opposite her. Bending hurt. "And she's not good."

Until now, Cessy hadn't noticed the shadow around Kim's eyes, exhaustion that seemed permanent, in contrast to her young, unlined skin.

"What do you mean?"

"I think she's depressed. I mean, I know she is. She barely comes out of her bedroom. And when she does, it's to tell me she's going to call the police."

"Really?"

"And then she changes her mind. I've never seen her like this. Not even after Dad died." She paused. "How are you?"

"Recovering."

Another pause.

"Should I talk to her?"

Kim looked at Cessy doubtfully. "You really think you can help?"

"Probably not."

Kim smiled at that.

Cessy reached into her handbag, pulled out a small USB drive from the side pocket, put it on the table.

Kim didn't move to pick the drive up, just eyed it. "What's that?"

"These are some violent-ass pictures," Cessy explained. "Don't look at them. Just keep them in case you need them. They're the pictures Hector took. I have another copy."

Kim took the USB drive, almost reluctantly. "Do we still need these?"

Cessy saw the concern, the moment of fear, on her face.

"We shouldn't," she assured Kim. "But just in case."

"Okay."

"How are you doing?" Cessy asked.

"Me? Why?"

"Your dad was murdered, you were kidnapped, your girlfriend dumped you, and now you have to take care of your mom. That seems like a lot to deal with."

Kim let out a small smile. "Well, when you put it like that . . ."

"So how are you?"

Kim traced the nail of her index finger over curved grains on the wooden table. "I still miss my dad, and I miss Rebecca. But I guess I'm okay. I guess I am. Nothing seems real. Then again, I didn't get stabbed in an IHOP."

She kept tracing the curved grain.

Cessy watched her.

"I mean, it seems like this is all temporary, and we're going to go back to the way things were. Or maybe not exactly back to the way things were. I know my dad is never coming back. All this stuff happened, and he wasn't there for any of it. You know? If he wasn't there for any of this, then he must really be gone."

Cessy nodded.

Kim touched the tears starting in her eyes, turned away.

"I'll be okay," she said, her voice small.

"You sure?"

Still turned, Kim nodded.

Cessy left Kim in the kitchen, walked out into the garden.

She saw Deb curled up on a bench, a blanket covering her, phone in her hand.

Deb looked toward Cessy, unsteadily. And if Kim was roughened by everything that had happened, Deb was defeated. Her hair was a tangled mess, clothes worn, eyes red-rimmed.

"Cessy. Are you okay?" Deb asked, noticing her limp.

"I will be."

"I'm sorry I didn't visit you in the hospital."

"That's okay. I wasn't there long."

"Have you heard anything?" Deb asked.

"About what?"

"About what I did?"

Cessy shook her head. "Just what they said. That Temple was mixed up with some bad people and ended up paying for it. Nothing beyond that."

"Bad people," Deb repeated softly.

"They pinned everything on Seth. Turns out he's got a criminal record, and it's not exactly helping him out."

"He didn't kill Levi."

"But he killed my brother. And tried to kill me." Cessy lowered herself to the bench, on the other side from Deb.

"I want them to arrest me," Deb said quietly. "Or I want a man with a gun to knock on the door and shoot me. Like I did to Levi."

"Do you?"

Deb nodded, and the nod helplessly turned into a shrug. "Maybe? I think I do. But then I think about Kim, about leaving her the way her father left her, and I can't do it."

Deb paused.

"But if Kim wasn't here, if it was just me, then I couldn't keep all this a secret."

"What do you mean?"

"It's eating me alive, Cessy. It really is. The guilt. I always feel so close to calling the cops and telling them what I did. I killed a . . . I need to be punished. I need to be punished."

"Why?"

"I killed someone."

"He would have killed you. He killed others. You did it to protect yourself."

Cessy felt an uneasiness stir as she spoke. A sense that something inside her, some firm root that had taken hold, might be pulled loose.

"You had to do it to keep Kim safe," Cessy went on. "She'd be dead now if you hadn't. Those three men needed to die. There was no other way. There wasn't a chance for forgiveness."

She saw Deb's fists clench, nails pressed into palms.

"Did you tell Kim?" she asked.

"Yeah." Deb stared forlornly down to the ground. "She was shocked. But she said she understood. She said what you said."

"Have you told anyone else?" Cessy asked.

"No."

"That's good."

"It's not *good*."

Cessy had thought Deb might be shaken, but not to this extent. Deb seemed on the verge of cracking, lost somewhere in a confusion of guilt and fear.

"Do you really think they'll blame it all on Seth?"

"I think so."

Deb was ashen. "But it's not his fault."

"And it's not your fault either. Those men killed my brother. They burned down my friend's safe house. Killed her and three other people. And who knows how many others? The world's better off with them in jail or dead."

"That's what Kim said. But are we?"

"Are we what?"

"Are we better off?" Deb asked. "I think about Levi, and I think about Kim, and when she was a baby, and then a little girl, and how I used to fall asleep with her. I think how Levi had someone who held him that way, who comforted him when he cried, who loved looking into his big wide eyes. I killed that baby."

"You killed the man that baby became."

"There's no difference between the two."

"Yes there is. That baby wasn't hurting anyone. It didn't make any choices. Levi made choices. Lots of them." Cessy paused. "Mostly bad ones."

"I can't rationalize this like you can. I did something unforgivable, something I can never come back from. I can never return. And I don't think I can live with it."

Her words were sharp to Cessy, the suicidal warning she used to look for when talking to women in Rose's halfway house. "What does that mean? What are you going to do?"

"I don't know," Deb replied miserably. "I think I was someone before all this, and I don't know if I can get that person back." Her voice lowered to a whisper. "Because sometimes I'm glad he's dead."

Cessy's wound ached.

"So am I," Cessy told her. "And I'm glad you and Kim are alive."

Deb's voice, still a whisper: "I'm not who I was and I'll never be again."

"Mom?"

Cessy and Deb turned, saw Kim standing at the entrance to the garden, her expression nothing but concern.

"I love you," Kim told her. "I love you no matter what. No matter who you are, no matter what you had to do."

"But I don't want to be this person," Deb said again. "I don't want to be this person. I don't want to be this person."

Deb sank to the ground, still repeating that small, simple line, the paved tiles on her knees and then her palms and then her forehead. She kept saying it until she cried. She kept saying it until shadows passed over her, and she kept saying it until her voice was hoarsened by tears, and she kept saying it until she felt Kim and Cessy holding her.

Like Kim and Cessy were holding her on one side.

Death on the other.

Both holding her. Pulling her.

CHAPTER

67

Ten Years Later

KIM SLOWLY BACKED her Subaru down the driveway, mindful of the neighborhood children in the yard next to her house. For some reason, the boys in the neighborhood liked to dart behind cars, screaming as they ran, much to the chagrin of adults. The neighborhood's social media group had recently been full of pleas for parents to break their children of the habit, along with articles posted of kids being hit by cars in other cities or states.

Kim wasn't worried about that happening to Diane. For one thing, her daughter was thirteen months old, so she wasn't running anywhere, although she could crawl faster than Kim or her husband Sean expected. They'd sit her down in the kitchen, and before they knew it, Diane was in the living room, dangerously close to the stairway they desperately needed to block off. Sean was supposed to call a contractor to do that today, and Kim planned on texting him later to remind him. He'd forget, which Kim used to find ruefully amusing, but now, five years into marriage, exasperated her.

She shifted the car from reverse to drive, glanced into the backseat at her daughter, the way she always did, worried she'd forgotten to put her daughter inside and the car seat was somewhere on the driveway or, terrifyingly, on top of the car. Of course Diane was always inside, but Kim couldn't help her concern or paranoia. And didn't really mind it.

She drove through Fairfax Station, eyes constantly roving either side of the neighborhood's streets, mindful of the remains of ice on the road. Funny how living in the suburbs had made Kim realize how much she didn't like children. She liked her own, of course, just not any others. She loved Diane beyond all reason and understanding, especially now that those first hard months of sleeplessness had passed, and they were on a schedule. Those ruthless first months, coupled with exhaustion and a quick vicious wave of postpartum depression, had filled her days with tears. But the schedule helped, and so did the eventual full night of sleep, and so did Diane's first smile and laugh. That baby laugh had softened everything inside Kim, filled her with the type of unimaginable love parents often tried and failed to describe. A helpless, consuming, necessary love.

She'd made a video of her daughter laughing, sent it to Sean at his office. He'd replied with an *lol* but didn't say anything else.

But Kim watched that video a lot.

She finally left the neighborhood, the snow-covered houses giving way to stores.

She and Sean hadn't expected to live in Fairfax. He'd grown up in Spokane, moved to Virginia for work after college, and they both had hopes of moving back to Washington state eventually. After the last vestiges of the pandemic had passed, the attractions of Northern Virginia's congested area returned. Her mom and her best friend were here, and DC didn't lack for attorneys, so Sean was almost always guaranteed to find work. And schools were a factor now that they had Diane, and the public schools in Fairfax County were among the best in the nation. Kim loved Spokane, thought it was so pretty and calm, but she'd begun to accept that she was going to spend the next phase of her life here. If not her entire life.

She turned onto I-66, quickly glanced into the backseat again, headed toward the city.

Diane was asleep. Riding in the car always made her drowsy. The heat circulating through the car helped.

It still felt odd for Kim to be home weekdays. She'd worked her first few years out of college, but her marketing position had been eliminated. "Marketing is always the first to go," her boss had told her sadly as he packed up his desk. Pregnant at the time, she hadn't thought about looking for other work, and she and Sean were fine on his salary. Not forever, of course, and Kim had never pictured herself as a stay-at-home mom, but she actually ended up liking this first year. It was alternately fun and boring and tiring, but she'd been surprised at how little she missed corporate life.

She reached the city of Falls Church. Kim parked on the side of the road, pulled out her phone to check her texts. A note from her mom, some college girlfriends asking about a dinner they'd been scheduling and rescheduling for weeks, a reminder about an upcoming grocery delivery.

She put her phone away and stepped out into the chill. Opened the back car door, pulled out the heavy baby bag filled with diapers and toys and blankets and clothes and food and wipes and bottles and sippy cups and biodegradable waste bags and sunscreen and pacifiers and tissues and rash cream and hand sanitizer and a folded changing pad—and, despite all this, somehow something for the baby was probably still missing. Kim swung the bag over her shoulder, lifted her daughter to her chest in the crook of her other arm, and headed across the street.

*   *   *

Deb opened the door to her condominium, saw her daughter holding her granddaughter, and couldn't help smiling.

Impossible, really, for her to see the baby and not smile. Even that first month, when she'd temporarily moved into Kim and Sean's house to help take care of the baby, and had dutifully helped out with the late-night awakenings, the horrific diapers, the exhausted strain between her daughter and son-in-law, she'd still felt joy at seeing or holding Diane. The kind of joy that could bring her to tears, that reminded her of when Kim had been her baby—a small, simple, untouched being; a warm ache of soul.

Deb hadn't realized how much she'd missed that.

How long it had been since she'd loved something so simply, without reservation, without complication.

She cleaned her hands and whisked baby Diane into her arms and carried her into her condo. Barely had time for Kim to call out, "Hey, Mom."

"How's my girl?" Deb asked, the question to both Kim and Diane.

"She's fine," Kim said, setting the oversized bag on the floor next to a chair, then collapsing into another. "She just woke up and she's chatty. Has *a lot* to say."

And Diane was gurgling happily, beaming up at Deb in a way that warmed her heart.

"Definitely happy to see her grandmother," Kim said with humor.

"I told you not to say that word," Deb said.

"I keep forgetting."

"No, you don't. Technically, fifty-two is too young to be a grand-mother. Legally, you can't be a grandmother until you're in your sixties."

"Uh-huh."

"I'm just going by what the law says." Deb held Diane up to the window leading out to her deck, let her look outside. She knew the baby liked that, found it mesmerizing to stare at cars on the street below.

"How's Nicole?" Kim asked.

Deb frowned. "I barely hear from her ever since Jack. We're sup-posed to get drinks sometime."

"Did they figure out a date yet?"

"No, but I think they're going to do it in Vegas or something. Nicole keeps saying she doesn't want to spend much on her second wedding; that way she can really blow out the third."

Kim laughed. "Are you busy now?"

"Not really. I was shutting down for lunch anyway. Told everyone I'd be back online in an hour or so."

"When is ADA going to know if they got funding?"

"Tonight or tomorrow," Deb said. "I sent the proposal out yester-day. Now we're just waiting."

"I see. But that's not what you were working on?"

"No. Turns out everyone needs money. I've been juggling clients." Deb set the baby in a jumper, let Diane bounce around in front of the window.

"What if," Kim asked, her voice hesitant, "someone needed money for part of their business? Like a security guard? Is that the kind of thing a grant could help out with?"

"These grants are for everything," Deb replied. "Copy machines, staff, travel, meetings. Security would definitely fall in there. Why do you ask?"

"Just wondering. I have a friend who could use some help."

"Who?"

"A mom in the neighborhood."

"Oh. Well, let me know if I can help."

"I will."

Kim still sounded uncertain. Deb noticed it. "Is everything okay? Are things good with Sean?"

"They are, yeah. We're okay. I've just been thinking about something."

"What's that?"

"I guess it's something I've been thinking about more, since the baby came and Sean and I are figuring out how to adjust and everything."

Now a note of hesitancy in Deb's voice. "Okay."

"It's just, I don't want to ask about this, but I thought you and Dad were happy. Did you ever know . . ."

Deb's attitude turned harsh and cold. She felt it, didn't fight it. "I told you, I'm not going to talk about what happened."

"But it's just . . ."

"Is there someone else?"

"No, I don't think so. He just seems to have a lot of work."

"I meant for you."

"No. And Melissa and I don't talk anymore."

"You finally ended things?"

Kim nodded. "We couldn't really keep in touch after I got married. Too hard."

Silence.

Kim didn't tell her mom about Hannah, the married woman down the street from her house who had a daughter Diane's age. Who had mentioned to Kim that she'd also dated women and men when Kim revealed her past during an afternoon playdate. Who had grown more affectionate in their friendship since then, long smiles and playful laughing touches on the arm.

Kim didn't want to acknowledge it yet.

And she didn't want to acknowledge that if this attraction was there for her, maybe there was someone else in Sean's life too.

"I just want to know," Kim said slowly, "if you ever knew Dad wasn't happy. Could you tell?"

Deb's face grew hot, and she struggled to keep her emotions down. "I don't want to think about it."

"I know." Kim saw her mom's expression, saw the pain behind her eyes. "I'm sorry."

Kim and Deb helped Diane out of the jumper and put her on the floor. The baby played with some animal-shaped blocks Deb had set out.

"Why do you want to know?" Deb asked.

"I guess I just worry. I never thought about it until now. Now that I'm in that same place."

Deb didn't reply.

The two women watched Diane lift and drop the blocks.

* * *

Later that day, as the afternoon was ending, Deb turned off her computer. Leaned back in her chair, rubbed her eyes.

She couldn't stop thinking about what Kim had asked.

Truthfully, she'd never been able to stop thinking about it.

The guilt was still there, somewhere buried under the surface. Along with the memories and pain of those frantic, hellish weeks a decade ago. Like a murdered corpse in a shallow grave, with the chance the slightest rain could expose the body.

And sometimes that guilt did rise in Deb. The feeling of the gun in her hand, the way that after she pulled the trigger, Levi's head snapped back to the ground. Like the bullet was a nail driving his head down.

And when those images haunted her, she remembered what she'd told herself. The excuses she'd turned into reasons. Levi would never stop coming for her. She had to keep Kim safe. He'd killed Grant. He and Temple and the rest of their friends had trafficked an untold number of people. He'd lied to her. He was probably going to die from Temple's shot anyway. She hadn't meant to pull the trigger.

The face of the killer.

She stood from her chair, walked to the window. Peered through her reflection out to the wintry city of Falls Church.

The small shops and restaurants, the people hurrying through the cold, doing their best to step carefully on the ice, habit still keeping them distanced. Dogs trotting ahead of their owners.

Deb pulled on her coat and boots, headed outside.

It had begun snowing again.

Flakes floated down peacefully, lingering, touching the ground as tentatively as a cat's nervous paw. The streets were quiet, and the early evening atmosphere lent winter's blue romance to the neighborhood.

It really is lovely, Deb thought.

She walked through the snow, felt the cold flakes melt on her face. It was cold and it was pretty and it was her life, and she had to keep moving forward.

She wanted to.

And at that moment, warm in the winter, snow melting in her hair, still feeling the memory of her granddaughter pressed against her body, Deb never wanted anything more.

*　*　*

Kim undid the car seat, notched it in the crook of her arm, carried it and her daughter through the falling snow and into the coffee shop.

Saw Cessy Castillo sitting at a booth, sipping from a tall plastic cup of some sort of iced coffee.

"Hey, fucker!" Cessy cheerfully called out, and then her hand flew to her mouth. "Oh, shit, can Di understand swearing yet?"

"Not yet, dumbass," Kim replied good-naturedly. "But soon. You have a few more months. Give me a hand?"

Cessy was already sliding out of the booth, wiping her hands with a sanitizing cloth. She took the baby from Kim, held Diane tight to her chest, hoping she didn't wake up. If she did, Cessy knew from experience she'd have no luck calming the baby down.

"I'll be right back," Kim said. "Let me just get my bag from the car."

"I got her," Cessy said. "Sort of. Hurry back."

"You're fine."

Crap, Cessy thought, eyeing Diane. *She's waking up.* She watched the baby's expression turn troubled, the closed eyes squeezing, mouth puckering.

Fortunately, Kim walked back in and took the baby; at this point, Kim didn't need to ask Cessy if she still wanted to hold her. Not that Cessy disliked Diane—she actually liked her a lot, to the point that her affection was a surprise—but she was more than happy to let someone else handle her.

"How are you?" Kim asked as she set Diane in the seat.

"Good! Nothing's changed since last month."

"Are those new bruises on your hand?"

Cessy involuntarily glanced down, surprised Kim had noticed. "Just a couple."

"Another difficult dude?"

"Sometimes they don't take no for an answer."

Kim glanced at Diane, smiled at her sleeping child. Then she took a sip from the coffee Cessy had ordered for her. "Tell me about it."

Cessy shrugged. "He showed up at the office when his wife was there. Screaming stuff. I asked him to leave and he wouldn't."

"So you led him outside?"

"Someone had to."

"And it had to be you? I know we've talked about this before, but aren't you ever going to hire security?"

"Security would probably want to be paid."

Kim frowned. "I know I've said this to you from day one, when you told me you were starting this organization—"

"And every month since."

"And every month since," Kim agreed, "but I'm worried about you. It's just you alone helping these women. And they have people in their lives who want to hurt them, or have hurt them."

"Someone's got to do it."

"I know," Kim said. "I just wish it wasn't you."

She reached across the table. Cessy reached back, squeezed Kim's hands.

"Take care of yourself?" Kim asked.

"Oh yeah," Cessy said. "I got this."

"What happened?"

"I walked him out of the office, turned around, and he slammed me into the door. Grabbed my neck."

"Oh, Cess."

"So I punched him a bunch of times, kicked him in the head. Thank you, six nights a week of Muay Thai."

"I really should have started taking classes when you did."

"I *told* you to. Anyway, he ran out the door after that. Cops picked him up an hour later."

"I hate that you do this," Kim said. "I mean, I'm glad someone's doing it, but I hate it."

"Honestly," Cessy said, "I'll be fine. Angry spouses don't usually show up. That was kind of a rare thing. And even if they do, I usually put their families in touch with someone who can help them better than I can. I'm just the go-between."

Cessy let go of Kim's hands, wiped her own hands down, drank a long sip of coffee.

And wondered if Kim could tell she was lying.

She wondered if Kim knew that her story had been invented on the drive to the coffee shop.

Cessy had gone to that man's house after talking to his wife. Saw him carrying the garbage outside late one night. Pulled down a ski mask and jumped him.

One hit in the back with an expandable metal baton had dropped him to his knees. A quick crack from the baton to his chin knocked him flat, and the way his chin jutted to the side told her that the bone was smashed. Cessy fell on him, let her fists do the rest until his face was buried in blood.

Took his wallet to make it look like a robbery.

Cessy could never tell Kim that.

She could never tell Kim that she liked it. That she did it because of what his wife had told her, what his daughter had told her.

She did it because, someday, Seth would be out of jail. And Cessy needed to be ready.

She did it because it felt good.

"I'm not giving up," Kim said. "I'm going to keep bringing this up."

"Yeah, yeah. How's Deb?"

"She's good. Saw her earlier today."

"Did you make sure not to tell her about me?"

"Oh my God," Kim said. "She'd freak if she knew we hung out."

"You should tell her we're dating. Really mess with her world."

Kim laughed. "Can you imagine? But no way—I could never date you."

"Why not?"

"Well, for one thing, you're straight."

"Details."

"And I'm married."

"For now."

"Sure. But also we'd fight and break up, and then I'd lose you. And I'm not letting my best friend go anywhere."

"*Fine.* I guess I'll just get used to not being invited over to, like, Thanksgiving dinner. Turkey sucks anyway."

"Maybe Thanksgiving dinner someday?"

Cessy shrugged. "As long as I still get to see you, I can deal. How's Di's sleep coming along?"

"She's doing a lot better," Kim said. "A couple of naps during the day, and most nights she sleeps all the way through. It's so much better now than it used to be. The rough part's passed."

The two women sipped their drinks, kept talking about Diane and jobs and life. Cessy heard the rush of a siren as a cop car sped past the coffee shop.

Neither she nor Kim acknowledged it.

There are always sirens. They call through the night and day, the summer and snow, calling relentlessly. And someday, Cessy knew, those sirens would call for her.

She thought again about that man's broken jaw.

Cessy reached down, stroked Diane's sleeping face.

Smiled.

ACKNOWLEDGMENTS

Thank you to everyone at Crooked Lane Books and, in particular, Melissa Rechter; Madeline Rathle; and, of course, my editor, Terri Bischoff. I'm so happy to work with you, and this book couldn't have been in better hands.

Thanks to Michelle Richter for her sharp eye, sage advice, and unwavering support through the years. And to everyone at the Fuse Books family.

Thanks to Books Forward promotions, especially Ellen Whitfield, for helping my work find a wider audience. There couldn't be a better champion.

Thank you to Yvette and Yenny Lucero for their stellar work in helping me with translations and for not making fun of my rudimentary Spanish. And to Dr. Heather Calvert for her help with the medical sections of this book (pencil, eye).

Thank you to the folks at my day gig, who have been so enthusiastic and supportive of my writing. I'm lucky to have known you all these years and to be part of your family.

I've been fortunate to be a member of a number of wonderful organizations—Crime Writers of Color, the International Thriller Writers, Sisters in Crime, the Mystery Writers of America—and they've all led to some wonderful opportunities and, more importantly, lifelong friendships.

Along that note, the entire gang at The Thrill Begins have been close to me for years, and will be for years to come. I truly love all of you.

Thank you to the Washington Independent Review of Books, particularly the tireless Holly Smith, for giving me a chance, years ago, to write a regular column in your esteemed pages.

Thank you to the bookstores, particularly in the DC/MD/VA triangle, that have tirelessly supported me and other writers, especially my neighborhood bookshop, One More Page Books.

Thanks to the Gaithersburg Book Festival, Fall for the Book, Washington Writers, ThrillerFest, and all the other writing festivals and conferences that do such a fantastic job of connecting writers and readers.

Thank you to the faculties at George Mason and Marymount universities, two of the best universities for writing and literature.

Thank you to all the writers who stand with and support other writers—Kellye Garrett, Eric Beetner, Alex Segura, Jenny Milchman, Sarah M. Chen, Hank Phillippi Ryan, Nick Kolakowski, Nik Korpon, Marietta Miles, Chantelle Aimee Osman, Shawn Reilly Simmons, KJ Howe, Jennifer Hillier (of course, Jenny), and so many more. I admire what you do, try to emulate it, and have the fortune to count those I admire as friends.

Thank you to the artists and musicians I've collaborated with in a number of projects—Angela Del Vecchio, DJ Alkimist, Sara Jones, Ayana Reed, Chantal Tseng, and so many more.

Thank you to my parents for always standing by me and believing in what I'm doing.

And no one is more important than my wife and son. Everlasting love and thanks to both of you. There's nowhere I'd rather be than with the two of you, no matter where we are.